Clear Line of Fire

Clear Line of Fire

Badrinath Nuggehalli

RUPA
PUBLICATIONS INDIA

Published in 2011 by
Rupa Publications India Pvt. Ltd.
7/16, Ansari Road, Daryaganj,
New Delhi 110 002

Sales Centres:

Allahabad Bengaluru Chennai
Hyderabad Jaipur Kathmandu
Kolkata Mumbai

Printed in India by
Nutech Photolithographers
B-240, Okhla Industrial Area, Phase-I
New Delhi 110 020

1

A wintry Virginia sun glinted off the guard booth windows. Allen Connolly stood by and watched the guards poke about his hired Ford. They seemed to be taking their time. Monday morning blues, he thought to himself. He pulled his jacket tight around his shoulders and rubbed his palms together.

The sergeant stepped out of the booth and handed his pass and ID card back to him. His morose expression reinforced Connolly's diagnosis. 'Tough week starting up for you, mac?'

The sergeant eyed him balefully. Then, relenting suddenly, he returned Connolly's smile. 'Guess you know how it is with us foot soldiers, eh, Mr Connolly?' He nodded companionably as his men finished their inspection and gave the car a light slap. 'Well, there you go then.'

Monday morning blues notwithstanding, the check had been thorough, and every man at the gate had been alert. With a grin and a wave of his hand, Connolly eased the Ford up the driveway towards the CIA headquarters building some hundred yards away.

He parked the car and strode up the steps into the long, low-slung building. Gleaming glass doors let him into a cavernous, octagon-shaped lobby dominated by tones of grey and blue. It had several passages leading off to either side at angles behind a grey and beige desk with a glass front. At the desk a receptionist tapped away at her keyboard, her eyes scanning the computer screen set below a glass-topped section. She smiled as he came up.

'Good morning, Mr Connolly. You're two minutes early for your meeting,' she said, showing him a perfect set of teeth. Her bright hazel eyes regarded him with calm assurance. He smiled in return and thought that she most definitely cheered the place up. She might be a black-belt in karate too, he speculated, just in case things got ugly. 'If you'd give me your pass I'll book you in. You might not have to wait long but, in the meantime, can I get you a coffee?'

Neat, real neat, he thought. The company's HQ at Langley seemed to have been hard at work trying to put on a more human face since he had last been here more than two years ago. 'No, thank you, miss . . . ?'

'Beauchamps, Mr Connolly,' she replied, taking the proffered pass. 'Amanda Beauchamps. Have a seat.'

'Allen to you, my dear,' he said, and turned towards the sofa in the waiting bay.

At five feet ten, Connolly was not a tall man by American standards. Nevertheless, he had the litheness of a jungle cat. His loose-fitting suede jacket and corduroys covered broad shoulders and a narrow waist – a frame which supported a light but hard-muscled body. The tip of an old scar from a knife fight in a Kabul back alley showed through the V of his open-necked shirt. Connolly had discovered that the scar was a big turn-on for girls and had gotten into the habit of wearing open-necked shirts to give them a tantalising glimpse. On the left side of his chest, but lower down, was another, larger, rosette-shaped scar – this one from a bullet that had torn up half a lung during the days before Desert Storm. Sheer grit had kept him alive as he had struggled for two days, alone and close to death, to get back behind American lines.

Connolly wore these experiences lightly. His deep-set, mirthful eyes belied years of fighting Uncle Sam's wars behind enemy lines all across South Asia and the Middle East. A shock of thick, black, curly hair covered his skull. His high cheekbones and swarthy, angular face gave prominence to his long, straight nose. He looked like an Afghan Pathan and, with his fluent command over idiomatic Pushtu, could pass off easily as a local in those desolate highlands – a fact that had been put to use in countless missions in Iraq, Afghanistan and Pakistan. He had also mastered several other South Asian tongues including Urdu, Tamil and Arabic – one of the many reasons he had been selected to join the agency to follow a career in addition to his original profession as a consulting geologist with several American and European multinationals with mining interests in Asia.

Connolly recollected the events of the past forty-eight hours as he waited. He had got the summons to HQ during a well-earned weekend in the north-western Pakistani city of Quetta. Bancroft from the embassy had run him to ground at the Residency Club bar, the only watering hole in those remote parts where an American citizen could find convivial drinking company without constantly being on the edge.

The state department attaché had driven up from Islamabad, braving a treacherous seven-hour drive through the mountains. That in itself was a cue that something important was up, else why wouldn't they have just sent a message to call him in? Bancroft hadn't had much information though, except to tell him that he was booked on the first available flight to New York and hand him his ticket. He had had just an hour to throw his things into a suitcase and grab a bite before setting off.

At JFK, he had been met by old Jacky Heinz, who had taken him straight to the airport bar and handed him his HQ entry pass and ticket to Charleston. He was to rent a car there and drive into Langley. Connolly didn't ask why he had to take such a roundabout route; he had seen enough of the games the HQ types played.

'Looks like this is a big one, old son,' Heinz had said as they sipped beer. Heinz had been his coordinator in Kuwait back in 1990. Connolly had taken a liking to this mountain of a man who also had a mountain of a brain and an uncanny knack for reading the Arab mind. After Desert Storm had wound down, Heinz had been recalled stateside to head an analysis project covering the Middle East as well as the Indian subcontinent. But Heinz was not really in on this one – he had merely been asked to meet him at JFK and hand him the papers. 'Matthews himself is in charge of this caper. Word is that he and Weinberger had a long rap down in DC last Friday. Here you are, and it's only Monday. Looks like they picked you out for this especially. I hear the job is out in India. But it beats me why they would want you there of all places. You're doing a good job in Afghanistan.'

'Maybe it's because I schooled there for a while,' said Connolly. 'But I haven't been there in fifteen years.'

'Yeah, that's what I figured. Ahh, it's probably just some static on the grapevine,' said Heinz, flapping his hand. 'Hey, you better get moving, your plane leaves in ten minutes.'

India

In the early seventies, Connolly's father had been an adviser to IBM in Delhi. He had been the liaison man for Big Blue in the labyrinthine political circles of that old-new country. When he became thirteen, Allen had been enrolled into the exclusive residential American school in Kodaikanal, a quiet hill station in southern India. That was where he had discovered his aptitude for foreign tongues. Mixing easily with the locals, he had mastered Tamil within months. The Connollys loved holidaying in the countryside and had been entertained regularly by the erstwhile rulers of old princely states on both sides of the India-Pakistan border. Young Allen had nurtured his talent for languages, picking up Urdu as well. Travelling widely, he had become acquainted with large portions of the subcontinent. He had inherited his father's love for geography and history, and had grown attached to the region which had seen a centuries-old civilisation flourish and mature despite wave after wave of marauding conquerors. More fascinating yet was the contrast – the country was still a political toddler grappling with the divergent pulls of spiritual wealth and economic poverty. By 1977, the year when a new government in Delhi had, in a fit of anti-US fervour, closed IBM and other American MNCs down in India, Allen Connolly had graduated from the Kodaikanal school. He decided to take up a career which would give him the opportunity to stay on and work in that part of the world and enrolled at Stanford to study geology.

His oriental looks, familiarity with South Asia and command over languages had attracted the attention of the CIA while he was in college back in the US. After five years of working with Exxon, Allen Connolly had been recruited by the agency as one of its field operatives in the Middle East. Over the next ten years, with considerable financial assistance from the CIA, Connolly had set himself up as a consultant geologist. The job gave him an excellent cover to travel to the remotest corners of those countries and maintain offices in several major cities in the region. Most of his assignments involved working with petro-majors and took him to various Arab countries. But so far, he had not been sent to the Indian subcontinent, barring a few clandestine visits to Pakistan while working with rebel Afghan tribesmen. He wondered what could be happening in India that the boys down there couldn't handle.

Or shouldn't handle. Was that it?

◆

Anton Konstantin groaned inwardly as he watched the ponderous old fogies file into the conference room. In the new dispensation within the Federal Security Service, which had taken over most of the operations of the disbanded KGB, the old guard had been completely reorganised. Formerly powerful men had been given sinecures where their outdated attitudes would do the least harm. Many of these were present today: Kharkov, director of the Institute of Inter-Regional Political Research; Zhivarev, head of the Socio-Cultural Analysis Department; Makarych of the Technology Transfer Wing and many others Konstantin had met briefly on previous occasions. They were relics of the cold war who had long outlived their purpose, if indeed, thought Konstantin, they had ever served any. He was part of a young breed of high achievers who were impatient to build a new and resurgent Russia, free of the parasitic lesser republics which had weighed down the erstwhile Soviet Union. But the fact that his boss and mentor, Major General Aliakhin, had called them in for this meeting meant that these old crocks served some purpose. So Konstantin kept his views to himself.

At thirty-five, Colonel Anton Andreyevitch Konstantin was the youngest ever section-head of the FSS. He was slightly built and always neat and trim. His small stature was more than compensated for by a live-wire mind and a hard-driving ambition. His pale blue eyes burned with a patriotic fire that made his less zealous colleagues nervous.

Konstantin did not tolerate fools gladly, especially not the current lot in the room. The gaggle settled themselves slowly into the chairs around the massive oak table. Huge and imposing, resplendent in his army uniform, Major General Yegor Aliakhin remained standing at the head of the table. Now there, thought Konstantin, was a member of the old establishment who had adapted himself well to the changed realities. Konstantin felt admiration tinged with an almost filial affection for this old soldier who had staked his life and more for his motherland, and under whom he had served with unswerving loyalty for fourteen years.

Konstantin was Aliakhin's protégé, in whom the older man saw himself as a youth. The only difference being that Konstantin belonged to the twenty-first century and was already beginning to be recognised as a potential head of the FSS. Apart, of course, from the obvious difference in size, but that counted for nothing in the special bond that existed between them.

It had been six months since Konstantin had been made head of Section K, the division of the FSS responsible for counterintelligence operations in the Indian subcontinent. When he first got this posting, the Kremlin had been abuzz with rumours that Konstantin had somehow run afoul of his mentor. The section was, from the FSS's standpoint, a low-priority one since it covered a staunch Russian ally. There were, to be sure, Pakistan and Afghanistan to keep tabs on, but neither was as challenging as assignments in the newly independent republics south of Russia, where Konstantin had spent three very successful years. His handling of the Armenian problem had marked him out as politically astute and tactically brilliant. For him to be shunted to the Indian subcontinent was, to all observers, an indication that his career had run into trouble.

Konstantin had been puzzled even more by the crash courses on Indian languages that he had been put through. If he was to be sent to the field – in a new sector to boot – at this stage of his career, this could not augur well. But he had implicit faith in General Aliakhin and waited patiently for the old soldier to reveal his plans. Surely, he told himself, there was a greater purpose behind Aliakhin's move. Konstantin had ploughed through lessons in Hindi, boning up on the topography of the key Indian metros, even making a few 'familiarisation visits' to Delhi and Mumbai before actually taking charge.

Aliakhin had been as avuncular as ever towards his protégé, even having him over for weekends of fishing and hunting at his *dacha* on the shores of Lake Baikal, complete with evenings of rip-roaring drinking and cards at the local inn. If Aliakhin had heard any of the rumours about Konstantin's career prospects, he betrayed no sign of it.

Konstantin had waited patiently. Now, he felt in his bones that Aliakhin's plans would be revealed.

'Gentlemen, let us begin,' said Aliakhin, bringing the meeting to order instantly.

'You are all familiar with the arrangement between the Indian and previous Czech governments for the supply of the Skoda 155-mm howitzer. This particular weapon from Skoda had several features which made it the most effective artillery piece for operations in the mountainous terrain of the Himalayas and Asia Minor. As you also know, that arrangement now stands cancelled. We had used our good offices with our Czech friends to terminate the contract. Consequently, the Indian government had perforce to choose between the British Vickers, French Caesar and Austrian Voest Alpine. All three are excellent guns, but none could match the tactical superiority of the Skoda.

'It has for some time been apparent that a matter which we had treated as closed has been reopened by our neighbours in Uzbekistan. This has been prompted by the return of one of Skoda's top ballistics experts, Dr Ismail Barkhatiev, an Uzbek national, to his own country.

'Uzbekistan has embarked on the design and development of this howitzer under Dr Barkhatiev's direction. What is most distressing is that they have not bothered to inform us.'

Images of Barkhatiev and his labs flashed on the screen behind Aliakhin as he explained the Uzbek initiative.

'In his most recent efforts in Samarkand, he has been assisted by one of his ex-students, Dr Rajan Swaminathan of India.' A grainy file-photo of Swaminathan followed as he outlined the Indian contribution.

Aliakhin wound up his recital of the facts with a detailed explanation of the Skoda gun and its advantages over the others. 'The question which I am sure is uppermost in your minds, gentlemen, is the most obvious one, and one that should strike any right-thinking Russian.'

Aliakhin's menacing glare scanned the room as the general's listeners bestirred themselves dutifully.

'Why are our good neighbours going through all this trouble to develop this weapon in such a secretive manner? Why should they share sensitive military secrets with the Indians?' Aliakhin's voice was rising with indignation. 'Why do they hide this from their Russian brothers? Do they not trust us?

'No,' he thundered, 'the Uzbeks have become ambitious beyond belief! And they think that this,' he scowled in disdain, 'this toy is going to give them power over their other neighbours in the South! Today Kazakhstan, tomorrow Tajikistan and then,' Aliakhin paused to scan the assemblage and finished with a dramatic stage whisper, 'then my friends, even Mother Russia herself will not be safe from their scrabbling hands.

'Now we,' Aliakhin leaned forward, his fists pressing down on the table, 'we are all here to see that the world is not subjected to the sprouting of a rash of regional powers. Powers who cannot be expected to act with maturity and a sense of perspective. I have called for this meeting, gentlemen, to ask you to monitor this disturbing situation through your respective departments and report to me on the first of every month without fail. The formats in which I want the information are in the dossiers before you.'

After a tirade like that, there was not even a hint of dissonance among those present. 'We shall then be in a position to take decisive action at the appropriate time. Thank you, gentlemen.'

The meeting was at an end and the old men began stuffing their papers into their briefcases. 'One last thing, gentlemen...' he said. Everyone froze.

Indicating Konstantin he said, 'This is Colonel Anton Konstantin, whom many of you already know well. He is in charge of Section K which, as you may know, covers certain key Russian interests in South Asia, and will spearhead our little operation. He is one of my most trusted aides. You are all requested to extend to him your fullest and most unstinting cooperation in his efforts to protect the interests of Mother Russia.'

There were some faint murmurs around the room, but no one said anything audible. This last announcement had caught them quite off guard.

◆

The smooth voice of the girl behind the desk cut into Connolly's reverie.

'In you go, Mr Connolly. Second floor, first corridor to your right and fifth door on your left.'

Connolly smiled his acknowledgement as he retrieved his pass and stepped into a long corridor. A guard was waiting to escort him to the old man's office.

They walked past a room spanning more than twenty metres and behind the frosted glass Connolly could barely make out the silhouettes of massive screens and ghostly white-coated figures of lab analysts flitting around. The intelligence network constantly fed the company's server farms billions of bits of information from every corner of the world. This was the nerve centre of the CIA. From here, Uncle Sam watched the progress of dozens of undercover operations in political and commercial capitals around the world. As he walked past, Connolly contemplated the analysts scurrying around with reams of printouts or peering at multi-coloured screens inside their sanitised cloister. Not for them the heat and dust and blood and sweat of arid Afghan mountains or teeming Asian bazaars. These were squeaky-clean automatons inhabiting these air-conditioned caves, fighting digital wars in a virtual world totally removed from reality. It was bizarre, almost grotesque. Connolly felt a shudder down his spine as he turned into the door of the lift held open by his escort.

Connolly's mood lightened as he stepped into the familiar office of the deputy director and chief of Section 3, H. Atherton 'Mad Matt' Matthews. At least this place hadn't been taken over by computer nerds. Here people dealt with people. The man behind the huge desk at the window knew what was going on in the real world. Matthews had been one of the best field operatives in his time, a man respected for his physical courage and feared for his ruthlessness. Now past fifty, he was a strong contender for directorship when Davies retired in two years.

'Come in, sonny,' said Matthews; to him, every junior was 'sonny'. 'Grab a chair.' There was one more person in the room – a middle-aged man wearing a well-cut navy blue suit and a quiet striped tie, looking very much the Wall Street broker. He was seated facing Matthews.

'This is Hawthorne from the Pentagon, sonny. He has an interesting story to tell. There's something going on in your neck of the woods which Uncle Sam wants you to check out. Well, not exactly your neck of the woods, but close enough. Now hear this.' Matthews leaned forward and jabbed a finger at Connolly. 'This job is completely hush-hush, see? Even our boys in the zoo (Zone of Operation) don't want to know about it. And we definitely don't want those teddy bears (Matthews' pejorative for the FSS) to know that we know anything at all about what you're going to hear, okay?'

Connolly felt uneasy. He was clearly being told that he was going in alone on this one. Not even the CIA would be there for assistance. He shot a sideways glance at Hawthorne and was met with a steady, appraising stare.

'He's yours,' said Matthews.

Hawthorne pushed a slim plastic folder along the desk. In a smooth voice and with carefully chosen words, he spelled out the scenario. 'In that folder are details of a strategic alignment for a 155-mm calibre self-propelled mountain howitzer now being negotiated between India and Uzbekistan. I believe that this weapon is known in common parlance as a shoot-and-scoot gun. In fact, this is a transaction which was being structured by India and the USSR since 1985. The Soviet regime had assigned the task of design and production to the ordnance factory at Skoda in Czechoslovakia. After the political disintegration of the USSR, India tried to get the Russians to take it forward but they politely declined as a result of some discreet persuasion from us. We had then considered that chapter closed.

'For reasons set out in the docket, Uzbekistan is interested in consummating the partnership with India on this howitzer. It appears that this weapon will have certain features which make it advantageous in military manoeuvres in the terrain of Asia Minor. India's interest is high because of the howitzer's capability to achieve tactical superiority in operations in the Himalayan areas bordering China and Pakistan.'

'You say "will have", Hawthorne. That means the gun's not ready yet?' Connolly interrupted. He noted with grim pleasure that Hawthorne could not conceal a slight frown. Connolly had him slotted for a nerd warlord, a commander from the electronic battlefield, and had taken an instant dislike to him.

Hawthorne cleared his throat. 'The gun, as you call it, is still in the prototype design stage. Again, for reasons set out in the docket, the Uzbeks are collaborating with the Indians in its development. For the last two years, we have been monitoring the progress more closely. We have reasons to believe that the project is now fast nearing prototype testing.'

'This mama is a real sweetie, sonny, mark my words,' Mathew broke in with a grin and a wink. It was obvious to Connolly that Matthews shared his dislike for Hawthorne. 'Now, in case you've been wondering how a couple of countries like India and Uzbekistan got their hands onto something so hot, it goes like this. The gun was to be made by Skoda. But once the Czechs got out from under the Soviet umbrella, they told every Soviet military "expert" to pack his bags and haul his ass out of there. One of these was an Uzbek ballistics scientist who had worked with them in designing this gun. Maybe the Czechs figured they could make this little thingamajig by themselves, maybe they just lost interest in it. But our little Uzbek returned home, bringing all his drawings with him. The gun is great for operating in those areas like Hawthorne here told you. But the Uzbeks had a little problem…'

Hawthorne took his cue, 'The superior shoot-and-scoot capability of this howitzer is only one of its advantages. It also features a so-called Variable Angle Recoil Dissipation mechanism which enables it to be fired from surfaces with greater inclines than any other weapon in its class. What this means is that the gun can fire from positions on mountain slopes steeper, and from terrain less firm, than other 155-mm guns. Which in turn means that for an army on the move in such terrain, the number of places this gun can stop to fire multiplies several times. The problem that Mr Matthews referred to, relates to the computer console which controls the gun. While the Skoda plant was working on the ballistics, the Soviets had been working separately on a state-of-the-art GPS-based software, the technology for which the Uzbeks do not possess. That was to be the other special feature of the howitzer.

'Now, the Uzbeks don't trust the Russians any more than we do. They wanted the howitzer for themselves but were constrained by their lack of software know-how. That's where the Indians come into the picture. The Uzbek scientist Mr Matthews referred to – Barkhatiev – had a bright Indian student whom he taught ballistics in the polytechnic at Patrice Lumumba University. This student,' Hawthorne frowned at his notes, his composure ever so slightly punctured, 'Sam, uh, Sam-Nathan or some such. Well, anyway this ex-student is now a prominent scientist engaged in software research at a defence laboratory called DRDO at Bangalore in India. I am given to understand that you are not unfamiliar with this city. This person is considered to be something of an expert in computer software for ballistics applications. Barkhatiev and his ex-student have got together with the blessings of their respective governments to complete the design of the gun.'

'Word is, sonny,' said Matthews, 'that these guys have finally cracked the design. So the gun is ready for prototype production.

And that's where you come in. The plum is ready for the picking, and we aim to have it.'

He lowered his predatory head and flashed the devilish grin Connolly knew so well. Mad Matt on the prowl was something else. It was the kind of thing that men like him were born to do. He made no secret of the fact that he enjoyed it. And Mad Matt had had the entire globe for his jungle ever since he hit CIA HQ after retiring from field work.

'Now hear this. You go to this Bangalore place and set yourself up as a consultant scouting the country for an American GPS software major. That's your cover. And like they say, Bangalore is the software capital of India. Christ, what a term – software capital! I hear they've got power blackouts half the time. Anyway, you shack up there and you're supposed to be surveying local talent, government policy, infrastructure, that kind of thing. I've set up a crash course for you to get up to scratch on the jargon.

'Your job is to get the design once the prototype is tested A-Okay. Maybe we'll snitch this Barkhatiev and maybe Swaminathan too.' Matthews certainly had no problems getting his tongue around the Indian name. 'Or maybe we'll just grab the designs and skedaddle. That's your call once you're out there. I'll brief you on your communication protocol immediately after this meeting.

'Questions?'

That last word was merely Matthews' way of calling the meeting to an end. Over the last ten years, Connolly had never known a question to follow. He knew enough not to have any. Not, at any rate, in the presence of outsiders like Hawthorne. There hadn't even been any question of asking him if he would do it. With Mad Matt there was no telling where questions would get you; he only wanted answers.

Hawthorne caught the signal and gathered his papers to leave. With a quick nod at both men, he walked out.

'That was just to get that pompous ass out, Allen. Now get this clear. I'm sending you in alone on this. But I don't want to risk losing one of my best boys just because the bloody goons up in DC are antsy about us being seen playing blind poker in India. Because it's embarrassing the hell out of the Pentagon that Uncle Sam doesn't know what the fuck is going on in a third world country. Can you beat the hypocrisy of those bastards? One of the reasons they don't want overt CIA involvement, they told me, is that it would be unseemly for us to appear curious about a hi-tech breakthrough in a third-world country!

'Okay, so I've got this detail of surveillance people flying out to India over the next few days. They'll all be there before you've landed, setting up their act. They'll give you the intelligence support you need on the field.'

He handed over a slim folder. 'The details of the operation are in this dossier.' He continued, 'Memorise and destroy as usual. Good luck, sonny.'

◆

Major General Aliakhin had manipulated the assembled officials superbly. Deliberately leaving Konstantin's mandate vague while pummelling them with a barrage of patriotic fervour, Aliakhin had obtained their obedience to Konstantin, several years their junior. Konstantin remained impassive, seemingly oblivious of the furtive glances of the men around the table as they filed submissively out of the room.

'They will cooperate fully now, General. There was not even a whimper of protest,' said Konstantin, looking with reverence at his mentor. 'You have been able to get the entire machinery of the FSS at our disposal without question. I wonder if these very men would have let go of their little fiefdoms so easily in the old days.'

The general's eyes had lost their fierceness, but they were tinged with sadness. 'My son,' he said, placing a hand on the younger man's shoulder, 'we have only bluff and bluster left to enforce our will on the world. The Soviet Union is dead and Mother Russia is not yet strong enough to take up her rightful position among the nations of the world. Take this gun as an example – we cannot do as good a job of designing it as the Uzbeks with the help of Indians will. Such is the sad state of affairs, Toni.'

Rarely had Konstantin seen the old man in such a melancholic mood. He was puzzled. Serving continually on field assignments, he had lost touch with conditions that existed within Russia. His main field of operations covered South Asian countries and, while many of them were democracies, the standard of living had never been anything to write home about. With those countries as reference points in his experience, Konstantin had little reason to believe that Mother Russia was not the paradise-on-earth it was made out to be.

The old man turned towards the window and looked pensively over the snow-lined streets of Dzerzhinsky Square. He saw his countrymen, huddled in their dark overcoats against the swirling snow, scurrying about their affairs. Aliakhin had long ago seen through the lie of socialism and anticipated the situation his country was now facing. His long military career had shown him the horror of wars that the inflated Soviet ego had dragged his people into. He had, for years, dealt daily with men drunk on power. Men who refused to change even after they realised that the socialist model was failing. Men who lacked the political will to alter the system because they feared change and the potential loss of power and privilege it prognosticated. The working man's dream had turned into something worse than a nightmare – a dull, demeaning drudgery with no end in sight.

He turned away from the window with a sigh and resumed the discussion. 'We refused to collaborate with the Indians on such a project when they asked us, not because we didn't want to, but because we couldn't, my son. Frankly, we were nowhere near ready with the GPS software. And obviously we didn't want them to know it. We didn't want the Americans to know it either. We made a great show of allowing ourselves to be persuaded to cancel negotiations with the Indians. And we told them that this gun represented an escalation of the very arms race that the new Russia would do all in her power to curb.' Konstantin took some time to absorb this.

'Don't look so shocked, Toni. You must be made aware of the levels of degradation we have to pull Russia out of, due to the mismanagement of our political masters. You have been exposed so far only to the realities of the field. Pull yourself together and face another kind of reality – one that exists in the corridors of power.

It's time for you to grow up some more. You are like a son to me and I feel almost like a tycoon in the US showing his heir the state of affairs of the company.'

Aliakhin turned his mind to the assignment at hand and Konstantin smiled as he saw the fire of combat return to his mentor's eyes.

Thumping Konstantin on the shoulder, the general said, 'But enough of this old woman's talk, eh, Toni? We have another battle to fight! Now the Uzbeks and the Indians are close to building the prototype and the moment is ripe for us to strike. I want you to obtain for Mother Russia the designs of this weapon. Though I referred to it as a "toy" so disparagingly a moment ago, it is critical that we equip our forces with it at the earliest.'

'The plum is ready for the picking, eh, General?'

The general chuckled as he gathered his papers. 'The very words that our friends across the Atlantic used while briefing their operative at Langley, Colonel Konstantin, the very words. Come into my office and I will explain in detail what I want you to do when you go back to your favourite hunting ground – India.'

2

Satyan Sharma rocked back on the balls of his feet, letting his body feel the balance. Eyes fixed to the spot, he swung the driver high over his head. His whole being was focused on the little white ball perched on the tee before him. Head still, he whipped the club down and gave it the full follow-through before looking up at the ball as it soared into the distance. He leaned over to pluck the tee out and grinned at his caddie. Par, or maybe just one over, looked eminently possible today. On this gusty morning and on the tough course of the Delhi Golf Club, that would be a great start to the weekend.

Satyan was in his early thirties. Tall for an Indian at six feet, his slim body moved with the grace of a dancer. In fact, he had been an amateur actor of some repute in Mumbai's theatre circles before his business interests began demanding too much of his time. He was good-looking and had deep resonant voice suited for a lucrative career on stage or, perhaps, even in the movies. Instead, he had opted to step into his father's shoes and take over the struggling, medium-sized electronics business.

He had been bitten by the electronics bug very early in his childhood and had, along with his father in the old days, spent many a weekend rigging up all manner of gadgets. One that he had been proud of was a long-range pick-up microphone, to listen in on the telephone conversations of the girl next door. This love of things electronic was the one thing that his father had bequeathed to him before letting his life slide away in a sea of alcoholic dissipation.

Satyan had discovered the depths to which his father had sunk only on his return from college in the US. The shock of learning that a man whom he had considered a god, a man whom he had chosen to place on a high pedestal all along, could no more command respect as any other man would, had wounded the junior Sharma deeply.

Satyan was the third in a line of entrepreneurs. Migrating to Mumbai from his native Bangalore in the thirties, his grandfather Seshadri Sharma had set up and nurtured a thriving electrical workshop. Word of his skill and dedication to quality spread quickly, and the Electrical Maintenance and Manufacturing Group (EMMG) prospered. The firm managed to land several contracts to service electrical equipment for merchant lines whose ships came calling at Mumbai harbour. Seshadri Sharma began to be consulted on difficult repair jobs by British naval ships based in Mumbai, and soon EMMG began getting contracts from the Imperial Army and the Royal Indian Air Force as well during the British rule in India, and was well-entrenched to serve independent India's fledgling military forces after the colonial rulers left.

Second in the line of succession, Jagannath 'Jugs' Sharma steadily grew the firm's revenues. Jugs, armed with a degree in electronics from the Massachusetts Institute of Technology and imbued with the American spirit of enterprise, turned EMMG into a thriving company manufacturing state-of-the-art electronic components. He built a design centre which enabled EMMG to maintain its cutting edge and retain the highly profitable defence contracts.

But a dark lining to the silver cloud finally tore apart both the business and the family. Jugs had earned his nickname during his college days due to his ability to imbibe and hold vast quantities of liquor. He had developed a strong partiality to bourbon during his years in the States. Everyone ribbed him about his love for the bottle, though it never got serious because Jugs consistently scored brilliant grades at MIT, graduating way up on top of his class. Back in India, he showed himself to be a dynamic business leader, and for many years, his fondness for the bottle continued to be overlooked. No one could say for certain when he began turning into an alcoholic. Through the seventies, his wife watched helplessly as the man she had once loved hurled himself inexorably towards destruction.

Satyan had been sent off to study at the Lawrence School, an exclusive boarding establishment in the picturesque Nilgiri Hills, so that the growing boy could rarely get to see the dark side to his brilliant father. He won an undergraduate scholarship to MIT, just like his father, and went over to study computer science, maintaining family tradition by passing at the top of his class.

He returned home, and to reality in 1980.

EMMG was close to bankruptcy, a situation stemming mainly from the negligence of his alcoholic father. Jugs Sharma had crumbled under pressure and become increasingly difficult to work with. His best people began deserting him and the company slid ever faster towards ruin.

To make matters worse, Jugs had begun to show his violent side at home. He would get physical with his wife whenever she tried to bring up the topic of his incessant drinking. Frightened and distraught, Mrs Sharma had withdrawn into a shell. Reluctant to upset her son as he pursued his studies in the US, she had not let on about the situation at home. She started keeping a secret diary where she would write imaginary letters to her son every other day, letters never intended to be sent but serving only as an outlet for her depressed thoughts. Ever the loyal Indian wife, she would end every entry with an appeal to Satyan to forgive his father because he couldn't help himself and to remember that in his darkest moods, the old man loved them both. In the end, her self-imposed deceit was too much, the bottled-up emotions too heavy for her to endure. She died, heartbroken, barely six weeks after Satyan's return.

And with her death, something died within Jugs Sharma. Quite inexplicably, the devil which had driven him to drink was gone forever. But gone, also forever, was the fire and passion which had ruled his life. He went to a sanatorium to dry out and came back, three months later, a cured but broken man.

But with her death, some dark force was born deep in Satyan's soul. At first, it revealed itself by way of irritation at small things that his father did, but over the weeks and months it turned in a raging inferno. He would castigate the weakened old man, raving at him for the mess he had landed the family and the business in. Almost every night, before he reached the boiling point that he felt coming on, Satyan would frog-march his father to his bed, clamping the now thin arms in an angry vise-like grip. After making sure the old man was firmly tucked into bed and would get to no further mischief, he would go downstairs to the darkened library and brood, sprawled out on his grey leather padded armchair, staring out over the swaying Ashoka trees at the egde of the lawn. By and by, he would be stirred by the faint scratching of the needle of the antique turntable, the acrylic LP record having run its course.

Left to pick up the pieces of a world he had thought solid and indestructible, the young Satyan Sharma vowed that EMMG would rise again. Bit by bit, he put together a crack team of computer engineers and modernised the operations. He called his father's old works director out of retirement and appointed him as a consultant to guide him in emulating the spirit of the days when Jugs Sharma had built a fighting-fit outfit.

Satyan immersed himself into getting the show back on the road. He began with the bankers and convinced them that EMMG was still a going concern. They had refrained from foreclosing on the loans advanced to the company which cost him a sizable chunk of equity and two positions on the board of directors, but it was a necessary price to pay for survival. Next he turned his attention to regaining customers, hiring managers for a newly formed business-development function. Finally, he turned his attention to the workers. While, on the one hand, he could ill-afford a labour problem, on the other, he wanted to clear the stables so that he could restructure his workforce according to the needs of a contemporary electronics and computer software powerhouse.

Fortunately for him, corporate India had discovered a new mantra – diversification. So, while the old EMMG was regaining its feet, Satyan spun off the electronics department into a separate company, christened it 'Next Gen Tech' and manned it with handpicked, younger workers. He invested in retraining them to adopt the latest work methods. He also invested in several joint ventures with European electronics firms who were only too happy to gain a foothold in the new and growing Indian market, stealing whatever chance they got against the Japanese electronics juggernaut whose invasion of Europe was well under way. Exploiting this eagerness of theirs, Satyan negotiated terms with them which cut down his cash outflows, yet gave his fledgling company the know-how to make critical electronic components in-house. This, combined with the advantage of low labour costs, gave him the ability to cater to many third world and iron-curtain markets. Within a few years, Next Gen had outgrown the stodgier EMMG and had become a transnational company competing successfully in the field of electronic components, a rarity among third world companies.

But the apple of Satyan's eye had to wait a few more years to be born, even though it had been conceived during his post-grad days at MIT.

Knowing well that the future lay not in manufacturing but in information technology, he founded a company which was devoted to developing computer software. This was his real love. This was where Satyan hoped to make a mark on the world stage. Indian software brains had begun to be recognised and respected the world over. He could see no reason why, if he could provide a world-class work environment and top-of-the-line pay packets, he shouldn't be able to realise his dreams. Hiving off a portion of the sprawling EMMG land, Satyan set up a top-flight software development group in a sleek new building. Springing out of a low hill, the bold, sweeping steel and glass curves of the structure brilliantly captured the spirit of this venture – Pure Space Networks (PSN). It looked as if a spaceship had crash-landed into the hillside, bringing with it aliens with technological prowess far advanced compared to mere earthlings. And the people manning it were chosen by him for precisely this quality – world-beating technological prowess. He scoured the world for crack Indian software experts who wanted to return to India provided the terms were good. By the mid-nineties, PSN had become an international landmark on the information superhighway. Obviously, it helped that the young entrepreneur was a whiz-kid himself.

One of the software experts Satyan roped in was his roommate while he was at MIT – a slim, soft-spoken and ever-smiling genius called Jacob 'Jake' Mehta. Jake had a prodigious ability to concentrate his mind on the problem at hand and had graduated from MIT summa cum laude. In the same year when Satyan enrolled for his MS course, Jake was starting on his PhD and, like Satyan, he was looking out for someone to share lodgings with him. Though several years older than Satyan, the two of them hit it off immediately when they met at the foreign students office and it didn't take them long to decide to shack up together.

Jacob Mehta was erudite and liberal in his views, much like Satyan. He had imbibed both Christian and Hindu philosophies deeply, which led him paradoxically to declare himself an intensely spiritual atheist. Physically though, Jake was quite the opposite of the athletically built Satyan; he never indulged in any exercise more strenuous than climbing the stairs to the third-floor apartment they shared for two years. They had stayed in touch after Satyan completed his course and moved back to India. Satyan often called upon Jake's advice while he steered EMMG through troubled waters.

Later, when Satyan called him to set up Pure Space together, he left a fast-track career and came over to India with alacrity, leaving behind his wife Maggie in Silicon Valley – a lawyer whose career was showing early signs of success – and their two very young sons. That was because Jake felt almost as much ownership in the vision of the global software powerhouse they had discussed over the years and which was finally going to become a reality. Satyan gave his friend complete charge of the technical wing of Pure Space and allowed him a free hand to scour the world for the talent they wanted. Jake's reputation ensured that many top-notch engineers joined Pure Space, willingly giving up lucrative positions in Fortune 500 companies. A couple of these new recruits had done cutting-edge work in NASA and other institutions at the forefront of science and technology.

'Jake, with you handling the operations we're going to win the world, buddy,' Satyan told him on the very first day he started at Pure Space. 'Tell me when you're ready to take over as CEO. I couldn't have got safer hands to put this baby into.' Satyan felt that sooner or later Gujarati commercial acumen would surface and combine with Jake's academic stature and philosophical mien to produce an outstanding business leader.

Jake grinned. 'Yeah, yeah, Satyan, let me get my bearings straight. I've got to convince Maggie to make the move to India and that may take a year or two. And what the hell, old man, what difference does a designation make between the two of us?'

Satyan wasn't too pleased with that answer because if Jake's wife Maggie wasn't convinced, it could mean divided loyalties for Jake, but he decided not to press the issue for the moment. They had more urgent tasks at hand.

He only said, 'Say Jake, why don't you get Maggie to come over with the kids when she gets her next break? Let India work its magic on her directly, eh?'

'Yeah, I'll ask her to come over this summer. Well, I needed to talk to you about IT set-up.' With that the two men got down to business.

It took seven long years for Pure Space to make its first major breakthrough. Jake Mehta and his team had designed a computer software product using GPS technology which could manipulate very large scale maps of vast areas and integrate them with a wealth of geophysical and meteorological data received on-line from satellites. Its capability of zooming in, from twenty-five thousand miles out in space, to a rock just five feet in diameter was one spectacular feature. The other was its ability to extrapolate data to visualise simulated weather, geophysical and vegetation features on the fly.

Satyan had tapped his father's wide circle of friends and associates to help identify the right people in the Indian government circles who would buy his software. He had also roped in Sambaran Bannerjee – the brilliant bureaucrat and his prospective father-in-law – who was, right at that moment, drawing a bead on his golf ball.

Bannerjee was approaching the apogee of a glitteringly successful career spanning almost three decades, rising to be the finance secretary to the Government of India. High-profile and constantly in the news, now that the push towards liberalising the Indian economy was in full swing, he was reputed to be among the ten most powerful civil servants in the country. His word could direct billions of rupees in government investment. He was part of a national 'brains-trust' which had shaped the financial architecture of India's re-designed economy.

The man himself wore the air of someone conscious of his role in guiding his country's destiny. Tall and spare of build, his sartorial elegance and intellectual genius were impeccable. His credentials, which included five very successful years at the Asian Development Bank and at the UN headquarters, prevented people from calling him pompous. Everyone knew that when he retired from the IAS in three years, he would be able to take his pick of plum jobs at the IMF, the UN or some similar organisation.

In the three months following the public announcement of the successful beta-testing of his product, Satyan had flown down to Delhi several times and Bannerjee had put him in touch with several ministers in the Central government. He had tried, without success so far, to get them interested enough to outlay the funds he needed to develop it commercially.

When the two men had settled down at the nineteenth hole with their beer, Satyan brought up the topic of the software.

'I spoke to the industry minister, Sam,' said Satyan, stretching his legs out into the warm December sunshine.

Even Rubita, his fiancée, always called her father 'Sam', unlike the typical Indian daughter. But then neither Sam Bannerjee nor his daughter were typical. Both were ambitious, hard-driving professionals and prominent figures in their respective worlds. And to Sam Bannerjee's delight, Rubita had selected a young man of as much stature and strength for a mate.

He looked over the rim of his glass at Satyan who continued, 'No bloody luck. The man is either a dolt or on the take. He just wouldn't spend more than ten minutes listening to me – and that was only because of your letter of introduction. And he couldn't have made it plainer that he was bored with the whole thing.'

'Hang on, my boy,' Bannerjee sympathised. 'You need patience when dealing with the government. Don't worry, we'll find you a buyer and then they'll all fall into line like so many dominoes.'

'The sooner, the better. I'm holding onto a very talented team of professionals back in Mumbai. They can always get better money elsewhere, but they're still sticking by me out of sheer personal loyalty. I don't know for how long, though. These guys were so charged up when the beta went through. Now it's been three months of no action. It's a wonder none of them has put in his papers yet.'

'This software of yours – you said it was a worldwide first, too, didn't you?'

'Yeah, Sam. There are others in the US which try to achieve the same results, but my Epsilon-6 has several features which have been created for the first time.' Then he looked up sharply, 'Do you have something in mind?'

'Well,' said Bannerjee, stroking his chin. 'I don't know whether we can pull it off, but I could try to explore possibilities with my contacts in the US. You know, what you need to do to click with those bumpkins who run the government in Delhi is credibility. It just struck me that there would be no better way to establish that than by getting American firms to buy your product.

'Nobody in India respects the white man more than the descendants of our freedom fighters who now sit at the helm as our lords and masters. In our country we have democratically created the tyranny of ignorance, eh, Satyan? This wall of ignorance can only be broken down by ramming it with certificates from the white man. If that is how the game has to be played to get things done in Delhi, so be it. What do you say?'

Satyan grinned. The old man had hit the nail on the head with his usual accuracy. Tyranny of ignorance – that was a good one. He looked up, his eyes dancing. 'Why not, Sam? If we can crack the American market, my boys will be only too pleased and so, for that matter, will I. More than the money it's the recognition as a world-class team. And who knows, after the Americans, the British, the Germans, the French…maybe even the Japanese?'

'Then I'll get on to it right away,' said Bannerjee with a decisive nod. He snapped his fingers to beckon a passing waiter. 'I'll ring up old Hank Sherman at Schlumberger tonight. It'll catch him in a relaxed Saturday morning mood, hopefully. We ought to be able to make some progress by next weekend.

'But what is this weak-minded attitude of yours, young man? Belittling the value of money? The trouble with you folks is that you allow yourselves to get carried away by your emotions. The Americans think big – and "big" to them means expensive. Pitch it right and you could be spinning money out of them. If you're smart enough to play with them, you have to aim to be a billionaire, not a piffling millionaire.'

'Seriously, Sam, I don't want to think too much about money just yet. My goal is to achieve more than that. I want to build a world-class software house in India.' Satyan had a faraway gleam in his eye. 'I'm in the investment mode right now,' he added.

'Tchah, you need to change your approach,' Bannerjee retorted with asperity. He leaned back with his replenished glass and continued, 'This country has long suffered from a heavy dose of spiritualistic self-denial. If you want to be one of those who makes the world go round, you need Vitamin M – and no one ever has too much of it.'

They were still arguing the point when they went into the club house for lunch.

◆

Satyan had hoped to get American mining firms interested in his Epsilon-6 software but was surprised that, after his first meeting with Hank Sherman, Sam Bannerjee's contact in Schlumberger, the US army also showed interest. In fact, it was the Pentagon which contacted him rather than the other way around, since Satyan neither had the intention nor the ability to initiate negotiations with the US military establishment. He wondered briefly how the Pentagon had got onto his breakthrough. He guessed that it may have been informed by Sherman. It wasn't a convincing answer but he felt that there would be time enough later to find out if and when the discussions went forward. In any case, the Pentagon's expression of interest was a confirmation, if confirmation was needed, that he had in his hands a world-class product.

Three visits and five weeks later, he was close to wrapping up a deal with the Pentagon for approximately five million dollars. He had tried to figure out the military applications his prospective client had in mind. By all accounts, the Pentagon already had surveillance systems that were decades ahead of the world. He couldn't imagine why they would be interested in paying such a huge sum for his software. In the end, he had given up on guessing their motives and decided to go with the flow.

On the third visit, ostensibly at the invitation of Princeton University, but really to have the next round of discussions with military officials, he had chanced upon Rajan Swaminathan, who was there to attend an academic conference. The two had immediately warmed to each other.

When Rajan heard about the software's capabilities, he was astounded by the scale of the breakthrough. More importantly, he was quick to see the immense value the software could add to the Indo-Uzbek howitzer's design. He immediately got down to convincing Satyan to hold back on the deal with the Americans until he gave his own country a fair chance to acquire the technology at a good price, even if it wasn't top dollar.

Jake Mehta's reaction when Satyan rang to tell him that evening from his hotel room about the new twist in the tale was not enthusiastic. Quite the contrary and to his puzzlement, Satyan found his technical right-hand man pointedly cold to the suggestion of calling off the negotiations with the Pentagon.

'Satyan, we know how corrupt the Indian government can be and this howitzer deal you're talking about can run into big time money. Maybe several hundred crores. Every minister and babu who can stick his dirty finger into the pie will try his damnedest to get into the action,' he warned. 'Man, those bastards will squeeze until the whole bloody thing is bled dry. Why get into a snake pit?'

'But, Jake, if my own country wants this then I'll be disloyal if I don't give it a chance first. Don't you see? And anyway, buddy, leave the dirty work to me. I've got connections and I know how to play the game.'

'Satyan, the Indian government, infact any government, has wheels within wheels and the files for big projects get pushed around from ministry to ministry until everyone has figured out how much his share is going to be. We could get stuck for years.'

Satyan pounced on the opening. 'Yeah right, every government has wheels within wheels. Same goes for the US, Jake. If we've got to choose between a rock and a hard place, let's go with our own people, man.'

'But, Satyan, the Pentagon is far more professional. They'll pay a great deal more, and if we close a deal with them our stock in the world market will rocket sky-high. You've got to stall this Swaminathan cat, man. For a few days, that's all I'm asking. Just see how fast the US army moves. And Maggie knows someone in the Pentagon who can push things, if that should become necessary.'

Satyan saw that the conversation was getting sticky. Jake, much to his surprise, seemed to be digging his heels in. Though he didn't want to, Satyan knew the time had come to pull rank on his close friend. 'Jake, I'm taking a call on this one. We'll go with the Indian government.' There was a strained silence that followed. Satyan decided to soften the blow a bit and continued, 'Okay, I'll give the Indian government a deadline to decide. Then we'll do what you say.'

'Come on, Satyan, how can you give the Indian government a deadline? They'll slam us, come down on us like a ton of bricks, just for thinking of something like that. Talk sense.'

A hard edge crept into Satyan's voice. 'Jake, I'm taking the call, okay? Let's drop this conversation.' Saying a hurried goodbye, he cut the connection off. He was feeling very upset and poured a stiff measure of Scotch to calm himself. Looking out of the window of his fifth floor hotel room, he cast his mind back over the last few years. This was the first major difference of opinion on a business issue he had had with Jake since PSN was set up. What was more galling was that he had not expected his deputy to take such a stand when his own country's honour was at stake. He decided that he must tell Jake to leave his wife Maggie out of any further discussions because the software could soon become militarily sensitive and she was still an American citizen. During her several visits to India, he had seen no signs of Maggie wanting to shift her base to Mumbai. He knew that with each passing year it was going to become more difficult to convince her to make the move. Over the years their sons had started school, made their circle of friends and got into the groove of life in the US. He knew that it would be hard on Jake, but Satyan could see no other option.

Once more Satyan felt irritated at Jake's intransigence. If there were potential military uses of his software, the issue went beyond business considerations. He was disappointed that Jake had not been able to rise above base commercial interests. A nagging doubt sprang up in his mind. Would Jake become susceptible to divided loyalties and become a vulnerable link inside his own team? With a shudder, he pushed the thought out of his mind. He convinced himself that it was just Jake's forthrightness that had led to the argument and now that the decision had been taken, his innate sense of right and wrong would cut off any dissension. He turned his mind back to the present. He was to meet the American military's chief negotiator the next day and wanted to go over his strategy with Rajan Swaminathan over dinner.

The next day he faced the US army officials with some trepidation. He needed a credible excuse to back out of the deal because playing games with an organisation as powerful as the Pentagon could be dangerous. In previous meetings, Satyan had sized up Colonel Braithwaite, the chief negotiator, as a tough nut to crack.

'Well, Mr Sharma, I hope you find our offer for Epsilon-6 good enough,' Braithwaite said, after they had settled themselves in the colonel's office. 'It's not every day that the Pentagon pays five million dollars for a piece of software. Here's the contract. I'm sure you'll find it in good order.'

Satyan leafed through the six-page document. 'I'll have to get this examined by my lawyers before I sign, Colonel,' he replied. And then he spotted what he was looking for. 'What's this? Why would you want the contract to be valid indefinitely, Colonel Braithwaite? I thought this was a straight deal for buying a user license of the software. That would most certainly have to be for a specified time limit. You can't make it valid for all time.'

'No, no, Mr Sharma. This is only to cover upgrades. In our experience, software can change beyond recognition within a few years as newer versions are released. And we must join hands to keep ahead of the commie wolf pack.' The colonel grinned.

'Sure, but I hadn't offered you the upgrades, Colonel. I haven't even planned them with any degree of clarity yet.' Satyan glanced at the colonel to see how the lie was going down. Braithwaite was barely able to suppress a frown. 'I need to think this through. Shouldn't you be offering me something extra for each upgrade?'

'Well, young man, remember you're talking to the Pentagon, eh? We always buy software at prices that include upgrades. If you want to do business with Uncle Sam, Mr Sharma, you had better learn that.' The colonel was puffing himself up. 'All the software guys we work with play by these rules. Even the big ones, I'll have you know. This condition is non-negotiable.'

Satyan's eyes had narrowed into dark pinpoints and he smiled grimly. 'Colonel, I have no particular compulsion to do business with the US army.' He knew that the message had gone home – the colonel realised immediately that he had gone a bit too far. 'However, as you say, I might like to do business with someone who wants to sock it to the commies. But I will have to rethink on the upgrades. I am going to reserve my rights on that one.' He was spoiling for a fight and the colonel fought down the urge to give him an excuse.

Satyan continued to leaf through the pages, taking his time, trying to bring his emotions under control. He needed more loopholes. He would have to cover the possibility of Uncle Sam deciding to cough up the extra money. Then he found one. Putting on a thoughtful frown, he jabbed a finger at a page. 'And this point, Colonel. This is also new to me. A first right of refusal to you if I want to sell Epsilon-6 to anybody else. Why would you need that?'

'Oh, just standard Pentagonese, Mr Sharma. Naturally, being a military organisation, the Pentagon would like to keep a tab on these things. Shouldn't bother you.'

Satyan shook his head. 'Colonel, I'm not sure I would like to tie myself down in that way. Look, this is the chance I and my team back in Pure Space Networks have been waiting for to break into the international market. There are dozens of applications, military and otherwise, that Epsilon-6 can tap. I can't sign away our rights on just one sale.'

Braithwaite had had enough. 'Mr Sharma,' he said, his voice low and hard, 'we have been very patient with you. Our influence permeates the entire globe. Bear that in mind. We will go all out to encourage you in marketing this product to legitimate, peaceful users once we reach an agreement on the sale. But if our negotiations should flounder...' He paused for a dramatic effect. 'Surely, you realise the implications for your business? Let me suggest that you don't do anything hasty. Uncle Sam is a straight-shooting partner once you come on board. But be assured that we expect the same from you as well.'

Satyan's smile was glacial. 'Colonel, Pure Space is perfectly capable of pursuing its best interests. But we do believe in fair play, you know. So, if the Pentagon needs all these clauses built in, surely you appreciate that we will have to rework our pricing?' The colonel could find no effective counter.

'Good day, Colonel, we'll be in touch.'

◆

Jamila Barkhatiev had the most beautiful eyes Rajan Swaminathan had ever seen. Looking at them across the table amidst the boisterous Saturday night crowd at the Black Cadillac, the most happening pub in downtown Bangalore, he was completely oblivious to the racket all around.

The light brown of her irises was flecked with delicate touches of dark amber. They reminded him of the autumn leaves that would float down as he drove Jamila around on her father's old Czech-made

Jawa along poplar-lined country roads near her native Samarkand. For the umpteenth time that day, Rajan found himself transported back to the long, lazy Sunday afternoons spent with her in the beautiful Uzbek countryside. Stopping on a whim, they would lie side by side in the tall grass, her soft hair nuzzling his cheeks as they snuggled together against the cold October wind. Or he would listen to her play the flute against the background of the waves whispering at the lakeside. He sensed again the fragrance of her body after they made love under the open sky.

In the three years since he began working with his old professor on the howitzer, Rajan had made several trips to the National Defence Research Facility, which had come up after Uzbekistan's declaration of independence from the USSR. The facility had been set up near Samarkand, the location chosen expressly for the convenience of the eminent scientist. While Barkhatiev supervised the ballistics, Rajan's team in India was working out the sophisticated computer programs which would control the operation of the gun. The gun was designed specifically to operate on the punishing slopes of the most remote reaches of the Himalayan and Hindu Kush mountains. Its onboard computer console was capable of mapping out trajectories under battle conditions with such great precision that it could fire a shell weighing twenty kilograms at a target as small as a foxhole from fifty kilometres away. But that was in ideal conditions. Now, in collaboration with Satyan Sharma's Pure Space Networks, it was being fitted with state-of-the-art GPS software, which would enable the gun to reproduce this accuracy regardless of terrain, ambient wind or weather. The crowning achievement of all their lives was now close to becoming a reality.

Rajan and Jamila had gradually but inevitably fallen in love. And while they had not yet discussed it with her father, there was a tacit understanding that when all this was over, they would get married. Old man Barkhatiev approved and he was sure that her mother would have too, had she been alive. He couldn't, however, stifle the pangs he felt at the thought that Jamila would soon leave him to settle in India. For the old professor, his daughter was one of the two reasons that made life worth living.

The other reason was his life's work which, with the gun's design almost complete, was close to reaching its most sublime expression. His path-breaking inventions in the field of ballistics and recoil dissipation, which had been rudely interrupted by political events nobody could have foretold, were now about to take tangible shape, thanks to the encouragement from his newly reborn nation's government. Barkhatiev was conscious of the fact that the Uzbek defence ministry supported him out of somewhat questionable motives. He was not too sure that he wouldn't be putting his inventions in the hands of trigger-happy governments run by gangsters rather than statesmen. But Barkhatiev was happy that it was his own motherland that would benefit from his efforts rather than a distant European power like Russia.

This time, it had been Barkhatiev's turn to visit India and the old man and his daughter had been camping at the Defence Research and Development Organisation in Bangalore for the past two weeks. Having seen the two youngsters off for a Saturday night jaunt, he settled down in his suite to work out the bugs which had emerged in the simulations over the past few days.

It was almost midnight when the headlights of Rajan's battered 1974 Fiat turned into the driveway of the DRDO guesthouse. Standing at the first floor window of his suite, Barkhatiev waved excitedly to the twosome as they got out and headed for the portico. They entered his room to find him so excited that he could barely contain himself. He grabbed Rajan's wrist and led him to his laptop. It was connected over a secure line to the computer in the research facility so that the professor could continue working from the guesthouse.

'I've been busy while you good-for-nothings have been wasting your time,' he said with a twinkle in his eye. 'I was wondering if you have the inclination to take a look at some of my calculations now, Rajan. I think I may have solved the problem of the tertiary orthogonal retractor.'

'Wow, that's fantastic, sir!' Rajan exclaimed. 'Of course I'll go through them now.' As they settled down to study the professor's latest breakthrough, Jamila went to the kitchenette to fix them a snack.

An hour later, the windows of the first floor suite continued to glow.

The watcher in the nondescript Maruti van parked on a hill about a quarter of a kilometre from the guesthouse gates sighed wearily. He decided to call it a day. On his way home, he pulled in at an all-night petrol station and then went into the phone booth to dial an unlisted number at the Russian Embassy in Delhi.

◆

The Sharmas' palatial 1940s bungalow had the old-world charm of colonial India. It stood on a quiet, tree-lined avenue in the upscale neighbourhood of Khar, a stone's throw away from Mumbai's busy Linking Road. A passerby strolling down the avenue could see, over the 15-foot high wall which surrounded the building, a line of Ashoka treetops which screened the upper floor from the sun's rays. The house faced west and only a single line of low bungalows separated it from the rocky shoreline of the Arabian Sea. Rattan chairs, long and comfortable, lay scattered about on the wide second-floor balcony which looked serenely onto the sea.

It was close to one a.m. when the large wrought-iron gates swung open to allow a black Lexus in. Satyan Sharma slid the car onto a driveway bordered by a wild growth of bougainvillea on the right, behind which lay a sprawling but well-manicured lawn. To the left was a long bed of flowers bisected by a rock garden. At the end of the flowerbed was a greenhouse. The flowerbed, the lawn and the greenhouse represented the only surviving passion of Satyan's widowed father, once the lord and master of 'Ashiana' – the Sharmas' home.

Operating the remote-controlled doors of the garage, he parked the Lexus between a flaming yellow-and-black Ferrari and a rugged green Land Rover. Leaning on its stand in a corner was a twenty-year-old Harley Davidson 500cc touring motorcycle, cared for lovingly by Satyan himself. He climbed out and stepped around to open the door for his passenger – a tall, slim girl in a shimmering evening gown. As she stepped out, the slit in the gown revealed the long firm curves of her legs.

Rubita Bannerjee had broken several hearts when she accepted Satyan's proposal for marriage. Few could deny, though, that they made a handsome pair. Since they had announced their engagement six months ago, scarcely a week passed when they did not appear in the city's society columns. They were sought after in every event where Mumbai's cognoscenti gathered. Both of them had hectic work schedules – she was a tv journalist and he was occupied in rebuilding the family business – which gave them very few opportunities to spend time together.

They had just returned from a quiet evening with very close friends at the Belvedere Club. Satyan held her hand as they walked to the front door and entered the house. They walked into the library for a nightcap and saw the slim envelope lying on the coffee table as soon as they turned on the lights. It had the large seal of Ashoka lions which meant that it was a document from the Government of India. Satyan's pulse quickened as he slit it open. It contained just one typewritten sheet. He ran his eye over the few lines and let out a whoop of joy. Turning to his fiancée, he swept her into his arms and did a little jig around the room.

'I've done it, Rubita! I've won! The gun has cleared the first leg of field trials. From now on, it will just be fine-tuning the details. We're going to show the world.' He laughed happily into her startled face as he swirled her around the room.

'Hey, hey, put me down! Look what you're doing to my dress!' She looked down in mock anger at his dancing eyes. He turned the lights off, leaving only the soft glow from the streetlamps to permeate the room through the bay windows. He hopped about in glee. Her evening gown had ridden up above her knees. Her elaborate coiffure had come undone in the sudden flurry, long strands flowing across his upturned face as she clung desperately to his neck. He swung her about, waltzing unsteadily around the coffee table.

'Unhand me at once, sir,' she said sternly. 'Is this any way to treat a lady?'

He brought her down gently and, thrusting a foot behind him, bowed with a flourish. 'A thousand pardons, milady. Your humble servant got carried away and forgot himself. Your smallest wish is my command.'

'It would be meet to mark this occasion with a toast,' she said, continuing in the same vein.

He snapped his fingers. 'An excellent suggestion, mademoiselle! As I recall, a bottle of Dom Perignon has been awaiting just such an occasion.'

Indulgently, she watched him potter about with the glasses. For a man who was the rising star of India's new breed of aggressive and dynamic entrepreneurs, Satyan could be ingenuously childlike when the fancy caught him. In the past few months, she had seen him getting carried away, more often than ever, while giving her updates on the progress of his new software. To be sure, there had been moments when she had seen dark pinpoints of rage appear in his eyes when he sometimes received calls in her presence from government officials, asking all types of puerile questions. Satyan seemed to have a visceral dislike of officialdom and its eternally corrupt denizens. Often it was the timely intervention of her father Sam Bannerjee that would defuse a potentially explosive situation.

But of late Satyan had become more buoyant as he neared the end of this long road and he would often slip into a happy childlike state. Many a time, she had to sit with a tolerant smile when a chance remark would set off a heated discussion about some technical point over dinner with his team of software designers. Formulae and flow charts would be put down on paper napkins, envelopes – just about any scrap of paper found lying around. Invariably, these impromptu sessions would stretch well into the small hours of morning. Rubita had learnt fast; after the first couple of times, she would make her excuses and beat a graceful retreat. Though, to her regret at such times, Satyan would barely notice.

She knew how much the project meant to him. For seven years he had struggled to turn the business around. Now, at last, the doors to global success were opening for him.

She put Duke Ellington on the CD player. The night air welled with the lilting tune. They clinked their glasses in a silent toast. Silently, their bodies entwined, they waltzed around the centre table. No words were necessary. His free hand caressed her hips, twisting her gown out of the way. Rubita tossed her long black hair off her face. She looked at him expectantly. He focused on her lips, glistening in the half light. He felt the rush return to his body, differently this time. He leaned in and pressed his lips against hers. She closed her eyes and pulled him tightly to her. His hand travelled up her waist and she trembled with anticipation as it brushed against her bra. She plunged her tongue into his mouth, gasping with pleasure as his fingers wrapped around her nipple, arousing her. The flavour of the wine mingled intoxicatingly with the taste of each other's lips. The glasses dropped from their hands, falling soundlessly on the thick carpet.

The dark night sky gazed patiently on the two lovers as they lay on the floor, locked together for a long time afterward.

3

The party to celebrate the first birthday of the first grandson of Shri Ram Niranjan Pandey, honourable Minister of State for Home and the number two man in one of the most powerful ministries in the country, was turning out to be an unqualified success.

The poolside of the Maurya Sheraton Hotel was glittering, as much from the coloured lights as from the diamond jewellery nestling in the deep bosoms of society matrons. 'Pandey-ji', as he was generally known, was very happy with the turnout. This was a clear demonstration of his rapidly growing influence among the political and business circles of the Indian capital. The first birthday of a scion of the family has always been a big occasion in aristocratic Indian families. That there was not an ounce of blue blood in his veins did not deter Pandey-ji one bit – he knew that he was part of the new aristocracy of independent India. He had ensured that at least three generations of his brood would live lavishly after him. He himself was a second-generation politician. His father had won his reputation during the struggle for India's independence and had been a Member of Parliament until his death ten years ago. Pandey-ji had reaped fully the benefits of his father's dedication and honesty. Basking in the aura of his father's integrity and unstinting Gandhism, Pandey-ji had capitalised on the faith the rustic voting public placed in him.

His massive face wore a genial look as he accepted the compliments of the assembled VIPs. After twenty-five years in politics, Pandey-ji had well and truly arrived, and the future looked exceedingly bright. A year ago, Pandey-ji had been given the post of the Minister of

State for Home. With the right moves, a senior position in the cabinet could be his before the year was out. He needed just one good opportunity to demonstrate his loyalty and usefulness to the nation's first family.

His eyes scanned the assembled guests for the Frenchman. He had clearly instructed Prakash-ji, his trusted aide from his hometown Darbhanga in Bihar, to ensure that Shri Leconte sahib would not miss this party.

Pandey-ji gathered the folds of his dhoti and, pursing his lips, directed a frothing red jet of betel juice at a nearby palm tree before bidding a welcoming 'namaste' to the tall, gaunt figure approaching him through the throng. It was Baba Sarvate who was in Delhi to preside over the South Asian Ecological Conference beginning the next day. The baba was a hermetical person and Pandey-ji considered it quite a public relations coup to have him attend this party. These days, people seemed to think that environment consciousness was the most fashionable movement in Delhi and that was enough for Pandey-ji. He had made it a point to demonstrate his solidarity with whatever was the current rage. And if he had to endure the boring company of environmental activists like Sarvate, so be it. Not two weeks ago, he had spent a whole Sunday afternoon with his youngest son, trying to commit to memory some of the jargon of what the firangis called the 'Green Movement'.

Checking quickly to ensure that journalists were within earshot, Pandey-ji smiled expansively and greeted Sarvate in a booming voice. 'Arre, Baba-ji! What a great honour to have you as my guest! Thank you, thank you so much for coming. How was your journey to Delhi? Why is your hand empty? What will you have, whisky or beer? Or some soft drink?'

'Nothing, thank you, Pandey-ji,' said Sarvate, who was a teetotaller and a devout Gandhian. He had come to this party for the sole purpose of petitioning the minister. Several attempts to meet the minister at his office had been futile, since Sarvate was not able to get past the indifferent underlings who infested every ministry.

Barely concealing his disdain for the man before him, he said, 'You see, I make it a point to retire early, at 8 p.m. every day. It's past eight already, so please excuse me if I come straight to the point. Pandey-ji, you must intervene and sanction compensation for all those poor villagers evicted because of the Sone Dam. The matter has stretched for seven years with no end in sight. The human resources ministry has raised some objection or other but the plight of these poor people continues. I am appealing to you since it concerns your home state. Surely you will not ignore the pleas of helpless villagers who live so close to your own backyard?' A couple of journalists began edging closer. Pandey-ji cursed himself mentally.

'But, Baba-ji, even the law ministry has yet to give the necessary clearances. As you know, the matter is still under their consideration.' Pandey-ji knew that this was a weak reply and stole a glance at the reporters to see how it was going down.

'That is precisely the point, Pandey-ji. We have appealed without success for interim relief pending the findings, which the government has consistently refused to consider.'

The pack of wolves was closing in and Pandey-ji decided he wanted out and fast. 'But of course, Baba-ji. If an eminent saint like you has taken up the cause, who am I to turn away? I will see what I can do. Let us meet tomorrow and discuss it,' said the minister, casting about for a tactical retreat. His trusted aide, Prakash-ji, stepped in quickly to divert the petitioner, working out the details of the next day's appointment while Pandey-ji ducked away with a cheery wave.

Some distance away, he spotted Mrs Goswamy, the wife of one of the leading real estate developers in Delhi. She caught his eye and smiled, weaving through the crowd towards him. She was in her mid-thirties and, arguably, one of the most desirable women on the cocktail circuit. Her deep-cut blouses and captivating cleavage were the toast of the corridors of power. She certainly knew how to make the most of her physical assets. Striding straight up to him, she leaned over to whisper urgently into his ear. Pandey-ji could see down her blouse and was mesmerised. He felt a surge of desire rush through his veins. At that precise moment, she looked into his eyes and smiled; there was no mistaking the open invitation. Pandey-ji knew that it was another tribute to his growing power that women like Mrs Goswamy welcomed his attention. Well past fifty, he knew that his obese body held no physical attraction for the opposite sex. He didn't give a damn. He understood the reason for her invitation. With an experienced and unerring nose for power, she had sought him out. And, as he knew, her favours were sought by the most powerful in the capital. Pandey-ji was climbing up the pecking order.

What pleased him even more was the whispered message: 'Leconte sahib is here, Pandey-ji, and he was asking for you just two minutes ago.'

Without waiting for a reply, she led him towards a group where the Frenchman was the centre of a circle of guests who were obviously angling for various favours. Pandey-ji allowed his eyes to linger on the sway of her hips as she made her way through the crowd. He made a mental note to tell Prakash-ji to get the farmhouse renovated quickly. A fling with her would be well worth the contract or two she would surely ask him to swing for her husband's firm.

'Pandey-ji, what a lovely party! Thank you for giving me a chance to meet so many *old* friends again,' Arnaud Leconte turned to meet his host in a tone which was pleasant enough, but conveyed to Pandey-ji's sensitive ears that he was being beleaguered by people he barely knew and would like to be rid of. Smoothly, Pandey-ji told the crowd of hangers-on that there was a sitar performance in the adjoining hall and that it would be a shame if they were to miss the performance by a maestro. Pandey-ji snapped his fingers and Prakash-ji materialised beside him, instantly took his cue and shepherded the crowd indoors. Mrs Goswamy had, with an elegant wave of her hand, melted away into the crowd. Leconte smiled his thanks and took Pandey-ji by the elbow, guiding him purposefully towards a couple of chairs in a quiet corner.

Arnaud Leconte's star had been on the ascendant ever since India's prime minister had begun the drive towards a liberalised economy. What had started long ago as a college acquaintanceship in France between his yet-to-be wife and an elegant and charming young French heiress had, over the last five years, become his ticket to ride the gravy train. For that young heiress had been going steady with the son of an Indian minister, who had risen in the hierarchy and was now the deputy prime minister.

The Lecontes had shifted to India when Arnaud took over as country manager for the French telecom giant which had been promised lucrative business in India. His wife, Fiona, continued her friendship with the lovely but lonely daughter-in-law of one of the country's most powerful families. The bond between the two families strengthened despite the persistent gossip that Leconte was using his position to gain out of turn considerations for a growing list of multinational corporations jockeying for prize government contracts. Leconte did not ignore such talk, nor did he ignore the sometimes uncannily accurate press stories about his financial shenanigans. He merely used his considerable tact and discretion to ensure that these stories were scotched and consigned to the dustbin of public memory. This was the way business was conducted in any third world country.

Leconte had survived in Delhi by walking the tightrope between commercial and political interests. It was as if he were operating in a specialised field of business, his competitors being other influence peddlers, each having built up his asset base of contacts through some special combination of skill and circumstance. He knew that, being a foreigner, one wrong move on his part could bring a swift end to his dream run. However, he had a great insurance policy. The deputy prime minister would be hypersensitive to actions which could be cast by the ruling party into an international conspiracy hatched by a readily visible 'foreign hand', so he could be depended upon to mount rapid and effective damage control before any scandals got out of hand. Fortunately for him, politics in India had become more and more commercialised and politicians at all levels had turned the whole business of governance into a vast money-spinning game. And, as in all thriving businesses, nobody in the establishment wanted to rock the boat – not even the so-called 'opposition parties'.

And now, the Indian economy had become large and diversified enough to support a steady stream of big money investment from all parts of the globe. Business opportunities were booming, new sectors were opening up. But the biggest business of them all, the one with the highest rate of return, was politics itself. Political parties were outlaying huge expenses to fight elections and were always under tremendous pressure to repay their patrons in cash or in kind. Powerbrokers were having a field day controlling huge flows of money.

And since Leconte had extensive contacts in the huge and booming Indian telecom sector, as well as the ear of several of the biggest political leaders in the land, his name inspired awe and a grudging respect among this tribe.

As they settled down in spacious cane chairs, Pandey-ji caught a fleeting look of sharp appraisal from his companion. He was instantly alert. This was not going to be a casual party chat. Snapping his fingers again, he gestured to a hovering steward who darted quickly towards the bar. Leconte sahib's preference for Campari on the rocks was too well known among the capital's five-star hotels to require any special instructions. Pandey-ji was partial to Black Dog.

Leconte had reverted to his genial self, making small talk with the minister as they waited for their drinks. His cautious manner indicated clearly to Pandey-ji that Leconte had a load on his mind. These white skins were so obvious, Pandey-ji thought. He did not waste energy trying to speculate on the nature of the Frenchman's burden; he knew that all would be revealed soon. He was sure that this conversation was going to lead to some critical juncture of his political career. He would have to gauge the situation carefully to use it to maximum advantage. And since a wise negotiator never opens proceedings, he waited for the Frenchman to reveal whatever agenda he had. A ripple of applause reached them from within the hall as the sitar maestro made his appearance.

When they had been served and the waiter had made a discreet withdrawal, Leconte finally said, 'So, Pandey-ji, how was your trip to Lakhimpur last week?'

So it was the gun deal, thought the minister, taken aback. Pandey-ji had been at Lakhimpur to witness the tests of the mountain guns that the defence ministry was considering for purchase. He had been invited by the deputy PM himself. But his presence had been hush-

hush since he did not have any obvious reason for being there, more so because the intense jockeying for position between him and the defence minister was well known. Funny thing was that he hadn't heard of Leconte sniffing around this one so far, yet the Frenchman knew. The deal had been cloaked in heavy secrecy and Leconte was not known to involve himself in military matters. Sign of the changing times, he reckoned. With the rapidly changing technology, telecom must be closely linked with armaments. He could think of no other explanation. He was quite ignorant about the global arms industry and it had been a mystery to him when the deputy PM had asked him to attend the tests. And here was the Frenchman, seeking him out with the express intention of discussing a matter that was far removed from both his jurisdiction and competence.

So, in his opening remark Pandey-ji played dumb. 'Leconte sahib, what can I say? Our country has so much to progress before we can raise our heads in pride. I am happy to inform you that I have secured the largest irrigation project in eastern India for my poor state. It is indeed fortunate that my honourable colleague, the agriculture minister, and I see eye to eye on this matter.'

'Yes, that's good news indeed. And how did you find the demonstrations of the 155-mm howitzers? I believe you were among those present.'

'Ah, yes Leconte sahib. It so happened that they took place while I was in the vicinity. The deputy PM sahib specially asked me to be present since I happened to be there. We have become very close nowadays as you have no doubt observed since you know him so well.'

'Yes indeed. The deputy PM is a very good judge of character,' said Leconte, playing along. 'Tell me, Pandey-ji, since you are a man of this world and your judgment is also one to be valued, what was your assessment of the Uzbek gun?'

'Leconte sahib, you know that I am ignorant about these technical things. The deputy PM thinks he belongs to the new generation – he is technically inclined himself. He knows best. I am his humble servant and follow his orders. I can only tell you what I could gather from the conversation. In fact, the defence minister sahib was putting forward to the PM sahib a case for a further sanction of a hundred crore rupees for the next stage of the development. This decision will probably be announced by the defence minister sahib next Friday.'

'Pandey-ji, the FIAM people approached me because their finance director is a good friend of mine. You must have heard of FIAM; it is one of Europe's leading military equipment manufacturers. It has been in the forefront of heavy artillery technology since World War II. Now, the finance director told me that, apparently, the test was not conducted under the most exacting conditions. Unfortunately, the honourable defence minister was not able to appreciate their point of view and told them that he would go by the word of the army committee. If such an important decision were to be taken purely because the Uzbek gun is cheaper, then it could only harm the interests of your country.'

'Leconte sahib, I know you hold the interests of this poor country close to your heart. But I fail to understand how I can do anything in this matter. The tests are over and the final report of the army committee is awaited. What can be done at this stage?'

Leconte smiled. 'Pandey-ji, I consider this country my adopted home. But, you see, I cannot be seen to be closely involved in a defence matter. The press is not mature enough to see that few arms purchases are made in the world today without the active collaboration of experienced transnational corporations. They would only create endless trouble for your dynamic PM, and India would lose on as fine a piece of weaponry as the world has ever seen. In fact,' said Leconte, dropping his voice to a barely audible whisper, 'the PM himself told me that he favoured the FIAM gun but the defence minister was not able to understand the larger issue involved. He seems to be toeing the line of the army committee, particularly Lieutenant General Sapru. The good general is a sound technical man, but he tends to view everything from a narrow technical perspective. He does not seem to realise that there are larger interests involved.'

In a few words, Leconte had shown Pandey-ji how the battle lines were drawn. What he had not known until now was that the PM was in favour of this foreign company. And now the Frenchman had as good as said that the PM wanted him, Pandey-ji, to intervene. Well, if the PM was depending on his faithful servant to tackle the intransigent defence minister, the pleasure would be doubled. Not only would he ingratiate himself with the PM but, with the same stroke, deliver a telling blow to the fortunes of one of his most important competitors in the ruling party's rat race. But how big were the stakes? And how could he, as a member of the home ministry, intervene?

As if reading the minister's mind, Leconte continued, 'Yesterday the PM told me that he was quite impressed by your proposals to make the paramilitary forces under your ministry, such as the ITBP and the BSF, more effective in controlling border skirmishes before they become serious. As you have also pointed out several times, insurgent groups today are being armed and trained by the armies of India's neighbours to the north and west. It is becoming increasingly difficult to maintain law and order in the border states without the direct involvement of the Indian army. The PM feels that this excellent force has always been conceived of as non-political but if the present situation persists, the army will continue to be dragged against its will into India's internal conflicts.' Pandey-ji was thinking hard now, wondering where this new line of thought was leading. 'Conflicts which, if I may add, the ITBP and BSF are best placed to handle. If only they were equipped and trained to act like military outfits.' Pandey-ji caught the drift. The role of his home ministry was now clear to him.

'Yes, Leconte sahib. As you say, modern equipment is essential for any fighting force, be it military or paramilitary. I think the PM would be keen to equip the ITBP and BSF with the latest weaponry, even big artillery such as howitzers, to ensure that the army need not get dragged into every little conflict on the border. It is a sad fact of modern India that terrorists and insurgents are so well-equipped and trained by countries seeking to destabilise their poor neighbours.' Leconte and Pandey-ji shook their heads in dismay at the state of affairs as they sipped their drinks. 'But tell me, Leconte sahib, maybe the home ministry will also have to be consulted on the choice of the gun but, with such a strong range of technical opinion lined up in favour of the Uzbek-Indian gun, what counterarguments can I offer at this stage to review the decision?'

Leconte leaned forward, sure of the kill now. 'FIAM is a company with a global turnover of more than twenty-five billion dollars, Pandey-ji. That, in Indian rupees, is nearly a hundred thousand crore rupees. Really, really big. They have experience dealing with many third world countries and understand the concerns of people who are involved in such decisions.' The two men exchanged meaningful glances at this point. Leconte lowered his voice again and Pandey-ji strained to catch the words. 'I give you my personal guarantee, Pandey-ji. FIAM will give serious consideration to all your requirements and nobody will be left unhappy. This deal is extremely critical to them. Not only will they be grateful for your cooperation, but so will be the PM himself.' The implication was clear that there was more than just money in this deal for Pandey-ji.

The Minister of State smiled at last. 'You are a man of the world, Leconte sahib. If the two of us can understand each other so well, what is left to be said? Come, I see that our sitar maestro has nearly finished the *alaap* and we will be just in time for the main part of his performance.'

4

The stream of workers pouring in through the gates of the EMMG factory in Andheri parted to make way for the Lexus. The young owner of the firm was always at his desk at eight a.m. Like his father in his younger days and his grandfather before that, Satyan Sharma took immense pride in being a hands-on manager. He headed his firm's design team himself, and spent a good twenty hours each week in the spanking new R&D wing of Pure Space Networks, the jewel in the crown for his group of companies.

With his boyish good looks, a genuine concern for his colleagues, and an increasingly impressive track record in the global software scene, Satyan had become something of a hero to his employees. As the car drove up to the main building of EMMG, the workers smiled and nodded at their young chairman. The car pulled up under the portico of the main building. Satyan got out and ran up the steps. He joined the little crowd of staffers in the foyer to take the lift up to the third floor.

As he strode into his office he found that Mr Agarwal, his admin chief, was already waiting for him. He was a short, paunchy man in his late sixties, and had been one of his father's most trusted lieutenants. Satyan relied heavily on his savvy and experience in dealing with his employees.

'Why, Agarwal sahib, you're here very early today.' Satyan ushered the man into his cabin. 'Surely the workers aren't giving you any trouble so early in the day.'

Agarwal looked worried. 'This is no laughing matter, Satyan. I think you are going to have some trouble from Lakhan Singh Yadav today.'

'Yeah, the new star on Mumbai's trade union scene. But tell me,' he said, setting up the electric coffee-maker, 'when I have revised the pay scales only last year, how come Yadav has any followers at all among my people? I hadn't known that he was looking at EMMG until last week.'

'He started operating within our group only ten days ago. And it's not EMMG he is looking at – that union is sewn up tight by Srikant Raut.' Agarwal was referring to the ringleader of the main union which accounted for over eighty percent of the five-hundred-odd labour force of the group. 'Lakhan Singh knows that he cannot gain entry into our group through EMMG. He has enrolled about a dozen workers at Next Gen Tech.'

'So, what are a dozen men compared to Raut's four hundred? They will have to toe Raut's line. And, right now, I'm okay with him. Where's the problem? You've got to try and talk some sense into this dirty dozen soon, Agarwal sahib.'

'Yesterday, Lakhan Singh enrolled two men from PSN.'

Satyan froze. There were only a handful of 'non-management' staff at Pure Space Networks and they hadn't been unionised yet. He and Raut had informally agreed that Pure Space would be outside the ambit of the union boss's activities for five years. In return, they had renegotiated deals for the employees of EMMG and Next Gen Tech last year. He had wanted Pure Space to be free of union activity during the start-up years in order to retain total control of the software group from the ground up – a policy which had already begun paying off, judging by the calibre of talent that Pure Space had been attracting from across the globe. And now with the howitzer project under way, sensitive defence work was also going to be taken up by him, so he did not want outside influences to queer the pitch.

'Surely Raut is not going to stand quietly by while Yadav moves in, Agarwal sahib? What has he done about this?'

'Raut and Lakhan Singh had a showdown last week, over at Cambridge Textiles. Raut's men were severely beaten up. I have heard that control of Cambridge may go over to Lakhan Singh within the next few weeks. Lakhan Singh is a Lok Seva Dal man and believed to be very close to the supremo. And you know that Raut has opposed the Dal all these years.'

The 'Dal' was a dreaded name among Mumbai's business class, well known for enforcing its diktat on the streets through the use of armed force, showing scant regard for the metro's hapless police. Its supremo was a legendary ganglord turned politician with a Robin Hood-like policy of giving wealth to the poor by extorting it from the rich. Extortion was hardly new in Mumbai and there were at least half a dozen large mafia-style operations in business. What gave the Dal supremo the edge was his ability to spot and encourage leaders from among the frustrated unemployed youth he recruited as his street soldiers. He organised his networks with these hand-picked young toughs manning the nodes. He gave them cars and mobile phones. With this masterstroke, he achieved two key objectives: he won their loyalty with status symbols and, almost overnight, created a winning underworld network strengthened by modern technology.

He made these strategic moves with far-reaching plans for himself in mind. He wanted to graduate from the relatively small-scale business of organised crime to the more lucrative business of politics.

He was readying both the money and the muscle power needed to collect vote banks. His starting point was the huge mass of textile workers in Mumbai, largely unemployed with mill after obsolete mill shutting down. In his fiery speeches, he put the blame for all their ills on the affluent class. What set him apart was that he followed these speeches up with decisive and spectacular action, often of the violent kind. His systematic targeting of prosperous builders, hoteliers and business tycoons gave him vast sums of money and immense popularity on the streets to boot. He now needed militant union bosses like Lakhan Singh to take over street operations, leaving him free to preach his political gospel to the voting public.

All these thoughts flashed through Satyan's mind as he focused on the new turn of events. 'No wonder Yadav has come up so suddenly,' said Satyan. 'We'll have to watch this guy carefully. What does he want now?'

'I've been told that he will ask for a meeting with you soon. Maybe today, Satyan. From what I have heard, he will ask for the same pay and working conditions that you are giving to the people in PSN. I suggest you let me meet him this time; otherwise you might send out a signal legitimising his position within the group. It's too early for that now.'

'Right, you meet him. Tell him that Pure Space has been set up as a completely different company and the productivity norms for that company are far higher than for EMMG or Next Gen. After all, that was the very basis for fixing higher pay scales for Pure Space. I had made this quite clear to all the workers personally. I even sat down with Raut to work out the details, even though the union didn't operate there, and offered these terms to any of the people at EMMG and Next Gen who qualified and wished to join Pure Space. Every man who wanted the option was taken on. Tell him that I have even offered shares at par to every worker in my companies. What can be fairer than that?'

'Satyan, this man is not interested in fairness. He wants to establish his reign over the labour force in Mumbai. He is not really interested in PSN; it is too small for him. But since he is still at the beginning of his career, he will use whatever platform he can to get noticed. He is sending a message to Mumbai. My feeling is that he will not go away easily. We can only drag the matter on for a long time, hoping that some other, bigger factory with a larger number of workers attracts his attention. He is also quite a violent man.' Then Agarwal lowered his voice. 'I have heard that he has been behind several kidnappings and even killings. That is how he has risen so fast in the Dal. This man is really dangerous and his success has only served to make him bolder in his methods. The only redeeming feature of the situation is that our total work-force is very small. He will probably lose interest the moment he gets some bigger fish to fry.'

Satyan nodded grimly. He could see no alternative but to go along with Agarwal's plan.

◆

After lunch time, Satyan drove to the labs of Pure Space Networks. These were cordoned off from the main factory compound by a high wall mounted with an electrified barbed wire fence. Guard towers at each corner were manned twenty-four hours a day. All the guards carried assault rifles and were trained in unarmed combat. Since EMMG and Next Gen had always had various defence contracts, armed security guards were nothing new. What was new was the state-of-the-art security and surveillance system which had been installed at Pure Space – a multilayered system as unobtrusive as it was foolproof. Even the guards were unaware of the electronic surveillance systems monitored around the clock by a separate team housed a few blocks away. Access to Pure Space was restricted at each stage of entry.

He felt his mood lighten as he stepped into the conference room. His team called it the 'bull-pit'. Here his team held their most invigorating brainstorming sessions and no-holds-barred arguments. Seniority and experience counted for nothing when a 'bull-session' was on and Satyan enjoyed the scrapping and wrangling during these sessions. Some forty feet in diameter, the bull-pit had about twenty chairs scattered around a long, low table which was used more as a common footstool than as a conference table.

This afternoon, he found Jacob Mehta and Rajan Swaminathan sitting in front of a giant plasma display set into the wall. The screen showed an aerial view of a patch of the Ladakh plateau. It was an enlarged view of the kind of terrain that would show on the console of the soldier operating the gun's FCU (Fire Control Unit). The two men were intent on simulating the effects of an artillery barrage mounted on a hypothetical enemy front.

Satyan had watched with relief as Jake and Rajan seemed to hit it off together. Each was a pundit in his own field and their meeting of minds had been crucial to the success of the project. If there was any trace of hesitation to work with the Indian government, Jake showed no signs of it once they got down to brass tacks. Satyan felt that Rajan's brilliance and his pleasant manner had won Jacob Mehta over. At any rate, the collaboration beween them was moving along swiftly.

'Hey, Satyan, how was the party last night?' Jake asked. 'Heard that Daler Mehndi was a big hit with all you supposedly culture vultures!'

'Yeah, he was OK. He's looking to win a Grammy sometime soon. Hmm...looks like you're getting somewhere with the fuzzy logic initialisation out here,' Satyan remarked, scanning the masses of data posted on one edge of the screen.

'Young Lekha here came up with a neat way to tap the data,' said Jake, nodding towards a short, bespectacled girl who had been standing quietly to one side. 'The error margin is now down to 0.5 percent.'

Satyan turned and gave her shoulder a friendly squeeze. 'Good show, Lekha.'

The girl shook her head ruefully before replying, 'Not canned yet, Satyan. The error margin is down only when you think of one gun operating by itself. According to my calculations, when this piece networks with even one more gun, the error margin shoots up to nearly five percent. Imagine what would happen if it were to be used in a battery of say four or five guns. Want to take a look now?'

'Yeah, let's do it.'

Jake and Rajan wheeled their chairs over to join them and the four of them went into a huddle.

The session broke up after several hours. The three men decided to hit the Sundowner Bar at the edge of Pali Hill, Satyan's favourite watering hole, for a drink to wind down. It was nearly seven p.m. when they got into his car. He drove through the factory gate and turned the car onto the road. It was dark. None of the streetlights were on. Cursing the laxity of the municipal authorities, he drove on slowly.

He turned the corner into a narrow side lane and braked with a jolt. Half a dozen toughs were systematically battering a middle-aged man with clubs and chains in the glare of the headlights of another car halted across the lane. One or two of them looked up at the new arrival before resuming the beating. Satyan's heart lurched when he realised that the car in front was Agarwal's. It took a long moment before any of the three men in the car could react. The blows were landing with calculated regularity. With professional thoroughness, they were covering every part of their victim's body. Agarwal made no sound, nor did he make any move to protect himself. The man was practically senseless, almost beyond pain. He was on his knees, his head down on his chest. With each blow, he sank lower.

When Satyan recovered from the shock, his bile rose and with it came a strong feeling of guilt. He hit the horn on the steering wheel with all his might, jamming it as it blared mournfully. Rajan and Jake were jolted into action by the blaring horn. They flung open the door and ran, yelling and screaming, into the glare of the headlights. Caught off-guard, the hoodlums jumped away from Agarwal. The banshee-like howl of the Lexus' horn and the two shadowy figures running towards them had the desired effect. The goons decided to leave. In any case, their job was complete.

They picked up the injured and bleeding man and loaded him gently into the back seat. Satyan drove quickly to a private nursing home in Santa Cruz. It was run by a close friend who could be depended upon to give him the best of attention with the maximum privacy. He sat by the bedside until the nurses finished cleaning and dressing the wounds. No bones had been broken and, with luck, Agarwal would get away from this with nothing more than a painfully bruised body. An assessment of the psychological damage would have to wait until he came to.

There was no question now of going to a bar. Seeing that the old man would be taken good care of, Satyan told Rajan and Jake to call it a day and carry on home.

◆

Agarwal's eyes were closed, his face shrunken and grey under the oxygen tent, his frail body fighting for life. Satyan watched anxiously as the nurses, with quick professional movements, took readings from the cluster of life-monitoring instruments.

After initial first-aid had been administered at the Santa Cruz nursing home, Satyan had got him shifted to the exclusive Breach Candy Hospital whose director, Dr Malkani, had been a good friend of his father and was an admirer of the younger Sharma. On arrival, they had taken the still unconscious Agarwal into an operating theatre, not a second too soon. The old man had suffered a cardiac seizure moments after they had shifted him onto the table.

Three days later, the admin chief was yet to emerge from danger. Satyan could not shake off the feeling that he had been too engrossed in the new breakthroughs at Pure Space and had not given serious consideration to the man's warnings about the union trouble fomenting in the factory. Now, Agarwal himself was a direct victim of his negligence.

Agarwal's pale eyelids flickered and his eyes opened a fraction. He smiled weakly as Satyan peered into the tent. His lips moved as he tried to speak and the doctor quickly made an admonishing gesture.

'The patient has shown remarkable resilience, Mr Sharma,' he said. 'It's only because of his fighting spirit that we have almost pulled him out of danger.' Satyan gripped Agarwal's good hand and pressed it in approbation. The doctor continued in a stern voice, 'But he is not going to help by pushing his luck so early. He must take complete, I repeat, complete rest for at least another three days. You have already stayed too long, Mr Sharma, and you must leave now. As you can see, he is doing better than expected. In another few days, he will be a lot stronger.'

Satyan nodded and, with a quick smile and another squeeze of Agarwal's hand, left.

He drove homewards. A few minutes later, his mobile buzzed. It was the union boss, Lakhan Singh.

'Sharma sahib, now that you have seen the old man, I think it's time you and I have a little talk.' The contemptuous tone grated on Satyan's ears. He fought down a surge of anger. 'Are you the bastard behind this cowardly attack on an old and defenceless man?' he asked.

'That was only a small lesson, Sharma sahib. I am a professional, just like you. I make my moves, you make yours.'

'Don't taunt me, damn you,' Satyan yelled. 'I'll see to it that you are broken and never get out of jail for this bloody crime.'

'Sharma sahib, calm down. If you continue to talk like this I will have to complete the job. The old man is still alive because I wanted to discuss our business first.'

Satyan pulled over, trying to regain his composure. The union boss was playing a deliberately calculated game. Losing his cool would only make matters worse and might endanger Agarwal further.

'What is it that you want to discuss?' he asked in a more even voice. 'And anyway, why with me? You could have discussed it with Agarwal, across the table, like a civilised human being. What kind of professional are you that you can't talk face to face, like a man?'

Lakhan Singh sighed wearily. 'Sharma sahib, please don't give me lectures. They bore me. If you force me to close this conversation here, the outcome will not be good for innocent people. If you have still not understood the kind of person you are dealing with, I will have to complete the lesson and you will have only yourself to blame.'

'Okay, okay, we'll talk. Call me up first thing tomorrow and we'll meet in my office.'

Lakhan Singh laughed. 'Sharma sahib, it's good to see you return to reason. But I am afraid I have other engagements tomorrow. We will have to meet tonight. Please listen carefully. On your way home, there is the Sher-e-Punjab bar and restaurant on Hill Road. It serves excellent Scotch whisky and tandoori chicken. And it is a good place to discuss confidential business matters. I shall expect you there in about half an hour. And please don't make the mistake of calling the police. You will find that I have many friends in the right places and I will not be able to guarantee the safety of the old man.'

Satyan sat in the car for a while, thinking. Lakhan Singh had planned this well. There would be no time to frame a strategy. Far from it, he did not even know what Lakhan Singh's objective was. He had not even met the man yet. And the threat to Agarwal's life had been made, none too subtly, twice in the conversation.

Satyan knew that calling the police, even to organise protection at the hospital, might be misconstrued by this thug, and the man had hinted that he might be immune from them too. Not surprising, Satyan thought disgustedly. Corruption had reached almost every level of the establishment.

Calling up his own chief of security, he arranged for some discreet surveillance at the hospital before gunning the car onward. He wondered about Lakhan Singh's motives. Could the control of the small labour force employed by him be so crucial? Or was it just that his group of companies had become a handy tool for an up-and-coming union boss desperate to gain a toehold in Mumbai? He was still puzzling over the viciousness of the utterly unprovoked 'lesson' when he pulled up at the Sher-e-Punjab.

A steward stepped forward from behind the counter as he walked inside. The place was reasonably well-appointed, though the lighting and decor was a bit loud. The clientele seemed fairly well-heeled.

'Mr Sharma? This way, sir.'

Satyan got the message immediately – this was Lakhan Singh's territory. He followed the steward through the open dining area. The place was filling up and seemed to be doing good business that night. They went up a staircase on the left, past the first floor which had rows of partitioned cubicles affording the diners partial privacy. On the second floor, there were rooms for those who wished to dine in complete privacy.

The steward turned to smile at Satyan. 'We have facilities to cater for every kind of party or occasion, sir. I hope you will return. Wish you a pleasant evening, sir.' Opening a door, he ushered Satyan into a small dining room and withdrew.

There was a table in the centre set for three persons. A waiter stood at a mini-bar in the corner, pouring out drinks for two men who were already seated. Both were dressed in the politicians' favoured white khadi. Their spotless kurtas crackled with starch. Both had chunky gold-plated watches on their wrists and heavy gold chains around their necks. The suavity of their dresses contrasted starkly with their bestial features.

One was a tall, rangy individual in his mid-thirties, with a deep chest and heavily muscled forearms. He sported a handlebar moustache and a week's stubble on his massive, weather-beaten face. A blood-red tilak bisected his forehead. He sat on a chair pushed away from the table to allow room for his long legs. Yet he wore a curiously deferential air as he played host to the other, older man. He turned his eyes towards Satyan. Their expression switched immediately to the arrogance of a man who had used violence successfully to bend people to his will. In his world, brute strength and ruthlessness meant power, which could then be translated into money if combined with politics. But, in politics, it was necessary to be able to switch from servility to arrogance in the blink of an eyelid. Satyan knew that he was looking at Lakhan Singh Yadav.

The second man at the table was vaguely familiar. He too wore the look of one who had climbed out of poverty, up the ladder of politics. He was small and lean, with angular features, a long pointed nose and beady eyes. He reminded Satyan of a reptile. He had a fixed smile on his lips—a politician's smile that did not reach the eyes.

Satyan could sense the small demon deep inside his soul stir. It had not raised its head for many weeks now. But he knew that many people's lives could hinge on what happened in this private room this night. He camouflaged his dislike of both men and moved into the room.

The arrogant union boss waved Satyan towards a chair. The smaller man remained still as Lakhan Singh spoke. 'Arre, Sharma sahib, you are bang on time. Very good, very good.'

He took Satyan's hand and squeezed hard in a bone-crushing handshake. Satyan had expected it and returned the grip manfully.

'I hope you did not make any foolish phone calls on the way, Sharma sahib. Well, we shall see. This is the honourable Central Minister of State for Labour, Shri Gulab Chand Yadav-ji.'

Satyan now recognised the face from photographs in the papers. The deferential note had returned to Lakhan Singh's manner. 'I happen to know him very well, Sharma sahib. He is a very great man. No other individual has served the people as well as him, in spite of many hardships he has faced in his personal life. People say so many things about him, but he is very forgiving in nature. You will never find a more helpful friend than Shri Gulab Chand-ji, Sharma sahib. Forgive me, Gulab Chand-ji, I could not help but say these things because I know you are such a humble and sacrificing man by nature.' He turned to Satyan and concluded his fawning introduction, 'He never talks about himself – that is his greatest failing!' Gulab Chand looked suitably modest and smiled down at his Scotch and soda.

'I am very impressed with your connections, Lakhan Singh,' Satyan said tersely.

Lakhan Singh guffawed. 'No, no, Sharma sahib, I did not call you here for that. In fact, Gulab Chand-ji asked me to arrange this meeting. But first tell me, what will you drink?'

'A whisky and soda, thank you,' said Satyan. 'I am pleased to meet you, Shri Gulab Chand.' Satyan shook hands perfunctorily. 'I do not want to disturb your evening, gentlemen, so I will be obliged if you can come immediately to the point.'

'See, Gulab Chand-ji, it is just as I said. Sharma sahib is a man who likes to hurry.'

'That is for you to say, Lakhan Singh.' Satyan rose, leaned forward and looked directly at Gulab Chand. 'Tell me what you have in mind and let us get it over with. I know that my labour force is too small to hold your interest for long. So why waste your time as well as mine in beating around the bush?'

Lakhan Singh laughed uproariously for the second time that evening. Gulab Chand's smile remained in place and a small chuckle gurgled its way past his lips.

'Sharma sahib, please sit down,' said the minister softly, speaking for the first time. 'I have come all the way from Delhi to speak to you. Not about your tiny labour force; it is of no consequence.'

Satyan bristled at the casual manner in which this slight had been delivered, but held his tongue and lowered himself gingerly into his chair. If this man was connected with the recent happenings, there was more to it than Lakhan Singh's machinations. The expressionless eyes and quiet voice of the minister held more menace than Lakhan Singh's loud-mouthed bravado. He took a gulp of his Scotch and soda. He felt he was going to need it.

Gulab Chand licked his lips and began after the waiter had gone. His reptilian head swayed gently as he spoke. 'Sharma sahib, for some months now, your factory has been working on the new gun to be procured by the Indian army.'

The atmosphere in the small room changed suddenly. Gulab Chand's expressionless eyes watched Satyan. Satyan sensed Lakhan Singh stiffen. He sat still, concealing his surprise. A cold bead of sweat formed under his armpit and trickled uncomfortably down his side. He waited.

'We in Delhi closely monitor every firm that has defence contracts awarded to them, for obvious reasons.' It was news to Satyan that the labour ministry was involved in such monitoring, but he held his tongue, intent on gleaning every little bit of information he could. 'When your recent labour problems came to our notice, I was instructed by the high command to investigate the affairs of your Pure Space Company with more attention.' There was pin-drop silence in the room as the minister paused before delivering his next words. 'Sharma sahib, let me inform you that the Central cabinet is very unhappy that you have not shared the full details of your fire control unit design with all the concerned parties. There have been rumours that your design is not up to the mark and that the field tests were rigged.'

His professional pride hurt, Satyan burst out in anger, 'How can they say that? I did not plan the tests; they were planned by the army and conducted under their supervision. My fire control unit came out with flying colours. I have letters from the defence ministry to prove it.'

'Yes, yes, I am aware of that, Sharma sahib. But what can I tell you about the goings-on in the defence ministry. They have issued wrong specifications, just to show the Uzbek gun and your fire control unit in a better light. You don't know the things people are saying in the Centre about how the army is being taken for a ride by corrupt people in the ministry. They are laughing at the army and at all the people connected with the Uzbek gun – including yourself.'

'I can't believe this nonsense! The army's specs were very demanding and we at Pure Space have worked very hard to meet the highest standards in the world. I have seen the exercises in the terrain near Lakhimpur and in the plateau of Ladakh. They were extremely tough. The gun performed well. It will certainly do well in the third test in the Kumaon mountains, too. I am sure of that. How can you, who have not stirred from your air-conditioned office, say such things?'

If the politician felt angered at Satyan's barb, he did not show it. 'Have it your way, Sharma sahib. I am not a computer expert, but I know what is being said about you by people who matter. But that is not the concern. You have been most uncooperative with the other ministries who may, in the future, also buy the same gun that the army selects. You may have done a good job according to the specifications given to you but, if there is a judicial inquiry, then the specifications themselves will be reinvestigated. Who knows what influences may have been used to set them? You will also get dragged into the mess unnecessarily.'

'I can face any inquiry with a clear conscience,' said Satyan. 'My firm has done an excellent job and I know it.'

But now, a different train of thought had been set off in his mind – would the project really come through at this rate? Was he going to get involved willy-nilly in a political scandal? He had nothing to fear from a judicial inquiry. He was confident that he and his team at Pure Space would eventually emerge in the clear. But any investigation in India took ages to complete. The delay would surely kill the project. He remembered his argument with Jake Mehta. His technical vice-president's words seemed to have a prophetic ring to them now. Here was a politician from a completely unconnected ministry and he seemed to be surprisingly well-informed about the project, even though it was supposed to be top secret. How did these things happen? Should he have listened to Jake? Damn these political wheeler-dealers, he thought to himself. They had the ability to make him question a decision based on his conscience, sowing seeds of self-doubt in his mind!

Satyan drained his glass as his brain raced. He told himself to remain calm; that was going to be crucial in dealing with Gulab Chand.

'Why would the army want to favour the Uzbek gun over any other?' asked Satyan as he refilled his glass. 'If bribes were to decide the issue, surely the other multinational manufacturers would have much more money at their disposal.'

'My dear Sharma sahib, don't you know?' Gulab Chand's smile broadened mirthlessly. 'Uzbekistan has very high stakes in this gun. They have dictated the specifications because this is their only chance to acquire such a sophisticated gun, suitable for their special intentions, without paying prohibitively high prices. They want to use it against their neighbours in Asia Minor to gain power in the region. It should be obvious to anyone. They will go to any length on this project.'

It seemed credible enough. Satyan had sometimes wondered why Uzbekistan was embarking on such a major weapons acquisition programme when its priority should have been to build its economic infrastructure. He had put it down to bloated political egos.

Then, Gulab Chand made a proposition that took Satyan's breath away with its audacity.

'Sharma sahib, there is only one course open to you. Even now it is not too late. Cooperate with us and give us the detailed programs and drawings of your FCU. These will be examined and reevaluated by a joint authority set up by all the paramilitary forces concerned. I will see to it that your cooperation is given due consideration by the high command. In fact, if things work out well, I may even put in a word with the PM himself to treat your case as a special one.'

Gulab Chand reached out to pat Satyan's wrist. Satyan hastily drew his hand away, reaching for his glass. Gulab Chand seemed not to notice the snub. He watched his prey with infinite patience. Lakhan Singh had barely moved during the last half hour.

'Why don't you get them from the defence ministry yourself? If what you say is true and there is an investigation, surely the PM will back you in dealing with the defence ministry.'

Gulab Chand sighed. 'What do you know of the ways of people in the government, Sharma sahib? You are still young, you studied in a nice public school, went to a nice college in America. You are very naive. I have just told you that there are people in the Ministry of Defence who have a vested interest in this project. There are a hundred ways to block an official inquiry. And even if the inquiry took place, there are thousands of ways to cover up the facts.' He wiped his sweating face. 'We want to get the facts clear before an inquiry is set up. Then, after an inquiry has been ordered, a whitewash to cover up the facts would be difficult.'

'And what happens if I do not cooperate? After all, my loyalty is to my country and I have a contractual obligation to the Ministry of Defence. These other paramilitary forces are not my concern.'

Gulab Chand exploded. 'How dare you cast aspersions on our patriotism? Are we not loyal citizens of India? I have been very patient with you, Sharma sahib,' he snarled. Startled, Satyan almost dropped his glass at this sudden outburst. The man was virtually spitting his words out. 'It seems,' he continued, 'that the lesson taught by Lakhan Singh has not yet been learnt by you. I will not be responsible for the consequences if you refuse to cooperate, Sharma sahib, I warn you.'

And there it was, out in the open, the threat of physical violence. Lakhan Singh had been a mere pawn in this game, the ostensible motive of making it big in the Mumbai union scene merely an opening gambit. Now bigger powers were moving in.

After a while, Gulab Chand resumed in a quieter tone, 'Think it over, Sharma sahib. You will not find a more reasonable friend than me in Delhi when trouble starts. I am a patient man, so think it over. But don't delay until it is too late. Then even I won't be able to help you. I shall be visiting Mumbai again next week. By that time your Kumaon field test will also be over and you can concentrate on my offer. Think it over carefully.'

The two men regarded each other. Their drinks remained untouched. Satyan knew that he was facing a very dangerous and confident adversary. They were sizing each other up, knowing that the next step was going to set the tone for future dealings. Gulab Singh was not to be trifled with. He had shown a quick and incisive grasp of all angles of the situation. Satyan knew that the minister was to be handled with care and circumspection. He had been subjected to a test of character and his next utterance would display how much control he had over himself.

'Mr Gulab Chand,' he said in a soft tone which did not conceal the steely determination underlying it, 'I will give your proposal good thought and if I am convinced that is the path I should follow for the good of my country, then I shall agree. But if I, at any time, discover,' he continued, his voice dropping to a low whisper so that Gulab Chand had to lean forward to catch the words, 'that you have not been totally honest with me, then I shall personally abandon all my other commitments and come after you. I have never deliberately indulged in violence, Mr Gulab Chand. But if I am provoked then, as god is my witness, I will hunt you and your associates down like rats.'

Planting his unfinished drink down with a sharp rap, Satyan pushed his chair back and left the room. The demon inside him writhed in silent dissatisfaction. It would have to wait for another time.

5

Satyan Sharma's jaded eyes drank in the cool greenery as the little jeep climbed steadily into the upper reaches of the Kumaon hills. The rapidly darkening sky was hung with thick, black, monsoon clouds. The heavy rain had let up momentarily, and Satyan had immediately pulled back the tarpaulin flap on his side. Though the cold wet breeze snapped at his face and whipped through his hair, he braced himself and leaned out to take in as much of the scenery as he could before the darkness took it completely away from him.

Beside him, Naik Kalyan Singh gunned the vehicle expertly up the winding road. He smiled indulgently. It was obvious to him that this likeable young sahib from Mumbai had been away from nature for too long. Kalyan Singh belonged to these hills and loved them dearly. He was only too happy to share them with someone who appreciated their beauty.

He had been detailed to drive this visitor from the helipad at the Kumaon Regimental Centre HQ at Ranikhet to the spot where, some sixty miles away into the foothills of the Himalayas, the 12th Artillery brigade had set up camp to carry out some exercises. What a civilian was doing at the army exercises, he did not ask. Nor did he ask about the several other visitors he had heard about, both civilian and military, who had also been driven up to the same spot. He was a simple soldier who carried out orders without bothering his head with too many questions.

They had been on the road for more than two-and-a-half hours. Despite the almost incessant rain, they had made good time. A few minutes later, they spotted the rows of pitched tents.

The jeep ground to a halt at the checkpoint. Satyan could make out the dim glow of lights from about a dozen or so tents. Off to the right was a large clearing with a long, low tent in the foreground. That was probably the camp HQ. Behind, barely visible, were a pair of massive, dark and menacing tarpaulin-hooded silhouettes – the guns.

Over the next three days, the two prototypes would be put through a gruelling field test, moving and firing continually. It would be an acid test under the toughest conditions.

Satyan had been on hand at Ladakh and then at Lakhimpur as an observer. As far as he could make out, the Indo-Uzbek gun had passed the tests with flying colours. For the last leg, the Indian army had chosen completely different, yet equally demanding, conditions. The Himalayan foothills in these parts were steep and thickly forested and the rain-soaked ground soft underfoot. The mist and the torrential rain, at times, brought visibility down to a few metres. The army had chosen the time and place well, he thought, nervously hoping that everything would go well.

He followed a sentry to his allotted quarters where he found that Rajan, Prof Barkhatiev and the observer from the Uzbek army, Major Sulemanov, had already arrived. They waited while he unpacked and splashed some water on his face before trudging through the slush to the HQ tent for the briefing.

A low trestle table stood in one corner of the tent, with several army officers around it. A large-scale map of the area had been spread out on the table. Brigadier Dilawar Shaikh, commanding the 12th Artillery brigade attached to the 34th Mountain division – a short, barrel-chested, bull terrier of a man – was in charge. Standing at the map was one of his battery commanders. The brigadier ran through the introductions while they were handed tots of rum in large enamel mugs, which they accepted gratefully; rum was the only thing that could thaw their freezing bones on that cold, rainy mountainside. Satyan's attention focused on three of the seated officers he had not met before as Brigadier Shaikh completed the introductions. There was Baichung Rampal of the Indo-Tibetan Border Police, Calvyn Gomes of the Border Security Force and Major Ashank Kumar of the Directorate of Military Operations, Army HQ, Delhi. Apart from a pair of Artillery Corps staff officers, he had met only the Uzbek Major Sulemanov. These were the people on whose reports so much depended.

Jabbing at the map periodically, Brigadier Shaikh explained in detail the maneuvers planned for the next three days.

Indicating several orange-headed pins alongside the route that the guns were to take, he addressed the civilians, 'So here, gentlemen, are the points from where you will observe the proceedings. You may not be within sight of the guns while they are firing, but my battery commander will be in touch with you over the radio periodically. Please refrain from initiating communication while on the field. Kindly address any questions or remarks you may have to me over dinner each day. Please remember, once the operations are underway, my battery commander is in complete control. We will therefore follow these simple rules so that he can operate unimpeded.' He glowered at each of them in turn and they hastily murmured their acquiescence.

'To conclude, gentlemen, let me emphasise that you are here as privileged guests of the Kumaon Regimental Centre, so I enjoin you to conform to the codes of conduct of this fine fighting force. Lastly, you may have noticed that the guns are parked in a fenced-off clearing just behind this tent. Until four hundred hours tomorrow, when my battery commander takes charge of them, they have been entrusted to a special squad of the military police who, as even my civilian friends must know by now, can be easily distinguished by a white band around their left upper arms. If any of you is taken by the urge for a breath of fresh mountain air during the night,' at this moment he was interrupted by a loud crash of thunder, 'you might bear in mind that the only authorised personnel near the clearing are the MPs themselves, and that rule applies to me and my men as well.

'And now,' he was almost smiling as he raised his mug, 'I salute my three civilian friends here who, I believe, have worked hard for several years to make this operation possible – a toast to you, sirs, and my sincere wishes for a successful test.'

They filed out after draining their mugs, bidding each other goodnight.

'Quite a sense of humour the old son-of-a-gun has,' Satyan said to Rajan, out of the corner of his mouth, as they walked away. It was starting to rain again.

Rajan grinned. 'But a kindly soul under his rough exterior, don't you think?'

They began jogging towards their tent. On the way, they passed the one which had been allotted to the three observers from the Services. The entrance flap had been pulled back, giving a clear view of the interior. The ITBP man was deep in conversation with his counterpart from the BSF. Sulemanov had been allotted a tent for himself. Major Ashank Kumar paused outside before going in, directing a steady gaze at them.

'The major seems to be a bit of a loner, eh, Rajan?'

'Yeah, a man of few words, too, it seems to me. By the way, did you know that he is an expert computer programmer? One of the reasons he is here is to evaluate your fire control unit and its rapid reprogramming capability.'

The rain had stopped. The sudden silence woke Satyan. He looked around the tent. The other two were fast asleep. It was almost half past twelve. He peered through the plastic window stitched into the entrance flap. The sky was clear. The clouds seemed to have rolled back for the time being, allowing the heavens to cast a magical spell on the pristine mountainside. It was too good an opportunity to lose. He rose, put on his parka and boots, and went to the entrance. Stars could be seen by the thousand in the clear mountain night. Though there was no moon, visibility was good. Pulling his parka tightly around his shoulders, he stepped out for a snatch of the Brigadier's 'fresh mountain air'.

He passed by darkened tents where the soldiers were resting, each capable, he estimated, of accommodating a dozen men. He counted ten tents in two rows of five each. The lights within the tents had been dimmed, throwing vague shadows, leaving the campsite with a dull glow.

He strolled slowly through the silent camp, savouring the stillness. Not since his schooldays at Lawrence in the Nilgiri Hills had he experienced the quiet solitude of night time at high altitude. A hectic work schedule had allowed little time for holidays far from the bustle of modern civilisation. Here, alone with himself, he felt the joy of communion with nature.

He reached the perimeter of the camp and turned to follow it along the fence. Lost in contemplation, he found himself at a sentry box next to a gate set into what he now saw was an inner fence cordoning off the guns. An MP stepped up to him, assault rifle at the ready.

'Who's that? State your name and ID number,' the MP barked sharply, in Hindi.

'I'm sorry. I couldn't sleep so I took a little stroll. I'm Satyan Sharma, a civilian observer deputed by army HQ. I didn't intend to come so close to the guns – I must have missed my way in the darkness. I'll go back to my tent.'

The MP paused, in two minds about what action to take. Satyan stepped back, but as he turned to go, the MP dug the barrel hard into his ribs. 'I will come with you,' he said in a harsh voice.

Satyan was about to protest when he caught a fleeting movement behind the MP. A shadowy figure stood inside the sentry box. He could make out an officer's epaulettes on the man's shoulder. Satyan opened his mouth to appeal to the officer, but the MP gave him a hard shove down the pathway.

Still, the officer chose to stay in the shadows. Why was he not intervening, thought Satyan, if only to investigate? Only when he reached his tent and was about to go in, did he see the dim figure stepping away from the sentry box. Something about the man's uniform seemed out of place, but he couldn't put his finger on it.

'I wasn't reported,' he said to himself, 'and the MP could have reported me to his superior officer who was standing right there.' Puzzled, Satyan pulled off his boots and tumbled back into bed. Thankfully the guard had left, satisfied that Satyan would not cause any more trouble. Suddenly he sat upright. He realised what had been amiss about the mysterious officer's uniform. It didn't have the white band around the arm that the MPs were supposed to be wearing. So, if he was not an MP, what was he doing in the prohibited area? It was now useless to go back outside. He would only land into more trouble and the guy was probably long gone anyway.

Satyan lay back on the cot, trying to unravel the significance of what he had just seen. The brigadier's rules had been unequivocally stated. The officer in the booth had been a trespasser. The MP had clearly intended to prevent him from seeing who that officer was. If, like Satyan, the guy had been on a midnight stroll, he wouldn't want to be identified, especially by a civilian. But even in that case, the MP's behaviour did not seem to be right. In fact, the MP should have reported both of them to his commanding officer. And if the mysterious officer was up to no good, then the two of them had to be in it together.

The question was – in what?

Satyan tried hard to recall the man's features. He drew a blank – the man had remained hidden in the shadows. He thought of the uniform. He would have to start with the rank. He concentrated on the memory of that split-second glimpse from over the MP's shoulder, trying to recall the number of pips the man had on his epaulette. Gradually, Satyan became convinced that there had been only one. So he was probably either a second lieutenant or a major, the only two ranks in the camp which had single pips on the shoulders. He hadn't been able to see clearly enough to decide which.

He then tried to figure out the man's motive for being there. He didn't seem to be carrying anything on his person when he had stepped away from the sentry box – at any rate, nothing heavy or bulky. That was about as far as Satyan could get. Not far enough, he realised ruefully, for him to do anything about it.

Satyan finally convinced himself that he was just another soul getting his ration of fresh mountain air, and that the MP had probably acted quickly to cover a minor transgression by a soldier from a civilian's prying eyes. Tossing and turning, he drifted off into a fitful sleep.

◆

It seemed to him that he was awakened almost immediately. Outside, he could hear the camp already buzzing with activity. He checked his watch with bleary eyes. Half past three. The others were sitting up, trying to wipe sleep off their eyes. Pushing themselves off their cots, they quickly washed and pulled on their jackets and boots. They walked out and headed for the mess tent, passing soldiers milling through the slush, getting set to move out. Sodium lamps, powered by a portable generator, lit up the entire camp. The guns' covers had been removed and they sat behind their enclosure, brooding. A squad of soldiers had fallen in nearby, preparing to take possession of the guns from the MPs.

After a quick breakfast, Brigadier Shaikh assembled all his officers for a final word. Scanning them as they crowded around the map, Satyan examined the shoulder epaulettes of each man. He counted two majors and two second lieutenants. He looked at the artillery major appraisingly as he leaned over the map, focused on the brigadier's words. Satyan discounted him; he seemed to be a bit too broad-shouldered. His gaze shifted to Major Ashank Kumar who was a much closer fit. The height was about right, too. At that precise moment, Kumar turned his head around to look directly at Satyan. With a sudden jolt Satyan knew instinctively that he had identified his man.

He turned his gaze away, trying to collect his thoughts. Maybe Major Kumar was apprehensive that, if Satyan reported last night's activity, he might be reprimanded by the doughty old brigadier for a breach of discipline. Worse, the brigadier may expel Kumar from the camp and send him back to HQ. No wonder the major would want his midnight stroll to be kept under wraps. But Satyan couldn't shake the feeling that there was more to it than what met the eye.

It was then that he came to the decision.

He took Rajan quietly aside once the briefing was over. 'Do you have a backup of the software for the fire control unit?'

'Yes, of course. Why?'

'And spares for the control panel?'

'Of course. There will be a thorough check of the guns and the systems before we move out. Is something the matter, Satyan?'

'They will check for physical damage, yes. But will there be a check on the software?'

'That has already been checked during installation in Delhi. You were there, too. And you know the installation takes ages because of the GPS. Only the USB key needs to be inserted by the battery commander before we move out of the camp.'

'The USB key!' There was an edge to Satyan's voice . 'Can you re-programme it now?'

Rajan was taken aback. He hesitated before replying, 'Well I can, but it will delay the start by at least half an hour. The brigadier will chew me out. But why–'

'Listen, and do just as I say.' Satyan's tone brooked no argument. 'Convince Brigadier Shaikh – I don't know how – but just convince him to allow you to change the key. Do it now and don't ask me why. Trust me. I know what I'm doing. Maybe you can tell him that you have been instructed to test out how a last-minute change can be done on the field. Or that you want to run a last-minute check on viruses or something. Or both, I don't care. Just make sure you change it. Basically, you have to ensure the only communication the guns receive from satellites is through a new password. Also, except Brigadier Shaikh no one should come to know about this, or be present when you change it. Do it now, before the guns move out of their enclosure.' The urgency in Satyan's voice surprised Rajan. His panic was communicated to the young scientist in that instant. 'Now go. There's not much time left. Hurry!'

Rajan stared uncertainly at Satyan for a moment before walking quickly towards the brigadier.

◆

More than anything else, the president reminded Major General Aliakhin of a silver-furred bear. Idly, he wondered whether such bears roamed the vast forests of Siberia, terrorising other animals, or whether the only specimen alive was dressed up in a suit, sitting in the chair of arguably the second-most powerful man on the planet.

The president's slant-eyed stare bored into him steadily. In spite of having given similar treatment to hundreds of people himself in his long career, Aliakhin found himself feeling a tad nervous. Even though the president had replaced the old guard in a modern, democratic Russia, he had won his political spurs in the earlier Soviet regime. Of course he knew all the old tricks, even those used by the FSS. And right now it was Aliakhin under the scanner, having just made a progress report on the Indian adventure which had little to show by way of progress. Konstantin had yet to come up with a viable plan to achieve the Russian objective though the Indo-Uzbek howitzer was already in the last stages of its field trials. And now the president had begun taking personal interest in the project.

He was not mincing his words now. 'I am extremely distressed, Yegor Aliakhin. This matter has stretched longer than we had planned for and what do we have to show for it? Nothing! I am a man who likes rapid action, my dear Yegor. You know that as well as anyone in the Kremlin. You are a man after my own heart and we have grown well together – so far.' Aliakhin's ears did not miss that ominous pause. 'I had thought that the department would deal swiftly with this, especially because the two countries involved are so backward. What resources can they have to match ours in counterintelligence?'

Aliakhin knew that though it was a rhetorical question, the president needed a response. It was his way of putting people on the defensive. Aliakhin weighed his words carefully.

'The Americans have been thwarted from stealing ahead of us, president. We know who their operative is and are keeping a close eye on him. Nobody is watching Colonel Konstantin.' Aliakhin waited with bated breath. Surely the president couldn't find fault with the department now.

'Operative? Only one? How do you know that they have only one operative on this project? And am I to understand that we have only one on this project as well? Do you understand the strategic importance of this exercise to Mother Russia, Yegor Aliakhin?'

'But of course, President. The design should not be allowed to be implemented by underdeveloped countries like India or Uzbekistan. I also realise, President, that Uzbekistan would also be tempted to sell howitzers to other Central Asian republics which would strengthen them against us. Maybe even Chechenya. I assure you, President, we are not lagging behind the Americans, even though it might seem that no tangible progress has been made so far.' He added, 'I have full teams of operatives to back Colonel Konstantin in Delhi, Mumbai and Bangalore. I give you my assurance, President, we will not fail.'

'That is a typical soldier's assessment, Yegor Aliakhin. Limited!' exclaimed the president, slamming the table with his huge palms. 'I want the designs not only for its military uses, but for its diplomatic value as – what is that term the Americans use – an ace-in-the-hole. We know the Americans want the designs as badly as we do. This means that they represent a truly significant breakthrough. They will be willing to pay handsomely, once we have it. I am willing to partner the Americans in spreading democracy in the world, but what's in it for Russia, eh? This is one of the little bargaining chips that I want. Now do you understand, Yegor Aliakhin?

'And what is this in your report about the Indian Minister of State for Home taking money from both us and the Americans? If they have only one operative on this project, how have the Americans been able to find a way to reach this minister while we haven't been able to do a thing about it? I am distressed, my dear Yegor. I am beginning to wonder if this project is really in the best hands.'

Aliakhin bristled. But he was too old a hand to allow his impassive exterior to betray his thoughts. He was sure that the best talent available in the FSS was at hand in India and that Konstantin was miles ahead of Connolly in field-level savvy. He, however, did not belabour this point and moved to another.

'We are not depending totally on one line of attack, President. I have arranged to have a suitable message delivered to Mr Pandey through one of his cronies who is due to visit Russia within the next two weeks. In fact, I have had this visit arranged myself, President, and a very special treatment has been planned. I am sure the message will be delivered unambiguously.'

The president looked sharply at Aliakhin and, even though not another word was said, his meaning was amply clear.

'Yes, yes, I think some stern message must definitely be passed on, Yegor Aliakhin. I am sure you will not fail to make a suitable impression. But that is not enough for us. We must have some way to exercise a greater hold on what is happening down there. We must leave nothing to chance. We must have that design to bargain with the Americans. And we must ensure that the Americans don't get their hands on it.'

'May I be permitted to use more direct methods on the field, President?' The president flapped his hand in an impatient gesture of assent. 'In that case, I shall instruct my people to intervene and take control of one of the…aces-in-the-hole…without delay. It's an old but simple move, President, but one that will not fail to get us the designs the moment they are certified as ready for production.'

The president grunted. 'The most powerful ideas in this world are simple, Yegor. We peasants understand that, don't we?'

The meeting was at an end.

Aliakhin rose and left, warmed by the president's closing remark, a reaffirmation of their common heritage.

◆

It was only when their vehicle was hit for the first time that they became aware of the jeep behind them.

They had not seen it because its headlights had been turned off. Even now, they could barely make it out in the rearview mirror, through the pouring rain. The jeep rammed them again, much harder this time. Their own vehicle leaped forward dangerously. With a loud curse, Kalyan Singh struggled to regain control of the wheel. There was a black chasm beyond the shoulder of the road on their left and an almost vertical rock-face on their right and they raced along, skidding and swerving madly down the steep wet road before he could bring his vehicle under control. Kalyan Singh pulled up and jumped out. Satyan got out too, stunned and shaking. But even after walking some fifty metres up the road, there was no sign of the stranger.

Puzzled, the two men stood looking at each other. There was nothing to see except the wall of rain, nothing to hear except its steady din. And they were getting colder and wetter by the second.

'He must have lost control and gone over the slope,' said Satyan.

'Maybe, sahib.' But the gurkha was uncertain.

'Let's go back and get a torch. We must see if he needs any help.'

They turned back down the road. They had almost reached their jeep when, with a loud grating roar, the assailant's vehicle raced out of the darkness behind them. The headlights flashed on and it hurtled down the road, flying at them.

In a desperate attempt to save themselves, the two men dived at the rock-face, scrambling to get out of the way. They clawed at the hard rock, hands slipping and sliding as the rain-slicked surface gave their fingers no grip. Losing their footing, both men came bouncing back onto the road, narrowly missing the wheels of the attacker's vehicle as it sped by.

Kalyan Singh was first off the ground, his gurkha blood boiling. He was gentle enough as he helped Satyan to his feet but, once he had seen to it that the younger man was all right, he was raring to go after the unknown maniac.

They ran to their jeep and got in. Kalyan Singh drove downhill, face grim. 'When I meet that demon, Satyan sahib, there will be only one outcome – either he will die or I will.' Too shaken to react,

Satyan could only hang mutely on, white fingers gripping the seat. Far below them, almost a hundred and fifty metres down the hill road, a pair of headlights showed the progress of their assailant.

Nearly a quarter-of-an-hour passed. Kalyan Singh was tearing wildly down the curves. Sometimes they could see the headlights below, sometimes a shoulder of the mountain-face would shield them from sight. A dead silence descended on them as their jeep kept charging on. Another quarter-of-an-hour passed.

They were startled when they were rammed from behind a third time. Going pell-mell down the hill in a single-minded chase, they had been caught off-guard. The crafty assailant must have stopped at a lay-by with his lights off. He closed in again, this time with his headlights blazing. There was no need to be covert now.

Kalyan Singh leaned forward, tense with concentration. All his experience and nerves would be needed to get out of this alive. Satyan clung onto his seat, sweating despite the cold, teeth clenched. Gradually, Kalyan Singh began pulling away. The hillside flashed past, the trees, the rain, the clouds in one dim, grey blur.

At last they saw, far below, the few scattered lights of a small village. Kalyan raced on, edging closer to the lights. Their attacker would have to get them before they reached the sanctuary of civilisation. The two vehicles careered down the hillside, the lights of the village now less than half-a-mile away. Suddenly, the headlights behind them disappeared.

'He has turned off his lights and will try to get us after the village,' said Kalyan Singh.

'Why don't we stop and get help from the villagers?'

'No, sahib. That would only put the poor villagers in danger. See, there are only about a dozen small huts here. That is an army jeep. *Saala behn-chod*!' Kalyan's lips curled as he contemplated the lunatic behind them. 'He will definitely have a gun. If it is an assault rifle, he can kill everyone in this village within minutes.'

They rolled slowly through the hamlet, a ragged cluster of tiny huts with no electricity. The few lights they could see were all from kerosene lanterns. No one was about.

'But if he had a gun, he could have shot us back there,' said Satyan. 'Why expose himself to such risk if he wanted to kill us?'

'Maybe because he is mad. Or maybe he wants to make it look like an accident, sahib.'

'But why try to kill us? What have we done?'

'Not us, sahib. You. He is after you. It must be something to do with the exercises back there.' The image of Major Ashank Kumar staring coldly at him flashed in front of Satyan's eyes. He glanced at Kalyan, who broke into a wicked grin. 'But if that is his game, sahib, this time he has tried to catch too big a bear. I was born in these mountains. I know how to get him.'

As they left the village behind, they accelerated down the hill. Above and behind them, the other jeep would now be approaching the village. After a few minutes, they could see that the headlights had crossed the village and were now moving rapidly down the road.

The chase was on again.

Tearing around a sharp turn, Satyan saw a little clearing on the right where a small temple nestled in a recess in the rock face. The hills were dotted with such temples. Behind the little temple, the black mountainside rose steeply. To the left, over an ankle-high marker wall, the valley fell away steeply into a dark abyss. Kalyan abruptly switched off his lights, turned the jeep around and backed into the recess beside the little structure. Telling Satyan to get down, he kept the engine gunned at full throttle and the clutch pressed fully down as the vehicle crouched in the darkness.

Satyan felt uneasy. He understood the gurkha's intentions but waited, hidden behind the little temple.

They heard the high-pitched whine of the jeep's engine over the noise of the rain a few moments before it came tearing around the corner. Angry at having had to yield such a large lead to his prey, the jeep's driver was going so fast that he must have taken the curve at nearly seventy kmph. Timing his move perfectly, Kalyan Singh switched the headlights on, shooting their full glare directly into the onrushing driver's eyes. At the same moment, Kalyan Singh released the clutch, making the jeep leap forward and off the ground.

In the reflected brilliance of a thousand raindrops caught in midair, the thing must have seemed like an avenging monster lunging out of its cave, eyes blazing.

In that heightened state of awareness, Satyan saw every detail with absolute clarity. The killer was turning the steering wheel leftwards out of the turn. Involuntarily, his reflex jerked it wildly back to swing away from Kalyan Singh's jeep as it sprang out at him. Behind the wheel, Satyan saw Major Ashank Kumar's face, eyes wide with surprise. Almost at once, the major checked the rightward turn of the wheel and started to turn it back. But, at that speed, it was already too late. He saw the realisation dawn in the major's eyes, his mouth beginning to open in a scream. He saw the man throw up his hands, trying to shut out the last terrifying sight of his life as the valley opened its emptiness for him. The racing jeep hit the marker wall and cart-wheeled, bouncing high up into the darkness.

Kalyan Singh had braked hard as soon as their jeep landed on the road, bringing it to a skidding stop. Satyan remained still as it sat quietly in the middle of the mountain road. The twin beams of the headlights shot out into the darkness which lay like a shroud over the valley.

The drumming of the rain continued unabated.

6

It was raining hard as Satyan's train rolled to a halt at Delhi station. Sam Bannerjee's chauffeur was waiting on the platform to pick him up.

He leaned back against the cushions as the car negotiated the thoroughfare around Connaught Place. The official pennant on the hood had been covered with a plastic sheath. He glanced out at the capital's commuters huddled patiently under their umbrellas, waiting for their buses. A twenty-minute drive took him past India Gate standing in solitary splendour against the dark sky and brought him to the Pandara Road residence of the finance secretary.

Bannerjee was waiting for him on the verandah. He wrung Satyan's hand enthusiastically, face glowing with pride as he welcomed him like a returning hero.

'Great show, my boy, absolutely splendid! I got all the details from Kali.' Seeing Satyan's puzzled expression he added quickly, 'John Kalidoss, the home secretary, you know. We were batch-mates at Mussoorie. We're meeting him for dinner tonight at the club, by the way. It seems you have won an undying admirer in Brigadier Shaikh and I'm told that he's a grizzled old soldier who's nobody's fool. Fantastic! Rubita was on the phone from Mumbai just now. She wants you to call her right away.'

Satyan had never seen the old boy so effusive. Rubita was ecstatic, too. Satyan allowed her words to flow over him, savouring the moment. The world was at his feet and there would be no stopping Pure Space now. He hummed happily to himself as he showered and dressed for dinner. They were scheduled for a quiet celebration with a few select members of Bannerjee's civil service clique at the Willingdon Institute. Small though the party was, it was a significant gathering nonetheless, for the powerful ministries it represented.

The dinner was excellent. The chef had outdone himself on the entrée – steak frites and filet mignon capped off with something he called 'Brazilian Surprise' for dessert. As far as Satyan could make out, it was prepared with some kind of caramelised nuts in custard with liberal dashes of curaçao. It could easily have been bungled, but the club's chef had pulled it off and was duly called out to be complimented by all present.

Satyan sensed a camaraderie bordering on intimacy within that little circle. Though some of the bureaucrats were junior and from altogether unconnected ministries, the easy banter which they exchanged with Bannerjee and Kalidoss indicated that this was a special clique with a very exclusive membership – a kind of Masonic society.

After dinner, Satyan, Sam and Kalidoss settled down with brandy and cigars in a quiet alcove in the library. The others had politely taken leave, allowing the remaining men to have a quiet and confidential chat. When all three had their cigars going, Kalidoss broached the subject of the future of Satyan's software for the howitzer's fire control unit.

'Well, my dear boy, no matter what the outcome of the howitzer project, you have done the country proud. India has thrown its hat into the ring, eh, young fellow? Let's see someone top that!' said Kalidoss.

Satyan grinned. Then he caught the nuance and a shadow clouded his brow. 'But why should we doubt the outcome, Kali? The gun did well all around. It wasn't just the FCU. She excelled on the ballistics and mobility too. Yes, a couple of bugs need to be sorted out here and there, but that's only to be expected during field trials. I'm sure Rajan and Barkhatiev can handle those problems easily.'

'Hey, hey, relax, young fellow. Don't get so hot under the collar,' said Kalidoss with a smile. 'No one is saying that the gun is not technically sound. We are all tremendously pleased that we have been able to come up with a prototype that matches world standards in performance. Let that not be in any doubt whatsoever. Kudos to you and your team!'

Bannerjee leaned forward. 'You're bang on, Kali. Satyan, this marks a milestone for Indian enterprise, and we're all immensely proud of you, my boy.'

'Then where's the hitch?' asked Satyan, feeling a little out of his depth.

'No hitch, my boy. No hitch at all, my boy,' said Kalidoss smoothly. 'We are now ready to progress to the next stage of evaluating the whole affair.'

He glanced quickly over at Bannerjee, who had pursed his lips thoughtfully. Satyan was staring into his glass with a slightly bemused expression. Kalidoss shook his head almost imperceptibly. Bannerjee caught the signal and leaned back with a little sigh. The silence dragged on for a while. A wall seemed to have sprung up. Neither bureaucrat said so, but Satyan could sense that the gun project had, quite inexplicably, run into rough weather.

'Look,' he said, breaking the silence at last, 'let's think forward about this. What did you mean, Kali, when you said "whatever the outcome"? What are the issues now?'

'Nothing that you need to bother about just now, Satyan. We need to examine the proposals from the commercial angles, now that we have crossed the technical phase of evaluation. Let the generals put in their comprehensive technical reports, then we'll see how the balance tots up.'

'Listen, my boy,' interjected Bannerjee gently, 'I don't want to sound like a wet blanket, but there are a whole lot of angles to be considered before the cabinet can arrive at a decision. There is the financial package offered by the other manufacturers, for example. Then, of course, the help offered in productionising the gun in India. Then there is the issue of spare parts, training and all that. I mean, you must understand that the cabinet has to take a very wide view of the situation.'

'Now don't let that dampen your spirits and enthusiasm, Satyan,' said Kalidoss. 'We've shown the world what India is capable of and our negotiating position is all the stronger for that. Let's celebrate that, dash it, and let tomorrow take care of itself!'

Satyan was no more in the mood to celebrate but, putting up a brave face, he raised his glass. He would need the home secretary's support to push their case through the coils of red tape. The establishment loomed before him in all its immutable bulk. He saw, now, how naive he had been all along. He wondered what other bureaucratese would be thrown at them in the months ahead. These men were comfortable as they were, protecting the status quo from entrepreneurs like him. It was by patiently stonewalling new ideas and initiatives that they held onto the cozy club cultures they had become used to over the years. And by maintaining the status quo, their political bosses would ask no questions either. It was all so simple.

Satyan stifled a desire to stalk out. The weight of responsibility held him down. He would have to learn to play the game with these experienced campaigners. A wrong move here and months of effort could be rendered futile.

The home secretary spoke again. 'You know, Sam, Krugman met me on Tuesday. He returned from Vienna last week. He says the chancellor should be able to put in a word with the US Secretary of State on the Pakistan situation. He had conveyed this to the British foreign secretary also. That could be useful.'

'Yes, yes indeed. It remains to be seen now how FIAM reacts. They were talking about speaking to the Secretary of State about Siachen. Wonder which is higher on the PM's priority.'

Satyan registered the words as if from a distance. He was pondering the dramatic turn of events. Now he was sure that Sam Bannerjee had brought him here to show him a glimpse of the hurdles yet to be crossed. Shrewd man, he thought, making it seem as if the topic had come up quite by chance. He realised that Bannerjee was actually doing him a favour by forewarning him of the kinds of opinions that people like the home secretary held.

The field tests were over, other tests had begun. Would the gun move and fire as smoothly through the corridors of power in Delhi as it had through the slushy slopes of Kumaon? Would the gun win this battle before it got into the relatively simpler terrain of the battlefield? Much would depend on his keeping a steady head.

'The lad thinks too much, eh, Sam?' Kalidoss broke through his reverie.

Satyan recovered his wits and forced himself to smile over his brandy. 'Thinking is what Indians are better at than anyone else in the world, Kali,' he said with a wink. 'A toast to Indian brains – the best they are!'

◆

Back in Mumbai, Satyan held a quiet celebratory dinner at the Land's End hotel for the core team that had worked on Epsilon-6. Now that the gun had passed three stages of field trials, Pure Space Networks' technical role in the project had come to a brilliantly successful conclusion. Yet, Satyan couldn't throw a big party because of its sensitive nature. So it was a small foursome – Satyan, Jake and two other members of the team – who sat down at a secluded table in the Vista restaurant overlooking the Arabian Sea.

As they clinked their wine glasses in a toast, Jake Mehta announced happily that his wife Maggie and their sons were arriving at the end of the month for their annual India holiday. He saw his family three or four times a year when he went over and then again when they visited India for the summer. His excitement was palpable.

His assistant Lekha teased him gently. 'So, Jake, are you excited because your sons are coming or because of Maggie? It had better be Maggie or you'll be in deep trouble,'

'What! Are you going to rat on me, you little pip-squeak?' he replied with a wink and a chuckle.

'Yeah, buddy. If Maggie comes over you'll have to walk the line, eh?' Satyan chimed in. 'So what's the deal? When are they shifting to Mumbai?'

There was a tinge of moroseness in Jake's reply. 'Still working on it, guys. She's not too keen and now she says the boys are getting settled in school. The water here doesn't seem to agree with her.

Calvin, my elder one, also comes down with a bad stomach every time he is here. Let's see how it goes this time.'

'All the best, buddy. Hey, Lekha,' said Satyan, changing tack, 'I hear that a handsome hunk has moved into your building. And somebody we know is falling head over heels for him. Tell all, young lady.'

'Satyan!' Lekha burst out in a shocked whisper, though whether because of the insinuation or because she had been found out, wasn't too clear to the party. They all laughed. Easy banter continued around the table until they broke up a little after eleven.

◆

The next day Satyan headed for the studios of Pinnacle TV in Santa Cruz after work. Thinking things over, he concluded that if he wanted to get to the bottom of things, he would have to start with Gulab Chand and Lakhan Singh Yadav. Rubita could possibly find out something more about the two men. He walked into the newsroom to find the team of technicians and journalists winding up for the day. The nine p.m. news had been telecast and the eleven p.m. headline update had been taped. The people in the newsroom nodded to Satyan as he threaded his way past their desks towards Rubita's cabin. She was picking up her handbag when he walked in.

'Hi, prince charming,' she said with a smile, 'you're just in time to help a damsel in distress. My car is at the garage and won't be back until tomorrow evening. I was going to take a cab home. Now my handsome young knight has come on his great charger to protect his lady love from the night riders of the metropolis.'

'Beautiful damsel you are, but in distress you'll never be,' replied Satyan with a grin. 'If ever there was a capable young lady less in need of a rescuing knight, that's you. Okay listen, I need to know about two guys – Gulab Chand, the Central labour minister and Lakhan Singh Yadav, a local union boss of Mumbai who is trying to make it big. Can you find out their backgrounds for me?'

'How disappointing, darling. I thought you had come all the way because you were yearning to see me again,' said Rubita, sticking her tongue out at him. 'I'll ask Shekar in Research. But why these two? Is there some connection? Gulab Chand is from the ruling party at Delhi but Lakhan Singh is from the Lok Seva Dal,' she added, reaching for the phone. After she had given the necessary instructions, she turned to Satyan, who was lounging in one of the chairs in the small, well-appointed cabin.

He glanced out through the glass partitions to make sure there were no casual listeners nearby. 'I had a very interesting chat last week with these two gentlemen. After that I got busy with the Kumaon trip and couldn't talk to you about it. This Gulab Chand guy wanted to lay his hands on the FCU designs. He practically threatened to sabotage the gun project if I didn't give him what he wanted. He threatened to get a judicial inquiry conducted to probe some idiotic charges about the gun's technical aspects. Hell, the gun's damn good and can stand up to scrutiny by any inquiry, judicial or otherwise. But I couldn't help feeling that he's fronting for someone higher up. Obviously some political bigwig is trying to meddle with my project. Or trying to stop it. But that's not the point. Once an inquiry commission gets its teeth into the project, you can be bloody sure that's the end to all our hard work.'

'Hmm,' said Rubita, fingers drumming on the table. Her journalistic mind began to work in a flash. Here was surely something worth talking about. 'Tell me what happened from the beginning.'

'Not here. Let's go somewhere we can talk without interruption. Look, Rubes, don't start working this up into a story right now. You know that this is a top secret project and also one where I want to prove myself. Any public controversy now and the thing might get shelved. And if we want to find out what's really going on behind the scenes, we should play along with Gulab Chand for the time being. If we don't draw him on, we will miss the really big fish.'

Rubita considered this. He could sense the struggle within her, torn as she was between her journalistic instinct and her loyalty towards her fiancé. Finally, she smiled. 'Okay, Satyan, I guess a little patience might lead me to a bigger story. I'll wait.'

A few minutes later, they were in Satyan's Lexus, heading for Yoko in Santa Cruz, a restaurant which served the best steaks in suburban Mumbai. Quickly, he ran through the conversation with the minister from Delhi.

'What puzzles me is how come Gulab Chand has access to top secret projects? The guy was really well-informed about details which very few people, even within the defence ministry, should have known. He fed me some bullshit about the labour ministry keeping a special tab on all private firms which are handling defence work. And then, this business of the paramilitary forces not being happy about the specifications. How ham-handed can you get, for crying out loud! Either Gulab Chand thinks I am a fool, or probably feels that it doesn't matter what I think. The second possibility means that the jokers running this caper in Delhi are so arrogant, they think no one can touch them.'

'Yeah, that's typical. You and I belong to the small minority who can't really affect vote banks. And such people are considered irrelevant by most Indian politicians.' Rubita's eyes glinted with anger.

'So let's play the game out, Rubita. Let's lay a trap to catch these jokers. Find out what you can from your sources and keep me informed. I'll play hard to get with our friend – maybe the real big guns behind this will show their hand. Mind you, I got the feeling that he is quite a savvy customer and it won't be easy. Things could get rough too, you know. Look what Lakhan Singh did to poor Mr Agarwal.' His face reflected concern as he pushed the car along through the traffic.

'I'm not worried, darling,' she said, snuggling closer to him. 'After all, I've got my knight in shining armour to protect me. Talking about Lakhan Singh, I wonder where he fits in. He's not in the same party as Gulab Chand. He's rounding up the crowds for a massive morcha next week in Mumbai. It's going to be the first major public demonstration after he hit the Mumbai scene, where he can show his strength to his political bosses in the metro. And the grapevine has it that it's likely to be a pretty big show.'

Suddenly Rubita straightened up. 'I wonder if Gulab Chand is connected in any way to the morcha. I have heard some of the Seva

Dal party bosses don't approve of it. You know, the types who are going to feel their own position in the party hierarchy threatened by this johnny-come-lately.' She paused for a moment. 'Then again, maybe Gulab Chand is trying to split the Lok Seva Dal and gain a foothold for the ruling party in Maharashtra. You know, fishing in troubled waters to see what he catches...that sort of thing. Interesting possibility.'

Her cellphone rang as they walked into the restaurant. It was Shekar, the research head at Pinnacle TV.

'Know something, Rubita?' said the excited voice at the other end. 'Those two guys you asked me about just before leaving the office? Gulab Chand and Lakhan Singh? They're from the same village, Basantipur, in Bihar.'

Rubita pursed her lips. The information was interesting, but she failed to see why Shekar was so worked up by the discovery. 'Good work, Shekar. Thanks for getting on the job so quickly. We should find out more.'

'Of course, there's more, Rubita. I wouldn't have called you up otherwise. Why do you think I am still at the office? I found out that Gulab Chand is in town right now. He is here to plan a morcha by cotton farmers in Mumbai next week. Something to do with pushing for higher support prices for their crops. You know, the usual bullshit.

'Now here's the interesting bit. The Dal wants to embarrass the Central government but doesn't have enough clout in the villages. So they've asked Lakhan Singh to round up the villagers. And Lakhan Singh was seen leaving the Oberoi hotel, where the minister is staying, just this morning. Through the service entrance, no less. Now, why are Gulab Chand, a Central minister belonging to the ruling party, and Lakhan Singh, who's supposed to be a Dal hitman, planning morchas together? How's that for a story?'

Rubita's guess had proved right. But she remembered her promise to Satyan. 'Shekar, I think your information is very interesting, and it might tie in with another angle which I am working on. But we need more evidence. Keep digging. And do me a favour. Keep this to yourself for the moment, because I don't want a premature story. I'm going to cover the morcha myself. Let's see if we can get any concrete info on this connection before exposing it. There may be something bigger cooking and I don't want to scare the big fish away by taking it public too early, okay?'

Shekar sounded uncertain, but agreed to keep it quiet. Promising to let her know if anything else turned up, he rang off.

Rubita sat down at their table, deep in thought. She glanced at Satyan as the waiter hovered around their table. When the waiter had taken their orders and gone, she apprised him of the latest development.

He nodded. 'It jells. Gulab Chand is definitely a sticky character. But he's just a fixer fronting for somebody. For whom? Finding that out will be the real trick. How the hell do we break into the inner circle of this den of thieves?'

'Why not go to the defence minister himself?' asked Rubita. 'Surely he will start an investigation?'

'That's out of the question,' said Satyan. 'The very fact that a labour minister is so clued into what's going on, shows that there is a leak somewhere. Whom can I trust? How do I know that I am not talking to the very people who are behind this? The stakes are so high that they won't hesitate to use violence if we try to pull any stunts. They already have.'

They paused while they were served. Afterwards he continued, 'No, we will have to make the first move ourselves. Nobody will believe us unless we have some evidence. We need to find out who the man behind Gulab Chand is. Who is the mastermind?'

'Well, we have two links in the chain: Lakhan Singh and Gulab Chand. How do we get to the third link?'

'By cutting off the first,' said Satyan. 'See, they want the design of the FCU, right? And they're using Lakhan Singh and his goons to scare the thing out of me. If we can neutralise Lakhan Singh, they will have to try other methods. Maybe they'll show their hand that way.'

'Yes, you've got it! Cut off one link and another will have to surface. But how? Lakhan Singh is a violent customer. Satyan, I hope you aren't planning any rough stuff. You must go to the police. He is a known thug. I'm sure I can dig up something for the cops to put him out of action, at least temporarily.'

'No, Rubes. That won't help. He is a known thug, like you said. So exposing him as one means nothing either to him or to Gulab Chand. And it might lead to more violence. It might endanger Mr Agarwal's life. I can't risk that. No. We must neutralise Lakhan Singh's value to his hidden masters. If we can figure a way of doing that without showing our own hand, only then can we hope to get somewhere.'

They ate silently, thinking about the situation.

Then Rubita came up with an idea. 'I know,' she said. 'We must expose Lakhan Singh's political double game. Because that's what he's playing. For now, he's a Lok Seva Dal man. But he's hobnobbing with the ruling party on the sly. All I have to do is run a story on that and the Dal top brass will go after him. That will keep him too busy to be of any use to the people who are after your FCU.'

'That's it!' said Satyan, perking up. 'Fight him on our ground – the media. But, Rubes, I don't want to risk your safety. God knows to what extent these guys are willing to go. You have to be careful not to show yourself.'

Rubita laughed. 'Not to worry, darling. I'm not going to try any heroics. We'll do it so subtly that Lakhan Singh and company will not know what hit them. Take this morcha these two guys are planning together. I'm going to be on the spot to cover it. Now, this is bound to be Lakhan Singh's showpiece, right? If past experience is anything to go by, the entire crowd will be a set-up. Free transport, a joy-ride to the big city, some pocket money for each of the village yokels who attend – the works. If Gulab Chand has come down to Mumbai just to make sure the show is a success, then it's going to be a big one. I'll bet that his ruling party goons are fanning out as we speak, preparing to round up the *hoi-polloi* so that Lakhan Singh can get the crowds he needs. I'll ask the research department to get me photos of all the local gang lords in the districts where the poor folk are being rounded up.' She clapped her hands in excitement, 'I know just the way to do this, Satyan! It'll be brilliant!'

'Great!' he said as the waiter appeared to clear the table. 'Let's go home and work this one out.'

Rubita laughed. 'No, lover boy, I know too well what you'll get up to. It's back to the office for me. Be a sweetheart and send a car to take me home in an hour or so.'

Satyan sighed wistfully as he reached for his cellphone.

◆

Sam Bannerjee stood waiting at the top of the portico steps in a silk tasselled dressing gown. His regal bearing gave the drab government bungalow the aura of a provincial raja's *haveli*. Rubita bounded up the steps, two at a time, and flung herself into her father's arms. An orderly stood ready at hand, but Sam had come out himself in the nippy December morning to welcome his only child into the house.

Giving her shoulders an affectionate squeeze he said, 'It's only on these occasions that I realise how time has flown. Every time you go away to Mumbai you become, in my mind's eye, a little schoolgirl in pigtails. And every time we meet I realise what a pretty young lady you've turned into. Do you realise it's been more than a year since your last visit to Delhi?'

'Sam, you always talk as if you're some dowdy old matron,' said Rubita in mock reprobation. 'If only you knew how many women would die to snare you, you'd be too busy fighting them off to wallow in old memories.'

'Oh-ho, my own daughter will be my matchmaker! Your poor dead mother should hear you now.'

Rubita playfully dug an elbow into her father's ribs. Hand in hand, they walked straight into the dining room where breakfast had been set for two. Warm sunlight streamed in through the tall windows. The sun seemed to play hide and seek with the leaves of the gulmohar trees outside. Little golden splashes lit up an otherwise dull grey wintry lawn.

'Mmmm, what a heavenly smell! I knew Joseph's Sunday-morning spread would be delicious. I saved up my appetite – I had just one cup of coffee on the flight – and now I'm ravenous!' She tripped into the kitchen to give Joseph, their majordomo for seventeen years, an affectionate 'hello' and returned to the table. The bacon was, as usual, excellent and the masala-omelette fairly melted in her mouth. The bread had been brought fresh from the baker.

She waited until they were into their second cup of coffee and her father had lighted his cigarette before she broached the subject that was uppermost in their minds. The cabinet subcommittee on the howitzer contract had met until late the previous night, evaluating the financial terms of each bid.

'Sam, how did the meeting go last night?'

He grinned. 'Trust my daughter to rush directly into a topic. It's a wonder your interviews are so watchable what with your manner being as subtle as a bull in a china shop!'

'Sam, don't hedge. You know I'm dying to hear the news.'

'Well, Rubes, you've got to learn to be a bit more detached. The world is a continuous stream of opportunities,' he continued, waving his cigarette in the air. 'Satyan has a tremendous product in his hands; he ought to do well with it, the howitzer contract notwithstanding.'

'Sam! Don't throw ten-letter words at me. Are you saying that the contract is not going to the Indian gun? How can they turn down a golden opportunity like this to get Indian industry on the world map? All the other companies are foreign; doesn't that count for anything?'

'Of course, Rubes, that's the primary reason why the cabinet hasn't yet taken a decision. They want to give Indian companies as much of a leg-up as they possibly can.'

'Stuff and nonsense! The Indian gun is the best in the field any way you look at it! They don't need patronising by those farts in the cabinet to get the contract. It's theirs by rights!'

Sam Bannerjee winced at his daughter's language. Nobody could control his headstrong daughter when she was on the warpath – not even Sam. In this, she was a chip of the old block. That was what he had been like in his younger days – brash, abrasive and absolutely sure of his convictions. On several occasions in the past, father and daughter had clashed in heated arguments that lasted late into the night. Vicious as the arguments invariably seemed, the morning always saw them laughing together at RK Laxman's latest cartoon in the papers. The special bond that existed between them had been a source of mystery to Mrs Bannerjee. Devoid of any intellectual pretensions, she had been shut out of this aspect of their lives. But she had been the rock of the family.

Many a time, Bannerjee had chuckled when his daughter had torn apart a wayward politician or official on tv. But now, under the glare of his daughter's fiery indignation, he felt his own self-assurance wilt a little.

'Rubes, look, I'm trying to get a message across to you if you will only stop to listen. You have to realise that a government cannot look at an issue through a narrow perspective. This contract is not going to be awarded solely on the basis of technical performance. I, as finance secretary, frankly see the payment terms of the FIAM and Vickers people to be far superior. I can't afford to ignore that.'

Rubita's mouth dropped open. 'Sam, what are you saying? *You* are supporting the foreign guns?'

'Now look here, young lady,' Bannerjee shot back irritably, 'I only talked about the financial angle. You know how proud I am of Satyan's achievement – not just because he's your fiancé. Any Indian would feel the same about it. You know how much I tried to help him in marketing the thing by using my contacts, not just here in India but in the United States as well. But this is about national governance, Rubes, don't forget that. There are larger issues at play here.

'Now, if you had any sense, you would tell Satyan to stop banking on just this one contract and look to the other benefits that this breakthrough can give his company. I've tried to, in my own way, but I can't talk too freely about it with him now that other issues are involved, you know.'

'But, Sam, that's preposterous! We were depending on you to handle those goons in the cabinet. This is a chance that India cannot afford to lose. It's a chance to create history! Are you people so caught up with your issues and perspectives and debates that you cannot break with convention if only for the sake of our own country? Banking on "just this one contract"? Is that all it means to you people – a contract, like any other? Isn't this something that will make every Indian hold his head higher? Isn't it something that will inspire many more Indians to challenge the myth of the superiority of Western technology? Isn't it something that people like you, who have had to see India cow down to the West a hundred times in the past, have been waiting for all these years? I can't believe that this is happening! What's the big deal about these foreign guns anyway?'

'Don't go all self-righteous on me, young lady!' Bannerjee rasped, slapping the table. 'The country's governance is much more complicated than you seem to think. We cannot afford to let our emotions get the better of us. And since you're so keen to know, we have been looking at one or two golden opportunities to leverage our position with the Western backers of FIAM and Vickers to get political concessions India has been wanting for years. Our friends across the border are quite worried about our bargaining strength in the UN and other forums now.'

A long pause followed as Rubita tried to come to terms with her father's line of reasoning.

After a while, he continued in a gentler tone. 'Rubes, patriotism isn't the privilege of only the young. We old fogies have our uses, too. India has emerged stronger as a result of Satyan's breakthrough and the collective wisdom of the government is being put to use to leverage this new strength to its maximum. Obviously, levers will be applied at the highest level by other governments for a kind of return of favours. It shouldn't sound so strange to youngsters nowadays. You keep talking about package deals, don't you? Well, we're in the midst of negotiating a package deal, that's all. The only thing is that the public won't ever see the technical, economic, political and diplomatic components of the package at one go. If running a government were so simple, who would need the IAS, eh?'

'I think I get it now, Sam. The Indian gun is just a pawn that the powers that be in this country are using in the great political game. You don't really care about the FCU or anything, do you?'

'Now that's not fair, Rubes. That's just not fair. Nobody will be happier than me to see the Indian gun get the cabinet's approval. All

I'm trying to say is that there are other influences at play here. You and Satyan shouldn't attach any naive notions of national glory to this gun business. That's what it is in the end – a business. My end of the business is political and Satyan's technical. We all have to be rational about this. I think you can at least see some part of what I have been trying to say. I'm happy about that. Now make sure Satyan understands all this so that he is not disappointed if things don't turn out his way, okay?'

Rubita knew that she had run up against the stone wall of the establishment. She had seen it often enough in the course of her work. She rose from the table and walked towards the door. Bannerjee remained seated, watching her, a deep sadness in his eyes. He reached out for another cigarette from the pack.

She turned back at the door. 'Sam, tell me one thing. Is Gulab Chand being backed by someone senior in the cabinet?'

The question caught him completely off-guard. He pondered it, cigarette lighter frozen mid-air. He realised that it would explain many recent events surrounding the labour minister which had seemed very strange to him, especially in connection with the howitzer deal. It made sense for someone to use him as a front if he wanted kickbacks on the contract. Gulab Chand's position as a minister gave him a great deal of power to maneuver. And yet he was junior enough in the cabinet to need the patronage of a senior colleague, which made him more malleable. Was he earning that patronage by acting as a front-man?

Rubita watched her father from the doorway. His expression told her that he didn't have any answers to the other questions she wanted to ask. But she had seen enough.

◆

The morcha was a huge success. Thousands of villagers had been herded out of their villages from distant corners of the state and bundled into trucks for a joy ride to Mumbai and a hundred rupees each. Not one of them knew or cared what they were there for; all that mattered was that they were taking in the sights of the fabled city at no cost. It was slack season out in the fields, and so no work was going to be disrupted. The crowds bellowed the slogans they had been given as they roared through the downtown streets. The entire afternoon traffic of the city seemed to have halted to watch their progress to the government's secretariat.

Lakhan Singh sat among the VIPs on the *pandal* which straddled the busy thoroughfare. He was beaming. He had done well – he had met his targeted number of heads. The faction of the Lok Seva Dal which he owed allegiance to would reward him for this day. Maybe they would even give him a ticket in the next elections. What made Lakhan Singh smile even more broadly, as he surveyed the scene, was that a second bonus would surely be coming his way from the ruling party. He was having his cake and eating it too.

And the tv coverage! He had never seen so many tv teams covering such event before. They seemed to be everywhere. It looked like he was going to be big news. The cameras had taken every conceivable angle. He even spotted several satellite tv crews; he was going to be seen abroad! Lakhan Singh felt good.

He checked his watch. There were only two speakers left. An hour, an hour-and-a-half at the outside, and he could leave for his meeting with Gulab Chand in his Oberoi suite. Lakhan Singh had fixed a meeting for that very evening since Gulab Chand was returning to Delhi early the next day.

That other little matter had worked out smoothly, too. That pompous fool Sharma had not been able to swallow his pride even at the last. His voice over the phone that morning had sounded petulant in defeat, hinting vaguely of reaching an 'understanding'. The man had come around fast, just as Gulab Chand-ji had said he would. He must have checked with his friends in Delhi and they would have put him straight about Gulab Chand-ji. A truly great man, Gulab Chand-ji, thought Lakhan Singh as he contemplated his rosy future, with two godfathers to provide for him.

It was seven p.m. when he drove towards the Oberoi. He had not taken any of his cronies along, giving them their bonuses and leaving them to paint the town red after a day's good work. The Dal top brass would be in conclave discussing the morcha and their cronies would be out celebrating. Not much chance of his visit to the Oberoi being noticed. All the same, he took care to take the service entrance on his way in. It wouldn't do to be seen in the company of a top member of the ruling party, especially on this day.

He wasn't seen as he took the service elevator to the fifteenth floor. Padding down the carpeted corridor, he rang the bell at the door of the Orchid suite. An imperious voice bade him enter.

The minister was seated in regal style, a tall drink, half-finished already, by his side. Satyan was seated in a chair across from him.

'Come in, come in,' boomed Gulab Chand. 'We were just discussing you and the morcha. You have done well, Lakhan Singh. See, Sharma sahib? We are not joking when we say that the people are with us.'

'It was all due to your blessings, Gulab Chand-ji,' replied the strongman. 'If god is willing, this is but the beginning. You have only to give the command to see the wonders that your poor servant can perform for you. Your every wish can become true if you give the word.'

'I am pleased, Lakhan Singh. Delhi will not fail to reward you.'

'What happens next, Gulab Chand-ji?' asked Satyan.

'Next? Why, Sharma sahib, just you wait and see. The ruling party has not been able to regain its true place in Maharashtra for so many years. But now, with the help of our friends in various parties, and in the Dal particularly,' Gulab Chand winked at Lakhan Singh, 'we shall shortly return in great style. Today is a very significant day in Maharashtra politics, my friend, and I am proud to be associated with this great event. Pinnacle TV will report on it in a few minutes. I want to hear what they say.'

The telephone at his side rang. Gulab Chand picked up the receiver and listened intently. He turned to Satyan, his face solemn. 'There seems to have been an accident, Satyan sahib. Your father seems to have had a stroke and he is in hospital. There is somebody at the reception downstairs waiting for you.' He held out the instrument.

Leaping to his feet, Satyan grabbed the phone. He listened silently to the voice at the other end. Then he said, 'Wait for me there. I will come down immediately.'

Turning to Gulab Chand, he said, 'Gulab Chand-ji, you must excuse me for a moment. I will meet my man and return within ten minutes. Please do not disturb yourselves. My father is not in great danger, I believe. But I must verify the exact situation and give the necessary instructions. I will be back.' Satyan rushed out.

Gulab Chand flicked the buttons on the remote control and tuned into Pinnacle tv. The two men watched with rapt attention as shots of the morcha flashed on the screen, the lead story of the eight o'clock news bulletin.

'The morcha was good, Lakhan Singh, but you must be more discreet in future,' said Gulab Chand sternly. 'There was no need to have the ruling party workers so prominently visible among the crowd. There they are. See for yourself.'

A tiny prickle of worry sprang up in Lakhan Singh's heart. Were they so obvious? If they were easily noticeable on tv, might not they have been seen by the Dal observers? They had been necessary to control the crowds, who would otherwise have melted away to spend their hundred rupees before even reaching the secretariat. In fact, he himself had not been able to spot them from atop the pandal. And all the henchmen had been out-of-towners. He had been sure that the local Dal goons wouldn't know them. Yet, there they were, easily spotted on tv.

The newsreader gave way to the reporter on the field. The cameras dipped in and about the bobbing crowd. It seemed to be a detailed story. He should have been exultant, instead an uneasy silence gripped him. Dimly, he heard the words as the camera ranged about. Every time it closed up on the crowd, it seemed one or the other of the hired goons was bang in the middle of the picture.

'Are you sure they will not be known in Mumbai?' asked the minister.

Lakhan Singh could only manage a nod as he gulped several times. It would be a miracle if nobody in the Dal ranks spotted them. And then he heard what sounded to him as a death sentence: '...We have received unconfirmed reports that the ruling party machinery has been informally mobilised to organise this demonstration. Pinnacle

TV will bring you more details on this mammoth demonstration with in-depth interviews of the key players...'

Lakhan Singh's palms were clammy with the cold sweat of fear. It was next to impossible that the Dal bosses had missed that part. They would surely investigate to seek the truth of the 'rumours', and then the whole game would be out. Retribution would be quick; the Dal would deal summarily with this kind of double-cross. He was finished here, he knew. In one swift stroke of ill-luck, his dream world had come crashing down.

Gulab Chand was watching him closely. 'Lakhan Singh, I think this chapter is closed. In my opinion, you had better leave Mumbai immediately. Go back to Basantipur. Take Suraj Bhan's help and tell him I sent you. I will see what I can do for you in a few weeks. You have spoiled everything by taking such a foolish risk.'

'But, Gulab Chand-ji, none of the men is known in Mumbai,' Lakhan Singh was bleating, 'I swear on my mother! It is only because of the tv coverage...'

'Enough!' Gulab Chand shouted. 'You are endangering not only your life with every minute you delay, but mine also, you fool! You have already put to waste so many months of preparation, and now you want to create more problems by staying here in my room, squealing like a stuck pig! Get out! There is not a moment to lose. Go to Patel's farm in Panvel. I will arrange for a helicopter to take you from there. The pilot will tell you what to do next. Go back to Bihar and wait for my instructions. Now go quickly!'

Gulab Chand covered his eyes with his hands after Lakhan Singh left. Because of the recklessness of that dimwitted thug, not only had the ruling party's plan for making a comeback in Maharashtra been jeopardised, even the Satyan Sharma affair would have to be started afresh. Pandey-ji would be livid when he learnt of this.

7

Ketan Manwani, chairman of Manwani Holdings, was well into his sixties and wore the power of India's largest industrial conglomerate with an air of understated nobility. He had been intrigued when Satyan requested a meeting to discuss what he called 'one of the most ambitious projects to be taken up by an Indian'. He had been even more intrigued when Satyan requested that he be accompanied only by Dr Atal Shukla, a former dean at MIT who headed Sunrise Infomatrix, the largest software house in the country. Pure Space Networks was fast becoming Sunrise's most dynamic competitor. The chairman had acquiesced even though Satyan held back from revealing the agenda beforehand.

Manwani had first met Satyan some years before, when he was awarded as the country's most promising young businessman. Manwani had presided over that function and had been impressed with the young man's vision and drive. He had followed the growth of the EMMG group with interest. A lasting friendship developed, with Manwani on occasion providing advice and guidance, playing very much the fond uncle to a favourite nephew.

Satyan had brought Jacob Mehta along for the meeting. Mehta presented to the chairman their breakthrough ideas on GPS software and the myriad applications it could be put to in developing the industrial infrastructure of the country. The sweep of the presentation won Manwani's unstinted praise and Mehta's enthusiasm infected both listeners. Though the old man's mystification about the purpose of the presentation grew as it unfolded, he refrained from seeking enlightenment on Satyan's motives until it was complete.

After a marathon session, they settled down to tea. The late afternoon sun glinted off the nearby stock exchange building. The white-gloved steward made a discreet exit, having satisfied himself that all his charges were comfortable.

'Well, young fellow, you have had us spellbound for close to an hour. It's not often that I am asked to hold on to the suspense in a business meeting for such a long time. Satyan, would you care to enlighten me now?' asked the chairman.

Satyan grinned. 'Sir, I really appreciate that you have been able to contain your curiosity until now. And grateful for the faith you have placed in us. I assure you it was worth the wait.' He leaned forward. 'Sir, I am going to violate some very sacred tenets of confidentiality. I am probably putting my neck on the block – in fact, I could even be accused of high treason. I am also going to reveal some of Pure Space Network's most zealously guarded plans.' He glanced over at Dr Shukla meaningfully. 'We, that is Jacob and I, because we couldn't involve anyone else, debated long and hard on the wisdom of talking to you and whether or not we should invite Dr Shukla to this meeting. In the end, we decided that there was no alternative. We are facing an unprecedented situation and are in way over our heads. And we need your unqualified trust. So we are going to place all, I repeat, all our cards on the table, even though we have a competitor sitting across it.'

Manwani waved a hand in the air. 'I have been following your career for a while now, young chap. Pure Space won our admiration ages ago. I think I speak for Dr Shukla as well.' Shukla nodded gravely. 'And I personally assure you that your confidence in us will not be broken. We will not take undue advantage of information received here.

'Now, to the matter at hand. It doesn't take too much intelligence to guess that your new product will have some military uses. The howitzer contract is not exactly public knowledge yet, but I happen to know a little bit about it. Enough, at any rate, to know that you are involved.' He smiled indulgently at his guests' astounded faces. 'I also happen to know that you are in the market for a partner with a sizable investible surplus. So, while you were enthralling me with the absolutely delightful breakthroughs your team at Pure Space has made, I was putting two and two together. You've, in all probability, come here to suggest some sort of tie-up between our two companies, I would imagine. So go ahead, my dear chap, don't hesitate to tell me what you have in mind. But I caution you, you mustn't tell me more than you need to. Don't compromise any classified military information. I trust your judgment.'

Satyan was amazed by the older man's perspicacity.

'Sir, that's a relief to hear. Yes, we've had to restrict our presentation to the non-military aspects of our products. That was aimed primarily at convincing you that ours is a world-class outfit capable of standing shoulder-to-shoulder with the best in Silicon Valley.' He glanced at Dr Shukla, who smiled encouragingly.

'Now, sir,' continued Satyan, 'we have reached a stalemate. Maybe even a checkmate. We've got a successful prototype which we are sure can stand up to the competition. What we need now is commercial backing which can finance the government in the purchase of the guns.'

'Financing the government? To acquire armament for Indian defence forces?' Manwani was puzzled. 'But surely, if there is an Indian option which can stand up to the competition, the government will pitch in with finance by itself?'

'Precisely our own expectations, sir. We had taken finance for granted when we set out on this project. But I am sad to say that the government's thinking is different.'

Satyan looked uncomfortable. Mehta stared fixedly at his shoes. Finally, Satyan cleared his throat. 'Sir, we have a draft proposal for financing the whole project.' He held out a slim folder. 'I would request that you give it your consideration. That's all we have to say to you as of now.'

'How much would be needed?'

'Twenty thousand crores, sir.'

Manwani smiled. 'Well, well, well. Let's see what we can do.'

◆

The Friday night rave at the Quantango, the latest hot spot on the Juhu shoreline, was intense, throbbing and psychedelically overwhelming. Satyan and Rubita were beating themselves about in sync with the frenzied mob, clothes drenched with sweat after more than two hours under the strobes. Rubita attracted appreciative glances, from both sexes. Her shimmering maroon Balmain creation was open down the neck and tied up at the waist, and a chunky chain twitched between her swaying breasts. The hip-hugging satin skirt swirled about her legs, barely reaching her knees. She laughed as someone bumped against her in the semidarkness, throwing her against Satyan, who grinned back and grabbed hold of her by the waist.

'Let's check out RATC, Rubes,' he shouted over the din. 'This place is getting too full.' The Rock Around the Clock discotheque had seen better days, so the crowd wouldn't be as thick as in the Quantango, and breathing space was what they needed right now.

'Okay,' she replied with a nod, and they started to head out.

Outside, the moon threw a long beam over the still waters of the Arabian Sea. A few scattered tables had begun receiving early diners.

A voice stopped them short as they headed for the car-park. 'Mr Sharma, a moment please.' They turned to see a young man with sharp angular features, deep set eyes and a shock of dark, curly hair. He was dressed just like any other denizen of the discos, but his manner was earnest and deferential.

'Mr Sharma, Miss Bannerjee, please excuse me for intruding on your evening,' he continued. 'My name is Javed Butt, and I have been asked to speak to both of you about a very important matter.' Instinctively, Satyan and Rubita reached for each other's hands. 'I understand that you may be a bit startled, but I assure you that it's all right. Why don't we sit down at one of these tables and get to know each other?' Butt took Satyan by the elbow and guided him to a table on the far side of the wide lawn. Rubita followed, somewhat apprehensive, but she figured that no harm could come in such a public place.

The stranger seated himself so that he could keep an eye on the entrance. As a result the illumination from the garden lights around them fell on his face, and they could study his intense grey eyes as he started to speak in a low but sincere tone.

'We have been trying to get in touch with you in private for some time now, you know.' All traces of deference in his manner disappeared now. 'This business of the – ah – FCU,' he smiled as his listeners started at the mention of a top-secret project, 'it has become invested with certain, shall we say, complications, as you are no doubt aware.'

Satyan and Rubita had recovered from their shock quickly and were appraising the man. To Satyan he seemed to have had a public school education and he found himself warming to the stranger's sincere bearing. His circumspection marked him out as a bureaucrat: an official dressed up as a party animal for the night. His dress was pretty cool, thought Rubita.

'I am,' he continued, 'from the Ministry of Defence. I have come from the capital to investigate reports that certain antisocial elements were attempting to compromise the interests of our country. We had tracked them to Mumbai and I was deputed to keep you under surveillance to determine whether they had made any overtures to you.'

Satyan was immediately angry. 'Do you mean that you've been spying on us?' he asked. 'This is really too much. I am going to take it up with the defence secretary. What is the meaning of this?'

'Please do not misunderstand, Mr Sharma,' said Butt. 'We do not doubt your patriotism or your dedication. It was only to understand the modus operandi of these antisocial elements that we had to resort to this step. Quite frankly, we were also concerned for your safety, because the methods employed by these people are often fraught with extreme danger. But after yesterday, that is, after the morcha, we realised that you are quite capable of turning the tables on them. That was as neat a trick to neutralise Lakhan Singh's influence on matters as I have seen in many years of service. My compliments to both of you. Incidentally, I wonder if you are aware that Lakhan Singh's...ah...neutralisation...has been permanently guaranteed as a consequence of an incident at the Vashi bridge on the road to Panvel this afternoon. We have it from reliable sources that his employers, the Lok Seva Dal, did not take well to the fact that he was playing a double game, especially since he seemed to have them, rather than the ruling party, slotted as the sacrificial goats.'

Satyan and Rubita were dumbstruck. 'Do you mean to say,' she whispered, gulping at the thought, 'do you mean to say that...that Lakhan Singh has been killed?'

'As he was paying the toll at Vashi bridge, some gangsters from a car in the adjoining lane fired several dozen rounds from AK-47s into his car. Death was certain and immediate. He had been trying to leave the city after the morcha yesterday and his meeting at the Oberoi with you, Mr Sharma. The Dal had anticipated his attempt to flee and was obviously watching all the exits from the city. The operation seems to have been carried out with clinical precision. The killers got away without leaving even the tiniest clue – none that will be followed up with any seriousness by the local authorities.'

Satyan and Rubita exchanged glances. Butt seemed so blasé about the whole event. And it was their – Satyan's and Rubita's – actions that had, in part, led to his death. As if reading their thoughts, Butt spoke without looking up from the menu card in his hand, 'Please do not trouble yourselves with any feelings of guilt about this man. He had it coming to him. For one thing, he had the blood of several rival union men on his hands. He was a man who lived by violence. If not today, he would surely have met a violent death some other day. For another, we know that he was involved in underhand methods to obtain the secrets of your project. He would have ended up compromising the interests of our country. He deserved what he got.'

They stared open-mouthed at him for a long moment. At last, the questions poured out. 'And what about you? Who are you? How do you know so much about us? And how are we to believe you? Do you have any ID card or something?' Satyan asked him.

Butt smiled. 'I was wondering whether you would ever ask. I would have been very disappointed if you hadn't. Here it is. But please don't hold it up for everybody to see. It will attract undue attention.'

Satyan examined it closely before passing it on to Rubita. 'Well,' he said, 'so you have an ID card. What do you want from us? Mind you, I am warning you that *I* will decide whether or not to give you what you want. Don't try to force or threaten me.'

'I want nothing but the good of my country,' said the man. 'For the moment, let me assure you that I have been asked only to give you protection that is necessary under the circumstances. You see, while the manner in which you removed Lakhan Singh from the scheme of things was admirable, the powers which seek to disrupt your work on the FCU will probably decide to adopt more, shall we say stringent, measures to achieve their aims. This in turn means that undercover surveillance is no longer sufficient to guarantee your safety. That is why I have only today received orders to come out into the open and establish overt contact with you and make the necessary arrangements.'

'How do we know that we can trust you?' asked Rubita. She could see, peeping from the open neck of his shirt, the tip of a scar running down his chest. She found herself speculating on its cause and how deep down his chest it ran. She thought that Butt would be extremely desirable to girls and wondered briefly if he had a beautiful wife or girlfriend. Guiltily, she realised that she had been staring at him and hastily turned her eyes away.

Butt smiled warmly. 'I will be as unobtrusive as possible, madam. My presence will only be noticed by you whenever there is any apprehension of danger. I will also request you to keep me informed of any strange developments around yourselves which you may notice. Otherwise, I shall do my best to be discreet. Here is my cellphone number. I would advice you to memorise it and destroy the paper.' He handed Satyan a small slip as he reclaimed his ID card. 'Now, if you will excuse me, I shall take leave of you. Please wait for a few minutes before leaving, so that we are not seen going out together.'

He got up to go. 'And one last thing. As you leave this hotel, you may notice a white Hyundai parked some distance up the road. You'll be followed. He has been watching you for the last two weeks. He has a companion who is keeping a tab on your scientist friends in Bangalore. Don't panic. Act normal. I shall be watching him. We are waiting for the right time before taking action. Good night.'

Connolly allowed himself a thin smile of satisfaction as he turned and walked away from their table. So far they seemed to have bought his cover story. He was pleased that they had been quick to ask for identification and had examined his ID card closely, because now that his credentials had formally been established, they would be more comfortable dealing with him. He had taken this step because his earlier cover of a Bangalore-based software engineer would not give him the leeway to barge in on Satyan and Rubita whenever the situation called for it. Posing as an Indian intelligence officer, he could latch himself onto them under the pretext of protecting national interests and they would feel duty-bound to accommodate him.

They remained at the table for another ten minutes, staring out into the sea. It was Rubita who broke the silence. 'How did he get on to the trick about Lakhan Singh, I wonder? And how did he know that all this was connected to the gun deal?'

'Maybe they are on to Gulab Chand in Delhi. Being from the labour ministry, that reptile has no business poking his nose into defence stuff. They must have been watching him at the Sher-e-Punjab when I went there. But one thing is clear, Rubes, there are a lot of shady things happening in this project. And I'm damned if I'm going to let these goons get away with this nonsense. We'll find out what's really going on. I think we should continue with our original plan of flushing out the man who's behind Gulab Chand, that's the only real lead we have as of now.'

'Yeah, you're right. I'll continue to dig around Gulab Chand to find out who his backers are. One thing this Lakhan Singh affair has shown me – if there are only gangsters and thugs involved in this, they don't have the savvy to understand the way media can harm them. Remember what you said that night – fight them on our ground? Bang on!'

Satyan smiled as he rose to leave. 'I said much more to you that night, but you were too busy plotting the downfall of the high and mighty.' Rubita pulled a face and punched him lightly on his arm. They headed out to the car park. He glanced into the rearview mirror as he turned the car onto the road. 'Looks like Butt was right about one thing. There's a white Hyundai following us.'

'It could have been planted there by him. Can you see the driver's face?'

'No, it's too dark. Ah, why bother? We've had enough for today. If he doesn't bother us, we'll not bother him. Let's forget the RATC. I'm calling it a day. Let that goon go to hell.'

'You sound as if you're one of those animals one sees in wildlife documentaries, the ones with the "live and let live" policies. More civilised than man and all that.' She giggled.

He put the car into auto-transmission mode and slid a hand along her thigh. 'And wilder than the animals,' he grunted.

'Hold your horses, lover boy, we'll be home in a jiffy,' she said, laughing and guiding his hand gently under her skirt.

◆

Mrs Goswamy – her name was Pallavi – gasped audibly as Pandey-ji brought his thumb and forefinger hard together on the tip of her right nipple. She was lying snuggled up to him on the settee in the vast bedroom of his Ghaziabad farmhouse. The pallu of her dark green chiffon sari had slipped down and lay half across his lap. He could see deep into the cleavage between her voluptuous breasts. The fiery orange material of her blouse plunged down way past the heavy diamond-encrusted gold pendant of her necklace which rose and fell with her rapid breathing. Underneath the blouse, Pandey-ji could see the black lace of her bra. Shoving his hand in, he cupped her breast and, with a rough twist, jerked her blouse down. One lace-covered nipple sprang out, stiff in arousal.

She slid her fingers gently along his thigh. Lightly flicking aside the folds of his white cotton dhoti, she let her fingertips brush against the throbbing head of his member. With a hoarse cry, he flung the dhoti aside and grabbed her hands. He slid lower on the settee and pulled her roughly so that she sat on his lap, straddling him. He jerked at the cords which held his drawers. His paunch heaved and rolled in his agitation. She hitched her sari above her thighs to get at the waistband of her black lace panties. Her carefully done hair had fallen askew. The little string of jasmines, with its mild fragrance, was lying crushed under their feet. Kneeling over him she knew she looked a mess, no better than any whore. But she saw that these little niceties meant nothing to Pandey-ji. He wanted a gratification so basic that his entire being was focused on the imminent union and release.

'I am sure you will enjoy the taste of my manhood, Pallavi-ji,' Pandey-ji grunted. 'You will not be disappointed.'

She smiled thinly and licked her lips. Steeling herself she buckled down to it. She had realised that the only way they would make any headway was for her to get on top. Lifting high her sari, she spread her legs as wide as possible to grip the huge expanse of his torso. He could clearly see her wet vagina in the pitch black bush between her soft and milky thighs. Then it disappeared below the surge of his paunch as she lowered herself onto him. It took a bit of maneuvering for her to take him inside her. Pandey-ji's fumbling frenzy made the job more difficult and it was with relief that she at last got some rhythm into the final jerks. She watched with a detached air as he stared, hypnotised, at her breasts, which were bouncing up and down in front of his face. When he had achieved his release, she got off and slumped wearily by his side. Pandey-ji closed his eyes, waiting for his heartbeat to return to normal.

'How did you like it, eh, Pallavi-ji? Good, no? You look exhausted. Go and tidy yourself. Call for some cold beer from the kitchen. That will refresh you, eh? We can have another round of fun later.'

Pallavi Goswamy smiled meekly, struggling with her clothes. Pandey-ji laughed happily and slapped her bottom as she stepped towards the bathroom.

Mrs Goswamy pouted at her image in the bathroom mirror. She was not used to being treated so churlishly. Well, she thought, there's always a time and place for everything. And right now, she wanted to concentrate on getting her way with this new star of the capital's political circuit. This was a business investment. Quickly, she rearranged her blouse and sari. With quick touches, she brought a semblance of order back to her hair and makeup. Putting on a warm smile, she returned to the bedroom.

The minister was on the intercom, speaking to a servant downstairs. 'Tell Gulab Chand-ji that I will be down in a few minutes. Make him comfortable in the sitting room.' He hung up and smiled at her. 'Eh, my pretty, I think you enjoyed that, no? Wait, don't go away, I have some urgent matter to attend to and then we will continue, eh? If you want anything, just ring the bell, my servants will provide it. Stay here, I will be back soon.'

He looked down at himself to make sure there were no telltale stains on his dhoti. Satisfied, he hoisted himself to his feet and waddled to the door, smoothening his kurta as he went out.

Mrs Goswamy stepped through the French windows onto the terrace. A cool night breeze was playing, just strong enough to stir the leaves on the peepal trees nearby. The terrace was wide and had a balustrade at the edge. It ran all the way around the house. The tiles under her bare feet felt cool. She strolled along the edge, the soft breeze soothing her frazzled nerves. As she came up against one corner, she heard the voices of Pandey-ji and his visitor floating up to her. She stopped, cocking her head to listen. The visitor's voice had a whining, defensive note to it. In response, Pandey-ji's seemed to be rising in anger by the minute.

She was able to hear snatches of the conversation. Remembering the names mentioned was most important. She caught fleeting references to somebody called 'Sharma sahib'. And then, there were references to some Americans. These Americans were not going to be happy about something. She tried to get the first name of this Sharma; it was one of the most common surnames in India. Her frustration grew when, even after several minutes, no first name was mentioned. There was something about a gun and its design. She couldn't make out the details.

Pandey-ji's voice rose again. He was castigating his visitor for using a common thug to manage a sensitive operation. She heard Pinnacle TV being mentioned; they had apparently made a fool of Gulab Chand. That remark helped Mrs Goswamy connect the dots. She had heard of the morcha and the rumours that a conspiracy hatched by the ruling party in Mumbai had gone awry. It was obvious to her that these two men were hand in glove in that piece of political skullduggery. But what about the gun and the Americans – where did all that fit in?

Suddenly the voices downstairs faded from her consciousness as a dark suspicion began to grow in her mind. Her hands flew to her cheeks as she stood wide-eyed in horror. She was sure now that she had witnessed an episode in a treasonous venture involving the two men downstairs. Icy fear gripped her.

Then she heard the visitor taking his leave of Pandey-ji and rushed back into the bedroom, adjusting her sari. She knew that, unwillingly or not, she was involved in this plot – one which was far bigger and murkier than any she had ever hatched. Currying favour for a few business contracts was one thing, playing with military secrets of the country was something else altogether. Deep in her heart, she knew that possession of the information she had just received came with a responsibility. She had to take some action; what that should be she would figure out later.

For now, she would have to perform convincingly for the rest of the night. Pandey-ji should suspect nothing. She composed herself as the minister made his way up the stairs.

8

Jamila Barkhatiev left the guesthouse for her Sunday morning visit to Bangalore's crowded Johnson Market. Row upon row of meat shops festooned with sides of mutton and dressed chickens were packed into a long, low red-brick building. The weekend crowd milled about. The whole place was redolent of the local bazaar in her native Samarkand. She jostled through the shoppers to make her way to Corbett's Ham Shop in the corner. Corbett, a hulking man in his fifties, was extremely proud of his shop. It was easily the cleanest and best-stocked in Johnson Market and he had a large and loyal clientele among the city's growing expatriate community.

Konstantin had watched, with a deepening sense of unease, the growing closeness between the American agent and Satyan Sharma. He knew that, though the field tests had gone well for the Indo-Uzbek howitzer, there were still some stages of development before it could officially be sanctioned for full-scale production. General Aliakhin had corroborated his assessment based on evidence gathered from his sources in the Uzbek government. They had decided that the time was not yet ripe for them to strike. But with the American positioning himself for the end-game, Konstantin was under pressure to gain some form of advantage. Leaving a surveillance team in Mumbai to cover Connolly and Satyan, he had shifted camp to Bangalore for his next move.

Rajan was in Mumbai for the weekend, for a conference with Satyan and his team at Pure Space. This helped Konstantin in two ways: the girl was unaccompanied, and Rajan's absence from Bangalore could hamper pursuit and give them more of a head start. All by himself, old Barkhatiev could be relied upon to panic rather than think level-headedly.

The agents closed in for the catch. They had studied her routine well and knew just what to do.

Konstantin worked his way up to the counter beside her, elbowing her sharply in the process. Murmuring apologies in French, he smiled shyly at Jamila. She returned the smile and shook her head, not able to respond in the same language. Another operative moved in right behind her, fumbling with a large cloth bag. They had guessed right – the locals crowding around assumed that all three 'white-skins' were together. They made space for the three. She winced as something sharp poked into her midriff from behind. She turned to see another white man fumbling to manage a very large bag of carpenter's tools while trying to attract the attention of the shop assistant. The pressure of the bag and the crowd behind the man kept her pinned to the counter. Feeling a bit annoyed, she wanted to reprimand him when he too mumbled an apology in French. Shrugging to show his helplessness, he continued a barrage in the strange language, wearing a sheepish smile on his face. Other sharp objects in his bag prodded her back and she decided to get away from the shop, but she was hemmed in by Konstantin at her side, who had launched a voluble barrage of words of his own. Suddenly the sharp objects were pulled away and she could catch her breath again.

Corbett materialised in front of her and she smiled. 'Good morning, madam. Same as usual?' She nodded her head quickly and he rattled off instructions to an assistant.

In less than a minute, she began to feel giddy. She found herself groping for support, grabbing at the countertop. The Russians caught her as she fell in a faint. They asked the assistant for a glass of water, which was hurriedly provided. The crowd gave her room and her supposed companions plenty of suggestions to revive her. It was no use – the sodium pentothal dose was guaranteed to knock her out for at least two hours. They half-carried her, murmuring apologies, into the air-conditioned comfort of their waiting car.

Meanwhile, in her white Esteem parked around the corner, her driver was deep in conversation with another 'white-skin', a driver for one of the expats who had come shopping. The man had offered him a Marlboro and they were discussing the finer points of the car as they smoked. The stranger stood shielding the driver's view of the shop, throwing unobtrusive glances behind his shoulder. Finally, he saw the vehicle carrying Jamila take a U-turn and drive away, heading out of the city towards the exclusive locality of Koramangala. Finishing his cigarette, he told Jamila's driver that he had to fetch his 'memsahib' from a department store nearby, waved goodbye, got into his car and drove away.

The whole affair, carried out with precision, had lasted less than four minutes. Less than half-an-hour later, Konstantin and his team bundled their captive into a hired Cessna twin-engine eight-seater and took off for Mumbai. They had used diplomatic passports to cruise through the perfunctory security check. A heavily sedated Jamila had been pushed aboard in a wheelchair attended by what seemed to be a couple of medicos. The Russians carried medical records certifying that she was suffering from leukemia. They also carried tickets for that evening's Aeroflot flight to Moscow.

◆

The resort at Madh near Mumbai was a good place for a day-trip to the seashore. It was just a couple of hours' drive from his house in Khar, and Satyan and Rubita had chosen it for a soothing jaunt with Jake, Maggie and the kids. They had driven over on Friday evening in Satyan's Land Rover so that they could step out on Aksa beach in the cool Saturday dawn and have an invigorating time playing with Frisbees in relative privacy before the weekend crowds landed up.

They stepped out dressed in T-shirts; both women in billowing skirts and sandals, the men in cargos, their shoes in their hands. The boys wore shorts and all of them had bought straw hats to protect their faces from sunburn from a market near the hotel the previous evening. There was a scattering of holidaymakers on the beach at that hour, mostly guests from the string of hotels along the shoreline.

For an hour or so, the group had a long stretch of sand to itself. That early in the morning, there was thankfully little to be seen of the garbage that litters Mumbai's beaches. The dawn air was fresh and the damp sand felt cool to the revellers' bare feet. The two young kids, aged seven and five, had a rollicking time. Once the crowds came in, they were spellbound by the bursting activity all around them. They didn't get to see such hordes in the States and the riot of colours, noises and smells was overpowering. They watched in fascination as, one by one, the food and fruit juice stalls opened up and started a brisk trade. A loud-speaker began belting out raucous Bollywood hits that could be heard a mile away. One stall they passed as they strolled by was selling crushed popsicles doused with flavours from a range of syrups and juices sporting every colour under the sun. Its counter was covered with a large, damp red cloth. The boys cast a glance over their shoulders; the adults were deep in conversation and paid their pleading eyes no attention. The stall owner saw them and smiled through his yellow-stained teeth. Casting an appraising eye at the group of affluent elders accompanying the boys, he called them over to sample his wares.

'Taking try, taking try? No problem, you taking try,' he said loudly, hoping to catch the attention of the adults. Deciding to take a gamble, he grabbed two popsicles and poured liberally from two or three bottles. Leaning over the counter, he handed the popsicles to the boys. Enraptured, they had licked and sucked almost halfway through when their mother spotted them.

'Jake, oh my God!' she screamed, 'that man is feeding our boys that trash!' With quick strides she pounced on the boys and snatched the offending popsicles out of their hands and threw them into a dustbin.

'How you, you horrid man!' she yelled at the stunned stall owner. 'How dare you give that rotten stuff to my boys! Oh my goodness, this country!

'Jake, pay this man off and let's get out of here.' Satyan and Rubita tried to calm her down while Jake paid for the popsicles, but with little success. Maggie was quite visibly distressed. 'Here I am, being so careful of what we eat in India and in just one moment that beast has spoilt our holiday.'

Rubita tried to lighten the mood by saying, 'It'll be all right, Maggie, the poor children only had a few little gulps. And we're all here to...'

'Oh, you people don't understand. Look, Rubita, it's not your body, right? If we really have to come to India we don't want to spend all our time getting sick and throwing our guts out. Every time we've come here, there's one or the other of us who's fallen sick. So please don't tell me what's what.'

'Well, what's done is done, Mags baby,' said Jake. 'Let's hope the boys don't...'

'Now don't you start on me too,' Maggie cut her husband off, hurrying towards the hotel. She had caught both boys' hands in hers and they tripped forward with doleful expressions.

'And now that you're done with this software project I hope you'll shake this country's dirt off your heels and come back to where you belong,' she said over her shoulder, without a backward glance to see if the rest were following.

The others could only stare at her stiff back and quicken their pace sharply to try and catch up. Satyan and Rubita exchanged resigned looks and Jake only dug his hands hard into his pockets as they rushed along in silence.

◆

Butt found Corbett at the ham shop a tough nut to crack. He leaned heavily on him, threatening him with dire consequences if he refused to give any information which would help in tracing the kidnapped Jamila. The man obstinately refused to speak up. He continued to deny having seen anything even though he had admitted to being at his shop that Sunday morning. He pleaded that the shop had been too crowded and that he had been too busy handling customers to have noticed anything amiss. Finally, Butt turned away in disgust and walked out of the shop.

Hearing of Jamila's abduction, Satyan, Rajan and Butt had dashed to Bangalore on the next available flight. The same evening, they had walked into Corbett's shop just as it was shutting down for the day.

'He's not willing to talk,' he told Satyan outside. 'But I know he's hiding something. I can tell when a man's lying. He saw something, but he's not talking. I think he's too scared to talk.'

But Rajan wasn't ready to give up just yet. He stepped up to the counter with his palms joined together in supplication. There was a pitiful expression in his eyes. 'Mr Corbett,' he said. 'You might remember me. I have come here one or two times with the girl we are talking about. She is my fiancée.' The shopkeeper glanced keenly at Rajan, as if trying to decide whether or not he was lying. 'I beg of you, please try your best to remember. You must! You are our only chance of finding her...'

Corbett remained impassive for a long time. Then he nodded. 'I have seen you before,' he said. 'And I remember that you have come with that lady. She seems such a nice girl. Okay look, I'll help you. But you can tell that bum out there,' he jerked his thumb in Butt's direction, 'that I'm doing so only because I'm taking pity on you and not because he frightens me. I'm doing this only because you seem to be a nice young fellow and I believe you, okay?' Rajan nodded vigorously.

'So, this girl came and bought her regular weekly supply of ham and beef and all, okay? I usually attend to all the Western clients myself. So I was totalling up her bill when these men walked in. They were obviously Russian even though they spoke French. Then I thought that they were her friends, so I didn't worry when she fainted and they gathered around to help her. It has happened so many times before; the Indian weather, even in Bangalore, is sometimes too much for these Western people. And it can become very hot and suffocating when the market is crowded and all. Like on Sunday mornings. I held the door open for them and several people helped them to the car. It was a dark blue Maruti Gypsy. The number was 'CAN' something. I don't remember the numbers, but I'm sure of the letters.

'You know when I first told myself that something may be wrong? When I returned to the counter, I found that she had left the meat behind. And the change. And they did not come back for it. Then I remember telling myself – Kevin, if they were Russians and all, why did they speak to the young lady in French? Why not in Russian? For the life of me I couldn't answer that, so I told myself – Kevin, you better try and remember that Gypsy number, okay? It may be wanted and all. So I tried and tried, and all I could be sure of were the letters. There was a lot of panic and all, man, so I'm sorry but I can't remember those bloody numbers.'

'But how did you know they were Russian?' asked Rajan.

'Well, the young lady is Russian, okay? I know that; she's come so often to my shop. And these fellows were talking French. I know French because I have been attending the Alliance Francaise for three years now. And these fellows, they didn't know very good French. And people from Western countries like France and America are very stylish in their dress and all. Arre, man, you can make out quite easily. No, no, they were not French, I am sure of that.'

Rajan probed further. 'Can you remember anything else? Anything at all?'

'No, young man, that's all. But you do one thing. Give me your phone number and if I remember anything else I will call you, okay?'

While Rajan scribbled out his address and phone number, Satyan leaned across the counter. 'Why weren't you willing to tell this to the police?' he asked, nodding towards Butt who was waiting at the wheel of their car.

'Look, man, I wouldn't have told you anything if you hadn't brought this young fellow with you. He's sincere and all, I can make out. And now I remember him, he's come a few times with the young lady. Now that chap out there didn't frighten me one bit. But if you come and threaten an old soldier like Corbett, he's bound to get angry. I've fought in the Bangladesh war, man. I'm not going to get scared so easily. And let me tell you something else, okay?' He leaned forward with a knowing grin. 'That man is no policeman. If he was, he wouldn't have wasted his time pestering me for an answer here, you know? He would have taken me straight to the police station.'

'Well, thank you very much, Mr Corbett. Your information will surely be very useful. You've been a great help,' said Satyan.

He was looking speculatively at Butt.

◆

The visit had gone spectacularly well for Gulab Chand. Welcomed at Moscow airport by the first deputy minister for industrial relations – a sure sign, thought Gulab Chand, that he was moving up the ladder – he had been dined and feted for two nights and two days. The freezing winter, the driving snow on the streets, had been little more than an interesting spectacle for him as he sped from meeting to meeting in Zil limousines. The last two evenings had been given over to banquets in his honour. Parties later at night had been wild drinking sprees, and the girls provided to keep him warm in bed most satisfactory. Gulab Chand was quite mystified – all he had done to deserve this special treatment up until then was to divert a few contracts their way whenever he found the Americans or the Europeans not amenable enough to his demands. Nevertheless, he enjoyed the pampering, biding his time until the true purpose of this visit would be revealed.

It was now Friday night, the last of his visit and he was scheduled to take a flight back to Delhi the next day, after a meeting with the deputy prime minister himself in the morning. As the third banquet of the week drew to a close, Gulab Chand glanced at his watch. It was almost nine p.m. Piotr 'Petrushka' Vassiliev, his guide and interpreter, had promised him an unforgettable finalé at one of the classiest nightspots of Moscow. Gulab Chand marvelled at Petrushka's resourcefulness. Everywhere he seemed to know the right people and was able to summon the prettiest young ladies.

This night was to be the young aide's *pièce de résistance*. Gulab Chand squirmed around on his seat, barely able to contain his growing impatience, as he stared around the table with vodka-glazed eyes. He nudged Petrushka who, with a flick of his eyes and a quick stab of his head, indicated the host for the evening. Gulab Chand understood he would have to make his excuses if he wanted to leave early. He switched his attention to the pompous figure seated to his left. The director of the Karoly Institute of Economics was holding forth on the breadth of his own vision, as displayed in a recently completed analysis of the Russian economy. Gritting his teeth, Gulab Chand waited for an opening to get a word in edgeways. When at last he was able to break through the wall of words and confess to a splitting headache, the peeved director reluctantly called the feast to a halt and released Gulab Chand after the customary rounds of toasts.

Gulab Chand and Petrushka got into the black Zil which had been placed at the Indian minister's disposal. They drove swiftly through the snow-banked streets towards the sprawling Nevsky Prospekt.

'The minister can hardly contain himself, eh, sir?' An easy familiarity had developed between the two. Petrushka was a personable young fellow and knew by instinct just where the tastes of his charges lay.

'When you have said so much about what you will bring me tonight, how can I not be impatient?' replied Gulab Chand.

Petrushka laughed. A twenty-minute drive would bring them to their destination. Enough time to grab another quick drink from the car's mini-bar. They turned into Smolinskaya Street.

He had received his orders that morning. He was to take Gulab Chand to the Smiling Dragon, the high-profile nightclub where he was scheduled to meet Tania. Once there, he was to go to the men's room after the first round of drinks and stay out of sight for at least twenty minutes. Their guest from India would be in the charge of specially deputed guides that night, he was told. As they walked into the Smiling Dragon, he could not help feeling a cold shudder run down his spine.

Petrushka spotted Tania – a languorous redhead, clad in a filmy creation in several colours – sipping from a tall glass, sitting alone at the bar. A cigarette in an ivory holder dangled from her fingers. She caught his eye in the mirror behind the bar, turned around and smiled, waving a lazy hand at them.

Then he spotted them. Bunched together at a table in a nearby corner. The FSS hounds must have known that they stood out like sore thumbs in this elegant and boisterous crowd, but they did not seem to care. He glanced at Gulab Chand, but the man's rustic mind was trying desperately to take in the fabulous scene before him. The best and brightest of Russia's nouveau-riche were there.

He introduced Gulab Chand to Tania. She looked at him in quick, disdainful appraisal, then led them, sashaying sensuously, to a large round table ringed by a sofa set into a secluded corner. Potted plants provided privacy while allowing a direct view of the cabaret floor.

A magnum of champagne arrived unbidden. On the stage, a girl crooned softly in a husky voice. The number reached its crescendo; she pirouetted and, with a pout and a wave, exited to enthusiastic applause, twitching her bottom as she went. Gulab Chand's head was swimming. He was halfway through his third glass of champagne. Tania was whispering something to him in English, but her accent and his fuddled brain prevented him from deciphering the words. It did not matter – he had a great view of her creamy white cleavage, his hand was on her thigh and he realised with a jolt that hers was on his. He peered drunkenly across the table but Petrushka seemed to have gone off somewhere on his own.

He acknowledged a group of Tania's friends with a vague nod of his head as they joined them at the table. She seemed to welcome them, so that ought to be fine with him, he thought. They seemed to understand Hindi and this endeared them to him. More champagne arrived. A glass toppled – he didn't know whose – spilling champagne on to his lap. Tania laughed, picked up the glass and refilled it. Gulab Chand waved it drunkenly in the air. In this place nothing seemed to bother anyone.

Tania was asking him something – permission to visit the ladies' room. He waved his assent and turned to the newfound friend beside him. The man seemed to be suggesting a change in venue.

'What about Tania?'

'She will follow. We have two cars,' his friend said.

Outside, the sub-zero cold hit him like a sledgehammer. They bundled him into a waiting car and pressed a bottle of vodka to his lips. He drank gratefully, feeling it warm his insides.

The conversation in the car was now only in Hindi. 'Where are we going, friends?' he asked.

'You have just been to heaven, now where else can you go?' Gulab Chand joined uncertainly in the laughter. The car swept silently through the night.

It eventually turned into a dark street lined with warehouses. 'Have we reached our destination?' asked Gulab Chand.

'Yes, my friend, this is a good destination for you.' They bundled him out and shoved him roughly towards the doorway of a large, dimly-lit building. Again, the freezing cold was almost like a physical blow. Something in the voice had sent a faint warning signal through Gulab Chand's stupor, but it was too faint, too late.

He was pushed into the building and frog-marched to a desk. Behind it sat an official-looking man with a clipped beard. Gulab Chand's mouth opened in anger to protest against the shoddy treatment his minions were giving a valued guest of the state. A vicious blow landed on his soft belly from a huge fist wearing a brass knuckle-duster. He let out a frightened yelp and doubled over. Hands turned him around and he felt the impact of a leaden pipe across his shoulders. Three huge men had ranged themselves around him and he felt a barrage of blows on his back, legs, stomach and chest. An occasional slap on the back of his head knocked his brains about. He fell down to his hands and knees, throwing up the evening's excesses in violent convulsions. 'This is what happens if you become too greedy, you son of a pig!' More blows rained on him. He thought that there must be some mistake. He was an honoured guest of the state. He wanted to clear the confusion but couldn't make himself heard through the noise of someone's scream. He was too far gone to realise that it was his own.

Someone splashed water on him, jolting him awake.

'Tell Pandey-ji to deal with us Russians honestly, understand?' It was a different voice this time. The man was speaking in Hindi, but it wasn't an Indian voice.

He opened his eyes uncertainly. A face was scowling down at him, not two inches away. The voice belonged to the face with the clipped beard. 'Do you understand, you traitor? Deal with us honestly and we are your friends. Deal with the Americans behind our backs and there will be no one worse than us!' Someone kicked him at the base of his spine. The face with the beard came close again. 'Will you tell your bosses, you stupid fool? Did you think we called you to Russia to give you a hero's welcome? You are just a small pawn in this game, idiot.' More kicks and blows landed on his stomach and head. Gulab Chand was now sober enough to hear his own screams. 'Shut up and listen, Gulab Chand! This is only a small lesson. A small one! Tell Pandey-ji that this is what we will do to him and his family if he doesn't play straight with us! Understand?'

Gulab Chand held up folded hands and begged the face to desist. 'I will tell him! I will tell him, I promise! Please stop beating me, I beg you! Have mercy!' He grabbed the bearded one's feet and bent low in supplication twisting his neck to look up at his tormentor's face.

The face came closer again, appraising him. Finally, it nodded. 'Yes, you dirty rat, I believe that you will. Good! Now you will be taken back to your hotel. It appears that the meeting tomorrow with the deputy prime minister had to be rescheduled due to unavoidable circumstances.' Gulab Chand nodded woefully. 'That being so, a seat has been booked for you on an early morning flight to Delhi. Just remember to do as you have been told and you will not be touched again, understand?'

'Yes, sahib. As you command, sahib,' Gulab Chand whined. He kissed the boots in front of him several times. Then the bearded man turned and walked away, leaving him sobbing with relief that he was still alive.

◆

Connolly replaced the phone and contemplated his next move. He would need a credible excuse to get Satyan to accompany him to Belgaum.

The message from Matthews had puzzled him. He was to set up an emergency meeting with one Brigadier Kharbanda – a contact number in Delhi was given – to plan the CIA's response to the Jamila Barkhatiev abduction. The message didn't specify how much this new player knew about the howitzer project. Connolly would have to play that by ear. He had got on the line to Delhi and scheduled the meeting in Belgaum, a small town situated some five hundred kilometres south-east of Mumbai, for the next day.

He knew why it had to be Belgaum; the Russians would not have a small town like that covered. What he couldn't figure out was the reason Mad Matt had decided to introduce the Kharbanda factor. The name would be false, a cover for one of Matthews' operatives. Perhaps Kharbanda could add value to the hunt for the missing girl.

With a shrug, he dialled Satyan's cellphone number. Connolly wanted Satyan under his eye while he was away from Mumbai. The Russians had taken the girl to escalate the whole game and it would be stupid to leave him exposed at this juncture. Satyan's reaction was predictable; he didn't want to go out of town at such short notice. He had several business appointments and an important dinner engagement to attend the next day.

'Why can't Brigadier Kharbanda come to Mumbai, Javed?' he asked.

'Listen, Mr Sharma, I know you're a busy man and I'm sorry that you have to be put to this inconvenience. I sincerely request you to come along, it cannot be avoided. Brigadier Kharbanda – he's my superior officer in Delhi – feels that matters are moving rapidly to a different plane now. He wants a reassessment of the situation very urgently. He wants to meet both of us together. The brigadier doesn't want the meeting to be held in Delhi. He's coming to Belgaum tomorrow and says it's imperative that he meet you and brief you on an important development in the case personally. I'm getting a helicopter to stand by for us. I promise to get you back to Mumbai in time for your dinner engagement.' Connolly pressed on. 'The brigadier has organised a safe venue at Belgaum where we can chalk out our plans in detail, undisturbed. He feels that it would be beyond the reach of the surveillance of our adversaries. Mr Sharma, please spare the time. Your cooperation could be vital to our efforts in securing the release of the young lady.'

Satyan thought it over. He wouldn't be in any personal danger; there had been enough opportunity for that sort of stuff. He knew that Butt had been watching him, but Satyan hadn't been able to spot him even once. If they were that professional, there was no point in declining the 'request'. He also realised that if he turned Butt down and something untoward happened to Jamila, he would not be able to forgive himself. He agreed.

Butt picked Satyan up from his office at nine a.m. the next day, in an Accent. Satyan could feel by the car's power that the engine had been modified for extra speed. They turned onto the Western Express Highway, heading north. Butt slipped the car expertly into the fast lane and shot it forward at well over eighty. Satyan glanced sideways at the intense, serious face. 'Javed Butt – that makes you a Muslim, I guess. From where, Javed?'

Butt gave him a cheerful grin. 'Kashmir, Mr Sharma. Have you ever been there?'

'Yes. Not recently, though.'

'Oh, shit,' said Butt suddenly, the slang catching Satyan by surprise. He was looking in the rearview mirror. 'Don't look now, Mr Sharma, but we have picked up a tail. I thought I'd shaken off the FSS. Blue Maruti Gypsy, three cars behind us.'

'FSS? What's that?' asked Satyan.

'Oh, it's just the new name for the KGB.'

Satyan was startled. 'KGB?' he blurted, 'here in India? What the hell are you talking about?'

'Why not, Mr Sharma? Did you think that this game was being played by amateurs? We have confirmed intelligence that the Russians have lagged behind in the field your friends Swaminathan and Barkhatiev are researching. The designs for the fire control unit would put them ahead by at least two years in their plans to manufacture a state-of-the-art shoot-and-scoot howitzer. That's one reason why the stakes are so high. You remember the white Hyundai outside the disco the other night? You thought they were local gangsters? No, Mr Sharma, the Russians have been tailing you for a long time now.'

He slid the car into the right-turn lane at an intersection and stopped for the red light. Satyan watched as the Gypsy pulled up in the same lane. Two cars now separated them. He had a glimpse of a thirty-something face, very fair and clean-shaven, topped by long black hair combed slickly back. The lights changed for the cars going straight. With a sudden screech of tyres, Butt swerved and jumped lanes. In the melee of blaring horns and angry curses, the Gypsy, stuck in the wrong lane, couldn't follow. Satyan glanced back at an anxious face peering after them as they vanished before the startled traffic policeman could react.

Konstantin contained his chagrin with difficulty as he waited for the lights to change. Fortunately for him, the road ahead was straight as an arrow for the next couple of kilometres and he could still keep them in sight.

Butt told Satyan that they were headed for Film City – a sprawling mass of rocky hillocks – housing several of Mumbai's film studios. A helicopter had been organised, standing by in a remote lot. A bumpy road led off the highway. Satyan glanced back to see the Gypsy tearing over a rise but far behind them. They turned into the lots of Leo Films and raced down a dirt track, threading their way between sparsely vegetated hillsides. They were raising a small sandstorm as they went. 'This cloud of dust will surely give our position away,' Butt muttered.

'How would he know it's us? He doesn't know which particular studio we turned into.'

'Oh, he would know all right. We intelligence people have an instinct. And we take our chances. He'll know all right. We just have to get airborne before he can reach us. There's the chopper.'

An orange and white helicopter stood on top of a hill. Its blades were turning slowly, ready for an instant takeoff. They stopped at the foot of the hill and started running up the slope. They had to cover about three hundred metres with nothing for cover but a few rocks. A blazing hot sun beat down on them. Basking lizards scurried hastily out of the way.

They were halfway up the slope when the shots rang out. They dived for the nearest rocks and scrambled to safety as another burst of automatic fire sent splinters of granite flying in all directions. Satyan lay a little above, some five metres from Butt.

'He's trying to kill us!' croaked Satyan.

'AK-56,' whispered the intelligence man, 'we're dead meat!' An automatic pistol had appeared in his hand.

They looked around. The main buildings of the studio were half-a-kilometre away. There was no way the sound of the gunshots would carry that far in daytime. Satyan scanned the upper part of the slope. The helicopter could not be seen but he saw a capped head peer cautiously over the edge. The barrel of a rifle accompanied it, but that was small consolation to the two men pinned down on the slope because, at that range, it would be a difficult shot at best. A jackal, which had hidden itself when the shooting had started, scuttled out from under a delicately balanced rock and scooted off, letting loose a little flurry of rocks and pebbles. Satyan assessed the rock, an idea forming in his head.

It was about two metres in diameter. Centuries of erosion had chiselled away at its base and it now stood precariously close to tumbling down the slope. Satyan estimated that it would be almost directly above the Russian. It was some twenty metres above him, to his right. The only modicum of cover was a very slight dip in the hillside halfway to the rock. Above the line of the rock the cover got better. He felt there was no other way; it was their only chance.

'Javed!' he rasped, 'cover me.' He jerked his head towards the rock and made a pushing motion with his hands. Butt thought it over for a moment before nodding. The timing would be critical. He held up three fingers. Satyan nodded.

Butt began the count and, as the third finger came up, he reared up and let off two shots where the Russian lay sprawled. Backpedalling furiously, he scrambled some way up the slope to another clump of rocks just as an answering fusillade went whanging about him.

Satyan had taken advantage of the diversion and had reached the dip halfway to the rock. It wasn't deep enough. Konstantin turned his automatic towards the half-exposed target and took aim. Satyan could see him clearly and watched in fascination as the barrel swung around to point directly at him. Almost too late, the adrenaline burst into his bloodstream and, with a heave, he launched himself at the rock.

The burst from the AK-56 tore up a jagged pattern where he had been lying a moment before. Then Butt popped up again and fired, forcing Konstantin to duck. A split second later, Satyan dove to safety and lay there, panting. The hard surface had knocked out his breath and it was a while before he turned to look at Butt.

The intelligence man held up three fingers again. At the third count he dashed up the slope. Bullets kicked up dust at his heels as he went in a zigzagging run and scampered behind the next piece of cover.

Grunting with the strain, Satyan dug his heels in and shoved until the huge rock grated and slid, then rolled off its perch. Like a monstrous cannonball it bounced and crashed on the hillside, taking with it a gathering of smaller rocks and stones. Then it slammed into another large boulder and, before long, the entire hillside erupted with flying missiles.

The hunted men did not stay to watch the spectacle but sprinted up towards the helicopter, with the ground shuddering and rumbling beneath their feet. The Russian would be running for his life if he knew what was good for him.

They were airborne in seconds. As they lifted off, they saw their attacker stand gazing after them in the swirling dust, rifle hanging loosely in his right hand.

'None the worse for wear, I hope, Mr Sharma,' said the intelligence officer. He was brushing away the dust from his clothes. Satyan shook his head and smiled thinly. Butt's face broke out into a huge grin. 'You're all right, you know, Mr Sharma? You'll do quite well.'

'You're not so bad yourself, Javed,' he replied. 'You saved my life at the risk of yours. I'll never forget that.'

Butt laughed and shrugged in embarrassment. 'All part of a soldier's work, Mr Sharma. Why don't you make yourself comfortable here,' he said, indicating a seat, 'I'll see if there's any coffee.'

'But I wonder what caused him to attack us now. If he's been following us all this time, surely he has had his chances. Why now? I wonder if this is linked to Jamila's kidnapping in some way.'

'Yes, Mr Sharma. I think the Russians are moving in openly, now that the technical phase of the howitzer's development is complete. Though I must confess that a daylight assault was not what I expected. Perhaps our precipitate departure from Mumbai, which may have been perceived by them as an attempt at spiriting you away to some unknown destination, triggered a panic reaction.'

Satyan smiled to himself. Now that the pressure had eased, the man had returned to his long-winded way of speaking.

'I must apprise the brigadier of the latest developments immediately,' Butt continued. 'This seems to mark a new phase in operations.'

◆

Butt had warned Satyan that the brigadier was quite different from the stereotypical soldier. Brigadier Kharbanda was, in fact, a qualified doctor of medicine. Apparently, he had become involved in intelligence work during the 1965 Indo-Pak war while serving at the border as a young captain in the army medical corps. His courage under fire and his ability to assess the military value of information he came across from Pakistani prisoners of war had brought him to the attention of the military intelligence people in Delhi. Butt obviously held the man in very high esteem.

Brigadier Kharbanda was a short, pug-faced man with a kindly, bedside manner. He took them in for lunch after they had washed and freshened up. After the meal, Butt excused himself and the two men sat down to the briefing.

'The affair of the howitzer is becoming quite complicated, Mr Sharma. We at intelligence HQ in Delhi are quite pleased at the way you have handled the challenges so far. However, I must warn you of moves in certain quarters which will pressurise you to act against your conscience. We have been informed that the FSS is in an advanced stage of preparations to acquire the designs and drawings of the gun.'

'We were attacked by one of their men this morning in Mumbai,' said Satyan.

'Yes, I got a full debrief over the radio before you landed. Obviously they have decided to escalate matters. But what I have to tell you is about an operation which is unprecedented in its scale, at least as far as the Indian theatre is concerned. There is an extensive undercover operation being mounted simultaneously in three centres: Mumbai, Bangalore and Delhi. Since you are at the epicentre of the Mumbai sector, I want you to appreciate the gravity of the situation in its entirety. We have therefore decided to place you and your fiancée under increased security cover. Without your full knowledge and cooperation, we cannot thwart the enemy.

'The abduction of Miss Barkhatiev can only be an attempt to engineer an end-game. We believe that they intend to use her to force Swaminathan or Barkhatiev, or both, to trade the gun's designs or, perhaps, even defect to Russia to help them produce this gun. You will readily appreciate the embarrassment to our country. We want to put in place a contingency plan, so to speak, to foil these operations. But, you see, the situation is quite complicated. Not the least because India and Russia are such staunch allies.'

Satyan leaned back, considering what he was just told. He contemplated his next move. How could he help them?

As if reading his thoughts, the brigadier said, 'We are keeping an eye on Swaminathan and Barkhatiev for their own safety, but have not shown our hand yet. It may become necessary to bring them to Mumbai so that it will be easier for us to keep a watch over all of you until we find a better solution. We might need to call upon your hospitality, Mr Sharma. We might need to make use of any accommodation you can provide us at Mumbai. My main purpose behind meeting you here today was to initiate the necessary arrangements.'

'Of course. Anything to help, Brigadier. You wouldn't want the Pure Space guest house. Rajan stays there whenever he's in Mumbai, so I suppose the Russians might know it and have it covered.' Satyan pondered the problem. 'Well, a close friend of mine has a spare flat downtown. I might be able to convince him to loan it for a couple of months. But I would need a good cover story.'

'We had anticipated some such likelihood, Mr Sharma. Surely, any friend of yours would know that your companies often take up work for the defence ministry. You could perhaps tell him that your guesthouse is currently needed for visitors connected with a sensitive project and that, quite by chance, you have important visitors in connection with another defence-related project. Naturally these others cannot stay in the same flat. You might add that they would prefer not to stay in a hotel. This sort of thing normally doesn't get questioned too deeply.'

'Hmm...well, I'll give it a shot, Brigadier.'

'Thank you, Mr Sharma. Now, if you will excuse me, Mr Butt and I have some matters to attend to before we can discuss the detailed logistics. Why don't you have some beer while we finish up here? We'll sit down again after an hour or so.' With a little nod, the brigadier indicated that the meeting was at an end. Satyan stood up uncertainly, then left the room without another word.

Butt was waiting outside. 'Well?' he asked.

'Your brigadier certainly doesn't believe in wasting words. He wanted to use my contacts to get a hideout for your men in Mumbai. He said we'll meet again on the details later. He wants to see you now.' Satyan walked over to a sideboard and selected a glass. Pouring himself some beer, he sat down in the verandah with a magazine.

Butt went inside. 'Looks like you've done a good job, "Brigadier",' he said grinning. 'The man has been taken in completely. Mad Matt sure hasn't lost his touch. Where'd he pick you from?'

The 'brigadier' smiled. 'I am a Pakistani immigrant. It is always a pleasure to render my old country a service. And anything that hurts India helps Pakistan. Now, Mr Butt, I have a package to deliver to you from Mr Matthews.'

Connolly took the sealed envelope into an inner room and opened it carefully. All the seals he knew would be there were intact. The moment he saw the contents, Connolly realised why Matthews had used this elaborate deception. Lying on the table before him were instructions for a completely new communication protocol. Connolly scratched his chin thoughtfully before setting about memorising them. It took him nearly half an hour. Then he burned all the sheets and stirred the ashes carefully in the wastebasket. Matthews must have suspected a leak at Langley. Nothing else would have prompted him to change protocol in the midst of a field operation. He had done it once before, during Desert Storm. The Pakistani wouldn't know about all this.

He walked out to find Brigadier Kharbanda contentedly reading a magazine at the desk. Connolly spent another thirty minutes briefing him on how to brief Satyan on the 'rescue operation' for the Barkhatiev girl. It had to be convincing enough for Satyan to believe that this trip had been worth the trouble. Connolly wasn't unduly worried. The Pakistani had shown himself to be a good actor and the 'plan' could be made to run into 'unforeseen problems' after their return to Mumbai.

9

The day-staffers at Pinnacle TV were bundling themselves towards the waiting bus which would take them to Santa Cruz station. They mingled with the news-shift people coming in. The next few hours would see frenetic activity for them as they put together stories received from across the country on the day's events.

Shekar from the research department poked his head around the door of Rubita's cabin. She was going over the notes containing précis prepared by her assistants at the news desks, planning the day's primetime newscast in preparation for the seven o'clock conference. Lasting about an hour, it was the all-important meeting where the news stories and materials at hand would be reviewed with other heads of departments. This conference would set off a last flurry of events including the editing of clips, contacting correspondents across the world to have them standing by for live videoconferencing during the news bulletin, and filling in facts, figures and file shots from the research and archives departments. The two hours from the time the seven o'clock meeting began until Pinnacle News-Point at Nine went on air, were the most tension-filled and high-pressure moments a body could tolerate.

Still only five thirty, the interiors of Pinnacle towers wore a relaxed look. Rubita had just come back from an interview with the CEO of a multinational corporation. Shekar had waited until now to bring her his findings, knowing that she would be in a receptive mood for the next half hour or so.

Looking up from her notes, she smiled and waved him in. 'Hi, Shekar. How was your holiday? Did you bring me any *bebinca*?'

Shekar had returned that morning from a weeklong vacation in Goa. Grinning, he dropped a parcel on Rubita's desk. 'How could I forget a request from the most beautiful newscaster this side of Santa Cruz station?' Rubita glared at him as he plopped into a chair.

'But that's not the real gift I've got for you. Remember you had asked me to keep a tab on Gulab Chand? The day after the morcha his crony Lakhan Singh was gunned down at Vashi Bridge, remember? Well, I kept collecting material on his other cronies and as usual, I found a whole list of favours he gave them to keep them happy and loyal. Corporators, company directors, cops – the works. And you know the best part? They are mainly from Bihar. That's the pattern that comes through, see? Buying loyalty by dishing out favours, and making sure that the people around him are all from his home state. That way he can always have a gang of followers with whom he can vibe. Very clannish kind of guy.'

Rubita knew that Gulab Chand was small fry in the network she was probing, but she also knew that look in Shekar's eye. He had obviously stumbled onto something big. So she curbed her impatience and waited to hear Shekar out.

'Now, I had the pattern of how Gulab Chand built his network of loyalists. I asked myself – why shouldn't the same pattern apply to the people he, in turn, would be loyal to? So I began to hunt around for names of people who he would turn to for currying favour. Obviously, being a politician and all, he would have sucked up to dozens of people through his twenty-year career. I was looking for a name which was common to all his posts – one powerful person who would have been accessible to him wherever he went. An-nd…bingo!' Shekar said, snapping his fingers. 'Guess what? I found my man!'

'Stop all this suspense and get on with it, you jerk,' Rubita said with a grin. But she felt her heart skip a beat.

'Ram Niranjan Pandey, Union Minister of State for Home. He's the big man behind Gulab Chand. He's from Bihar, from Nawadah. He was in the Bihar cabinet as minister for social welfare when Gulab

Chand was an MLA. Pandey made Gulab Chand's brother the MD of a cooperative bank back home. This brother has been milking the bank for years and no one has been able to nab him. Then Pandey made Gulab Chand a minister in Bihar before leaving state politics to join the Central government in Delhi. And now he's got him elected to the Parliament, too. But you know what the clincher is? Pandey is related to Gulab Chand by way of a marriage! His favourite nephew – and the rumour is that this guy is probably an illegitimate son of Pandey – is married to Gulab Chand's youngest sister. This "nephew" is the chairman, at the ripe old age of thirty-two, of the Bihar Waterways Transport Corporation.'

'Ram Niranjan Pandey,' Rubita repeated. 'Makes sense to me. But what happened to Lakhan Singh? If he was backed by such a powerful clique, how could he get shot like that in broad daylight?'

Shekar grinned. He had anticipated this question. 'They were beginning to get too ambitious, Rubes. Bihar was OK, their own territory. And Delhi is open territory for political honchos from all over the country. Now, with the Lakhan Singh gambit, they were trying to set foot in the commercial capital of the country. Kind of natural, in a way. There are plenty of hoodlums from that part of the country floating around in Mumbai nowadays, you know. More coming in everyday, in fact. He was probably trying to break the Dal's stranglehold in Mumbai, first through the unions and then, other things.

'When Lakhan Singh's double-game was exposed during the morcha, I think the Dal saw what was happening and eliminated him. At least, that's the most popular theory so far and I must say it seems the most logical.'

'Okay, I think it's time I interviewed Mr Pandey on Pinnacle TV. But I don't know yet how I will use this info, Shekar. Let me think it over. But hey, you've been able to get a lot of good information even though you were on holiday. How did you manage it?'

'Trade secret,' said Shekar, winking at her. 'Enjoy the *bebinca*, it's Goa's best.'

She picked up the phone after he left the room. Glancing at the desk clock, she dialled her father's number in Delhi. He would still be in the office. She would have just enough time to check out some facts before the seven o'clock conference.

'Rubita, what's up in Mumbai? I hope there's nothing wrong?'

'All fine here, Sam,' she said. 'I had a free moment so I thought I'd give you a call and find out how you're doing.'

Bannerjee chuckled. 'I know my daughter well enough to know she won't call me up at the office just to chat. You've obviously got yourself a hot lead for a story and you want corroboration. Don't try to hoodwink your father!'

'You win, Sam. You're right. Can you talk?'

'Well, I've sent off all the boys and I was about to leave. There's an official reception tonight with the PM attending, but I've got enough time right now. Shoot.'

'Sam, you remember I had asked you if Gulab Chand had a godfather high up in the government. Well, I have information that this godfather could be Ram Niranjan Pandey. Do you think this could be true?'

'Well, they both are from the same state. It's possible that they maintain close contact, but this sort of thing is quite common in politics. Hardly the basis for a scoop, I should say. Do you have any specific information?'

'Well, not too long ago Gulab Chand had a private audience with Pandey at his farmhouse near Delhi. They discussed the gun project. And they are probably passing on information to the Russians or the Americans. Perhaps both. My informant wasn't clear.'

'My goodness, Rubes! Do you realise what you've just said? You're talking about a union cabinet minister! Can't you be more discreet? This kind of talk can get people into deep trouble – you, me, the persons you named. Who did you get your information from?'

'In this case, a disgruntled socialite who dispenses her favours to the high and mighty in the capital. You know what I mean. Impeccable source, I think you'll agree. And, Sam, I think this is somehow connected with Gulab Chand's Russia trip. I heard rumours that he had some kind of brush with the authorities there. And he's been nosing around Satyan and the gun deal. We felt that whatever he was up to couldn't have been on his own. Firstly, he's not in the defence ministry and secondly, he's too junior to have known so much. Unless he was acting as the front for somebody big. Somebody like Pandey.'

'Look, Rubes, this thing has now gone too far for you or me to influence in any way. Do you know that the PM himself has had closed door discussions with the FIAM people? What it means is that the matter is now at the very highest level, beyond even the Gulab Chands and Pandeys of this world.'

'Sam, are you saying that the PM himself has got his hand in the till? That's absolutely explosive!'

'Now, now, Rubes. You're letting your imagination run away with you. Who said anything like that? Don't jump to any half-baked conclusions. After all, the people have elected him. Shouldn't you respect that mandate before shooting off at the mouth?'

'You mean I should not do anything that will shatter the halo around his dear balding head? Do you mean that we should ensure that our great lord and master, the latest shining example of the dynasty that our country is proud to be saddled with, should always look squeaky clean to the sovereign multitude? Even if he decides to feather his nest while the voters are blinded by his halo?'

'Rubes, Rubes, sarcasm will get you nowhere. Our PM wouldn't be interested in feathering his own nest. Whatever he does would be in the best interests of the country and his party. And as for the "dynasty", the fact of the matter is that they are the only people around who have the charisma and vision to keep our country together and carry it forward.'

Rubita was dumbstruck at her father's words. The silence on the line lengthened as she absorbed the full meaning of what Sam had just told her. He was actually building a case for a decision in favour of FIAM. Was he preparing her in anticipation of defeat for Satyan? Or was he merely being the loyal government servant? No, definitely not that. She had, in recent months, felt that her father had drifted away from her, and not a little because of the gun deal which had all of them caught up in a maelstrom of confusing pulls and pushes. But surely he hadn't drifted so far away that he would hand her an official line in a private conversation. Was the conversation really private, then? Was it being monitored by the Intelligence Bureau? Rubita did not know what to make of it.

'Rubes, look, a statesman has to use whatever means are at his disposal for the benefit of his country. The ends justify the means in politics and our PM is a statesman, not an ordinary politician. After all, if the party doesn't win the elections, he won't be able to sustain the progress India has made in the last five years.'

The penny dropped. Sam was trying to tell her something and she had been so engrossed in her juvenile debate that she hadn't sensed it. She kicked herself mentally for being so obtuse. He was telling her very clearly that the parliamentary elections, due in a few months, were top priority for everybody in Delhi now. The campaigns were going to be expensive. Ergo, every political party was now focusing energies on collecting funds. If payoffs were happening or were going to happen on the gun deal at the PM's level, then that was a lever any ruling party would have taken advantage of. That meant an end to all technical arguments on the subject. The decision had as good as been made and Sam was telling her to get Satyan to salvage whatever he could out of the episode and plan ahead for Pure Space.

'Rubes, are you there?'

'Yes – yes, Sam,' she replied, 'thank you for putting things in the right perspective. You're right. Satyan should begin planning ahead, beyond the gun deal. It's been so exciting for him these last few months that he hasn't thought of anything else. I'll tell him. How has your health been, Sam? I hope you are watching your sugar.'

They talked on some more and rang off. Rubita sat there for a long while, her mind far away, dwelling on memories of her childhood and teen years, growing up with a father who was a tower of strength and a shining example of the best qualities in man: elegant in bearing, sharp of mind and resolute in his convictions. For some reason, she felt a nagging sense of loss, of bereavement almost. She felt sure that Satyan had lost the contract for the FCU because the Indian howitzer was not going to be selected. The timing was bad, with the parliamentary elections looming. She dreaded the moment when she would have to break the news to him.

But there was more.

She couldn't say for certain, but she got the feeling that her father had been holding something back from her. She had never felt that way about him before. There had been no secrets between them, until now. She knew that there was something her father had not told her. Not about the PM. Something more personal. Her father had been wary of her in a way she hadn't felt before.

She felt an intense melancholy overwhelming her heart. It took her a great effort to focus on the stories of the day.

◆

Ram Niranjan Pandey directed a red stream of betel juice in the direction of a large brass spittoon some four feet away from his swivel chair. The flock of officials filed out of his office, having just concluded the weekly Monday-morning meeting. Pandey-ji had been his usual genial self. With sharp, rustic commonsense he had disposed of matters he had deemed important with the speed and precision that had won him many admirers among his cabinet colleagues.

He kept on top of the goings-on in the ministry chiefly in two ways. The first was these meetings which lasted until well past noon. Considering that he rarely spent any time in the office if he could help it, both he and his secretaries kept to this routine religiously. It was the only way any work would get done at all in the ministry.

The second – and to Pandey-ji's mind more important – way was through his judiciously selected set of informers at various levels who had access to him night and day. These were hand-picked men, selected by him over the years based solely on unquestioning personal loyalty. They moved from ministry to ministry, following him faithfully. Over the years, he had cut them into several of his deals, ensuring that they did well by associating with him. His concern for their well-being was genuine and heartfelt. In return, their loyalty to him was undying, unswerving and had stood the test of many crises and ordeals.

All the officials went out of the room except John Kalidoss, home secretary and the ministry's top bureaucrat. Of all Pandey-ji's minions,

Kalidoss was by far the most useful. Pandey-ji had never forgotten the day when the suave, sophisticated bureaucrat had, due to one night's indiscretion at the gambling table, lost everything that he had owned, including his wife's jewellery and his sprawling coffee estate and ancestral villa in the deep south of India. Kalidoss had stripped his soul bare to Pandey-ji the next morning. For the sake of his wife and children, he had pulled himself back from the brink of suicide and decided, in his torment and shame, to sell his soul to the devil.

Pandey-ji had wagered on the man's loyalty and had won several times over in the last eight years. He had seen in Kalidoss a rock-like fealty which was his for the asking. Pandey-ji had bailed him out that day. Ever since, Kalidoss had become Pandey-ji's man, a fact the wily politician kept under wraps. Though Pandey-ji had joined the home ministry as the cabinet minister's deputy, he had deftly maneuvered to get Kalidoss installed as the top dog in the secretariat. From there on, Pandey-ji had wrested effective control of the ministry from his boss. Pandey-ji also used Kalidoss' position to keep himself informed of higher level cabinet affairs to which his present status did not allow official access.

Now Pandey-ji hesitated between the need to hear Kalidoss out and the urge to get into his waiting limousine ready to take him to his farmhouse in Ghaziabad. The previous evening he had made arrangements with the delectable Mrs Goswamy's husband for a three-day sojourn with her in the privacy of his retreat, conveniently located a couple of hours drive from his city residence, where he could be reached for emergencies or could sneak into the metropolis to attend the innumerable official parties he was invited to and return to its luxury for the night.

But if John sahib was waiting to speak, it must be important. With an inward groan he arranged his face into an encouraging smile and began the proceedings.

'John sahib, it has been a long time since you and I had a chat. Tell me, how are things with you? I hope the family is all well?'

Kalidoss laid his papers on the table and settled himself more comfortably. He smiled. 'With your blessings, all is fine with me, sir. My daughter has finished her final year exams at the medical college. We are all very grateful to you, Pandey-ji.' Pandey-ji had come through yet again when Kalidoss had wanted ten lakh rupees for a 'donation' to a leading medical college in Delhi, to secure admission for his daughter. In spite of having put away five lakhs for just this, Kalidoss had found himself short of the required sum and had been despondent that his daughter's cherished dreams were in danger.

The minister waved a hand. 'And how are things at the office, John sahib? I trust that everything is under control? With you in charge of my ministry, what is the need for me to worry?'

'That is what I wanted to speak to you about, sir. I just wanted to ensure that you are informed about the latest developments on certain new projects and contracts.'

Pandey-ji's antennae perked up. He eyed the secretary speculatively. 'What is it, John sahib? Have the Russians sent any more messages?'

Since Gulab Chand's return from that country, and his detailed account of the trip to Nevsky Prospekt, Pandey-ji had been waiting for some message from the Russians. None had been forthcoming. Yet, the Russians were known to be deliberate in their moves. They played their politics the way they played their chess – slowly and surely, decimating all opposition. He had been badly shaken by the treatment that Gulab Chand had received and had waited nervously for the follow-through. With the passing weeks, his equanimity had begun to reassert itself. However, what worried him about the gun deal was that he was now in too deep to be able to disengage from either the Americans or the Russians. He had decided to be more circumspect in the future.

He leaned forward to hear what Kalidoss would have to say.

'No, Pandey-ji, it's all quiet on the Russian front. No word from the Americans either. What I wanted to bring to your notice is something entirely different. Sir, you remember that I was to discuss the matter with Sambaran Bannerjee?'

'Yes, the finance secretary. I was told that he is satisfied with the financial package offered by FIAM.'

'Yes, sir, there is no problem there. But what was interesting was that he was enquiring about Shri Gulab Chand. He specifically asked if the minister had fully recovered from his trip.'

'So, the good secretary is concerned about the well-being of his political masters. After all, Gulab Chand-ji returned only recently from a strenuous week in Russia. What is so unusual about that?'

'Sir, despite all our efforts to keep things quiet, rumours have begun floating that the labour minister had an accident of some kind during his visit. But the way Bannerjee asked the question, I could sense that he was not asking out of casual courtesy. He was fishing for something more. Otherwise, why ask me, the home secretary, about a labour minister?'

Pandey-ji considered this. He couldn't see how the finance secretary could have guessed the special relationship that John sahib was referring to. To his knowledge Bannerjee had never worked with Gulab Chand. And the exclusive clique of IAS officers Bannerjee belonged to – he knew that Kalidoss was a member of this clique – would never socialise with the likes of Gulab Chand. Maybe John sahib had a point. But Pandey-ji needed to be sure before playing his hand.

'What did Bannerjee sahib want? Anything?' he asked, eyeing Kalidoss meaningfully. The implication was clear; was Bannerjee asking for a piece of the action?

Kalidoss smiled. 'No, sir. I can't imagine an officer like Bannerjee asking for anything like that. I think he just wanted information. The worrying aspect is that I think he wanted confirmation of something that he already suspects.'

Pandey-ji waved an expansive hand. 'I am sure you handled the situation with your usual tact, John sahib. For the moment I don't think we need to worry. The cabinet decision is almost finalised, eh? Soon it will all be over.'

With that, Pandey-ji hoisted himself out of the chair and left the room.

◆

Mad Matt looked up from the dossier on his lap and stared over his bifocals at the Pentagon man.

He had been summoned from Langley that morning to Hawthorne's spacious office which he referred to as the 'world's largest ant-heap of armchair soldiers' to talk about the 'fiasco in India'. The galling thing was that it was turning out to be just that – a fiasco of humungous dimensions. His adversary glanced around the table as he ticked the points off. Representatives from the state department and the National Security Council nodded grimly as each point sank in.

'Gentlemen, the facts are becoming embarrassingly clear to even the meanest intelligence. We have on our hands a potentially disastrous situation which could put the Bay of Pigs misadventure into shadow. Considering that, in the near future, we may have to reassess our basic stance towards the world's largest democracy, this incident could not have come at a worse time.

'I had, even at the outset, advised against sending an operative who wasn't up to scratch on the ground realities in this fast-changing situation. My advice was not heeded, and just such an operative was chosen for this sensitive assignment. He would have, in unfamiliar territory, been prone to errors of judgment. Sadly, this is exactly what he seems to have committed on the field, and I would be loath to blame him.' He looked across at Mad Matt, who seethed with helpless anger, as he said, 'Not being able to tap into our extensive contacts in India, this operative has had to operate almost completely in isolation. Hence we have no clue about the Russian game plan. As a result, we have found that, on more than one occasion, events have overtaken us, as in the case of the abduction of the Barkhatiev girl.'

'But we got on top of that pronto, didn't we?' said Matthews. 'We know where she's being held and we're preparing to intervene. We've sent in a team to back Connolly's play.'

'Yes, but only when the situation is on the verge of getting out of hand, Mr Matthews. I am given to understand that the sighting of the girl was out of mere good fortune. Further, Mr Matthews will not deny that the frenetic search exposed our operative's identity to the danger of being uncovered by the Indians. Thirdly, precious time is being lost in this unforeseen diversion from our main purpose to obtain the designs and drawings of this howitzer.

'It is also my sad duty to inform these gentlemen, Mr Matthews, that there was an abortive attempt to eliminate Satyan Sharma in a most crude manner during one of the field tests. Surely the CIA needs to control its urges to use extreme measures. I am sure the US would not like to be seen in the same league as the Russians in the crudity of their methods.

'Gentlemen, we cannot afford to allow this operation to continue to be at the mercy of lady luck. I propose that, henceforth, this operation be overseen by a committee consisting of all the people in this room. This affair needs to be viewed in the perspective of the country's diplomatic, military as well as intelligence objectives.'

Mad Matt leaned back, outwardly pensive, but smiling inwardly because Hawthorne had let slip his ignorance of the facts. The CIA had not been involved at all in the attempt on Satyan Sharma's life in the Kumaon mountains. He had also verified that the FSS had not been involved either. For several days, he had worried that another country had tried to butt in – the Swedes or the Swiss, or perhaps even the French, since all of these would face strong competition in the multimillion dollar global market for this class of weapon if the Indians succeeded. He had, after careful inquiry, satisfied himself that no other power was participating in this game. For now, he would have to ensure that Hawthorne did not hijack the operation from CIA hands. Definitely not now, when he had put the end-game into play.

'Gentlemen,' he said in a measured tone, 'I deeply appreciate Mr Hawthorne's concern for taking a holistic view of the situation in India. It was precisely for this reason that the president has asked the director to report to him personally on the progress in this project, and expressed the desire to see to it that the CIA took all precautions to keep the whole shebang under complete silence. We have confirmed that the orders to eliminate Satyan Sharma came from high up in the Indian government. We are even now in touch with the highest levels there to find out and expose the source of these orders. Our efforts have been well-received and I am certain that action will follow very soon.'

He stepped up the offensive. 'Now, gentlemen, perhaps you can understand why we have decided to depart from convention in this case. Any attempt to rock the boat at this stage can only result in a loss of time which could end up with the Russians gaining access before us to the designs. Not that we particularly need them; it would suit us just fine to make sure that the teddy-bears don't get them.

'Gentlemen, I suggest that you take these thoughts back with you to your respective departments and mull them over. You'll agree with me that our objective here is somewhat more limited than what Mr Hawthorne made it out to be. But he's spot on when he says that the US should not, at any cost, show its hand, particularly, when a major reversal of our India policy is on the cards. That's why we've got one of our best people out there and, luckily for us despite what Mr Hawthorne may say, one who knows India extremely well and is himself practically unknown in India. So, gentlemen, I would say that the operation is already in the best hands.'

Hawthorne glanced at the men around the table. One by one, each man expressed the view that there was no option at this late stage but to go by Matthews' line of reasoning. Eventually, Hawthorne gave in, deferring to the general opinion around the table.

With a cheerful nod all around, Matthews began gathering his papers.

◆

An extensive hunt had been launched in Bangalore for Jamila Barkhatiev. It had not taken the Intelligence Bureau much time to verify that she had not taken a flight to Moscow.

Rajan Swaminathan had pulled the strings at the external affairs ministry in Delhi, where his friend was an additional secretary, to get action. Several days passed by before the cooperation of intelligence networks across the country could be obtained. It took a while to impress upon the authorities that a potentially disastrous international incident was building up. The search had then fanned out across the entire country.

Ten days after the kidnapping, it had become abundantly clear that she had not been moved after the Cessna had landed in Mumbai. But just in case, the government put a team of para-commandos with training in urban antiterrorist operations on standby, ready to be deployed to any major Indian city within twenty-four hours.

Old Barkhatiev suffered a stroke in Bangalore. The doctors attending to him opined that if anything were to happen to his daughter, he would probably never recover.

Some two weeks after Jamila's abduction, the girl was traced to an apartment owned by the Russian diplomatic service in Mumbai.

The Bel Air apartments, off Mumbai's posh Carmichael Road had been chosen by the FSS as a safe-house despite the exorbitant rent. There were several reasons for this. Chief among them was the proximity to the Russian Information Centre on Peddar Road. It was also not too far from the beach along Marine Drive, from where the Russians were planning a night-time extraction. Guests staying at the flat would have the further advantage of anonymity amongst diplomatic corps from other consulates, most of whom maintained apartments and consulates in the vicinity.

A platoon of para-commandos staked out the apartment, hoping for an early sighting and positive confirmation. It was one of three on the eighth floor. There were only three men in there with the girl. Though the men went about their errands as usual, the girl had not stepped out of the apartment even once. They caught glimpses of her during the night, as they scanned the windows with night-vision glasses. Rajan was brought up one night and he gave definite identification. The next step was to get the girl out of the apartment unharmed. Unconventional methods would be needed.

They set up round-the-clock surveillance, looking for routines, patterns of behaviour and likely vulnerable points. It was Rubita who came up with the plan. She gamely volunteered to get the commandos an opportunity for a surprise attack. Satyan and Rajan discussed it with the platoon's commanding officer and reluctantly came to the conclusion that, though it placed Rubita in a spot of danger, there seemed no better option. Satyan tried to talk her out of it, but she wasn't having any.

When Sergeant Dmitri Spritsnik sauntered into the Carmichael Department Store at about seven one Wednesday evening, there were already about half-a-dozen European and American shoppers browsing about, mingling with a host of local residents. He went through his shopping list at a leisurely pace, tossing his selections into a little wire cart. The store specialised in catering to clientele who had the money and taste for cuisine from different parts of the world.

Rubita strolled in after the Russian soldier, watching what he picked up carefully. She put a few things from nearby shelves into a cart of her own as she followed at a discreet distance, making sure that her cart had fewer items so that she would get past the billing counter more quickly than he. She smiled thinly as he picked up a tin of Beluga caviar. The caviar was invariably on the list each time one of Jamila's captors went shopping. She picked up a tin herself. The team had decided that this would be the key to getting them into the apartment.

She cut through the store quickly as Spritsnik headed for the cash counters. They both paid at parallel counters but Rubita got through a few moments before Spritsnik. As he walked towards the door, he saw the attractive woman in front of him turn back absentmindedly, apparently remembering something on her shopping list at the last moment. In her preoccupied state, she collided with him, lost her balance and clutched at him to keep from falling down. Their shopping bags went flying, tins and packets spilling to the ground in utter confusion.

Rubita was profuse in her apologies as, down on their hands and knees among the bemused crowd in the shop, they scrambled to shove their purchases back. Spritsnik found himself staring straight into a charmingly contrite pair of eyes.

'Oh, I'm so sorry. You must be very upset with me,' she stuttered helplessly.

Spritsnik, startled by the frank stare, could only mumble an embarrassed reply. It took quite a while to sort out the mess and get the items into their respective shopping bags. He found himself talking to her, telling her that he stayed at Bel Air, was in India for a week before returning to Russia. He discovered that she stayed at Hastings Towers, a block of apartments up the road from Bel Air. He did not notice that as they stuffed their purchases back into the shopping bags, both caviar tins went into her bag. Her pleasant chatter tinkled in his ears as they walked out of the department store together and headed up the road.

A couple of hours later, the bell at 843, Bel Air rang. A young man opened the door. It wasn't Spritsnik.

'Oh, hi. I've come to return this tin of caviar.' Rubita smiled her most engaging smile. 'It must have gotten into my bag by mistake. It is yours, isn't it? Or have I come to the wrong flat?'

Four commandos, in two pairs, had stationed themselves on the landings of the adjacent floors, a few feet away but out of sight from the front door. They had teargas shells and stun-guns at the ready. All four wore gas masks.

They were aiming for a quick, decisive operation. They had planned on recapturing the girl unharmed before any of the residents in the building stumbled into the corridor and interfered with the line of fire. Nerves taut, they listened to the conversation at the open door leading into apartment 843, waiting for the prearranged signal.

'No, it's quite all right,' said the young man, taking his eyes reluctantly off her to glance into the flat. 'Dmitri, the caviar has been found. There's a lady here to return it.'

Spritsnik came to the front door. She smiled as she saw him, holding the tin out in front of her. 'I thought you might have planned a party or something, you know. So I thought I'll return it right away.'

'Thank you, Miss, uh, Bannerjee. You are most kind.' There was an awkward pause as they stood there uncertainly.

'Hey, Dmitri! What's happening?' yelled a voice from inside.

That snapped the frozen tableau into action. Rubita became flustered: 'I guess I must be on my way. Here, I'll give you my card. I'm from a tv company. Maybe we could meet up some time before you leave for Russia.'

The two young Russians gawked, shuffling their feet while she fumbled about in her handbag. Suddenly, she lost her grip and the bag tipped over as it fell, spilling its contents around their feet. All three bent to pick up the stuff – this was the signal the commandos were waiting for.

It was all over in moments. Stepping quickly and silently down the half flight of stairs, the team on the upper floor lobbed two teargas grenades in through the open door and stepped away from the door. Rubita dove sideways and rolled out of the line of fire as the second team reached the hall from the landing below. The two Russians were on their knees, their hands clutching the little odds and ends from Rubita's handbag. They looked up just in time to see the muzzles of the stun-guns before they were hit by blasts that put them out of action with the least amount of noise. The first team ran into the flat to mop up. There was no contest. The third man and Jamila were fighting their tears, coughing helplessly.

10

Arnaud Leconte greeted Chintamani Rao, the deputy prime minister's son and his wife as they emerged from their new greyish-blue BMW. The Lecontes had moved into a sprawling mansion in Delhi's West End the previous month. Chintamani and his wife came every Friday afternoon for tea and an hour of frolicking in the swimming pool in the backyard. In winter, they could play tennis on the neatly trimmed grass court instead.

Over the last few years, Chintamani Rao and his father Panduranga Rao had used Leconte as a conduit for arranging payouts for several multinational company contracts. Ever since the economy had been liberalised in 1991, India's booming telecom, information technology and defence sectors were completely in the elder Rao's grasp as far as kickbacks were concerned. Panduranga Rao tolerated his son's laziness only because of the close friendship between Chintamani's wife Jeannette and Leconte's wife Fiona, as a result of which it had become possible for the Raos to amass wealth way beyond their dreams. No matter which party was in government, Panduranga Rao was always contacted for channelising thousands of crores in slush funds for every major contract.

The Raos had hundreds of crores stashed in the British Virgin Islands, and a comfortable villa overlooking its capital, Road Town. The Islands were a tax haven to rival the nearby Cayman Islands and, with the US Virgin Islands just a hop away, the whole area was a playground for the rich and famous. Many a shady deal was struck in the villas and clubs in these islands. The family planned to migrate to the Islands once the elder Rao retired from active politics, though Chintamani Rao was eager to emigrate earlier because he had an international career as an art dealer in mind.

Chintamani Rao had built an acquaintance with a senior Swiss bank official who had access to vast stores of art lying unclaimed in vaults that had once belonged to Nazi officers during the World War II. In recent years, many of these Nazis had died while on the run, leaving the treasures in their vaults untouched. Untold wealth lay within reach and Chintamani Rao and the Swiss bank official had worked out a cozy arrangement to winkle it out through the underworld art markets. The Virgin Islands had a thriving art market and the Raos had built a tasteful collection, including a Matisse and a Monet. They were, by Indian standards, already immensely wealthy and were beginning to get accepted in the rarefied circles of billionaires.

Chintamani Rao was lean and athletic and had rakish manners that were a hit with women. He fancied himself as a debonair man of the world. So much so that he modelled his persona on James Bond: he had named his yacht 'Commander Bond', owned a bright yellow Aston Martin that he used very sparingly, and even owned a snub-nosed Walther PPK pistol which he often carried with him. Apart from being a passionate collector of paintings, the younger Rao was an expert sailor and scuba diver. His rave parties during the sailing season were getting recognised as a high point – all-night binges where the young and happening glitterati met and freaked out, and the orgies sometimes raged over entire weekends. His wife Jeannette knew about these flings but bore with them because she was quite frightened of confronting him or upsetting him in any way. It was, in any case, a small price to pay for the luxury in which she was maintained and the imperious way in which she was able to lord it in Delhi's social circles.

Tea had been laid out by the pool, in the shade of two mango trees. The deputy PM's son was looking forward to this particular afternoon. He wanted to discuss the plans for their holiday in Rao the following month. The Lecontes and the younger Raos were keen travellers and made it a point to holiday together at least once a year. Chintamani Rao had been taking Samba lessons the past few weeks, determined to make full use of his first visit to Brazil. He found to his chagrin that Arnaud Leconte had more serious things in mind.

After they had finished their tea, Leconte turned to his wife. 'Fiona darling, why don't you show Jeannette your new ferns? They have been brought especially from Alsace,' he explained to Jeannette, 'and Fiona is absolutely determined to see that they flourish in this hot climate. You must see her experimental nursery, Jeannette. I am sure Fiona will love to hear your ideas on the very special temperature control apparatus she has devised. It's really very clever.'

'Yeah, but why don't we discuss the important thing first, Arnie?' asked Chintamani. 'Let's get the ladies to tell us what they want to do in Rio before pottering about with plants. Then you and I can iron out the details together.'

Leconte was firm. 'But of course, Chintu my friend,' he said, using the nickname by which very few people in the capital felt free to address the deputy PM's son. 'We have the whole evening to do that. But first you and I have some other, more important, business to discuss. Ladies, I am sure you will excuse us.'

The deputy PM's son grimaced as the ladies started for the house. Reaching out, he poured himself another cup. Leconte resumed, 'Chintu, we need to talk about some disturbing new developments on the gun project. We may have a serious problem coming up.'

His guest frowned. 'What's the problem? I thought we had decided on FIAM and that the decision would be announced soon. All the financial arrangements have been agreed upon, haven't they?'

Leconte contained his growing irritation at his friend's flippant attitude. He needed this young man's full cooperation. What he was about to propose would be considered beyond the limits for a foreigner, influential though he was. He could not be seen to interfere in government so brazenly. Therefore, he needed to hold his guest's attention long enough to make him realise the gravity of the danger they were all in.

'Chintu, there's a storm brewing in the West. My principals have sent me a message that they are not happy with the way Pandey-ji has handled the affair so far. He has not been able to get this Satyan Sharma to back off from the project. In fact, even I think that Pandey-ji has been quite incompetent.'

Chintamani looked up sharply. Leconte seemed to have it in for Pandey-ji for some reason. He shrugged. 'Now that the deal is almost final, the Indo-Uzbek gun is out of the reckoning anyway. Even though it is supposed to be the best gun technically, we have all decided to make the financial terms and conditions of the contract the clinching argument, haven't we? And these conditions, the poor sods in Uzbekistan won't be able to match – leastways, I don't see that happening. Where's the problem?'

'Chintu my friend, there's more. The Americans have been negotiating with Pandey-ji to get the gun's designs for them.'

Chintamani smiled, understanding dawning on him. 'So, Pandey-ji has been trying to feather his own nest with a little extra on the side. Just because you haven't been able to get any of that action, that's no reason to go after him, Arnie.'

'Chintu, Chintu, give me credit for more intelligence than that. Pandey-ji is indulging in treason. Don't you see? He's skating on thin ice.' He glanced sharply at his guest. 'What the hell are you laughing about, now?'

Chintamani's shoulders were quavering with laughter. 'The very thought. Oh, my God! The image of that tub of lard on ice-skates! Arnie, you're a scream! Oh, that was too much!' He gave in to fit of giggling despite Leconte's stern stare.

'Here!' Leconte snapped, 'Pay attention, my friend, or else it will be the end of laughing for all of us. Now, for some reason, the Americans are unhappy with Pandey-ji. Enough to have told me about their little side-deal last week. If they make this deal public knowledge, the consequences would be disastrous for all of us. God alone knows what other skeletons will be pulled out of the cupboard. Your father would be first on the firing line. He would be sacked and possibly put into prison and face a long trial in the courts afterwards. And that would put paid to your plans of settling down in the Virgin Islands.'

'Come, come, Arnie. Things can't be so bad. Some solution will emerge. I'm sure you can find some way of placating the Americans.'

Leconte found it hard to conceal his annoyance. 'Chintu, look, we must think about the American message more seriously. We must think why they are so angry with Pandey-ji. In fact, they told me to get the message to the PM to have Pandey-ji removed from his post.'

'Who are the Americans to decide our cabinet?' his guest shot back immediately.

Leconte ignored the question. 'Now I tried to figure out the reason for the Americans' ire. Did you hear of the working over Gulab Chand got in Moscow?'

'Yes, there was some unfortunate accident, I heard. Otherwise he had a good trip and the Russians treated him grandly. But what does that have to do with the gun?'

Leconte explained patiently. 'Gulab Chand has been Pandey-ji's front-man while contacting Satyan Sharma. They have had a couple of secret meetings in Mumbai over the last few months. But he was not successful in getting what the Americans wanted. Then this Moscow incident. I found out that he went missing for six hours. On a freezing cold Moscow night. After a grand red-carpet welcome and a week of being treated like a VIP. And ever since his return, I have found Pandey-ji acting as jumpy as a cat on a hot tin roof. I wonder – has he been trying to double-cross the Americans? Are the Russians angry with him, too? Have they discovered his American game? In any case, he has become too dangerous for the rest of us to tolerate.'

'Arnie, tell me what you have in mind quickly. I know you won't let me go easily. So get it over with.'

Leconte spelt it out carefully, 'Chintu, you must tell your father about this entire conversation. Don't miss any detail. And tell him that Pandey-ji must go. He is making the whole game too dangerous for all of us. He must go – and fast.' Leconte punctuated that last sentence emphatically, tapping his guest's knee with each word.

'Okay, okay, don't get so excited. I'll tell him. Today, as soon as I get back, all right? Now, tell me, when do we hit Rio?'

◆

The blue-uniformed security guard snapped to attention as yet another limousine slid into the little arch above the street entrance of Manwani Plaza. The gentle roar of the Mumbai Stock Exchange conducting business in full swing emanated from the third floor of the Jeejeebhoy Towers nearby. It was the eighth limousine of the afternoon. The guard watched impassively as Jayant Khanwilkar, chairman of the Indian United group of companies, stepped out and strode into the headquarters of Manwani Holdings.

If the guard was surprised that so many of Mr Manwani's traditional business rivals had assembled here, he betrayed no signs of it. The *badey log* – VIPs – were obviously up to something. He hadn't seen such a gathering take place in all his twenty years of service. Must be something to do with the coming parliamentary elections, he thought. No other event could have brought all the leading corporate generals of the country together at one place. His friends in the Stock Exchange building had not told him anything that could explain it. The press had obviously not got on to it yet. They would, soon enough, though. He marvelled that such a high-powered meeting had been kept under wraps until the very last moment.

Some ten minutes later, the chairman of Manwani Holdings rose to address the people assembled in the conference room on the third floor.

'Gentlemen, thank you for sparing your valuable time. Let me, with all humility, accept formally the stewardship of the Fort Club that has been entrusted to me. I hope I shall prove worthy of the trust.' He glanced at the attentive faces ranged around the hundred-and-ten-year-old oaken table which had witnessed the making of so much of India's corporate history.

His grandfather, the patriarch of the Manwani empire, had heralded the dawn of the industrial revolution in the country by setting up the country's first steel plant. The grand old man had, in his own inimitable way, carried the torch of Indian independence, defying British colonial might with an aggressively dynamic brand of homegrown entrepreneurship. Ketan Manwani's father had consolidated this empire by providing an effective platform for realising the scientific and technical dreams of the Nehruvian era. With typical flair, he had put India on the world map by spreading the steel empire into South East Asia and by establishing the nation's first petroleum refining complex in Assam. The Manwani group had flourished, with only a handful of other business families to rival it.

Now the moment had come when the present chairman, having just completed a reorganisation of the group which had put him firmly in the saddle in the face of opposition from his father's septuagenarian satraps, would demonstrate that the flair for grand gestures had lived on in the family after his father's demise. What he was about to launch was a project which would enable India to compete with multinational corporations in that toughest of arenas – the global armaments marketplace. The stewardship of the Fort Club would give him the leeway in Delhi to influence government policy. The magnates sitting at his table knew that Manwani was best placed to oversee the Fort Club's first major initiative. The chairman's heart swelled with pride but he did not allow emotion to encroach on the solemnity of the occasion.

Straightening his tie, he continued, 'The memorandum of understanding and the articles of association of the Special Purpose Vehicle representing our consortium I take as read, gentlemen. I also have to formally ask if there is agreement on the terms set out in these documents.' Everyone nodded in reply. 'Thank you. Let us proceed then, with the main agenda for the day. I formally invite you to affix your signatures to these documents. Mr Khanwilkar, would you like to begin?'

One by one, the eight magnates, collectively representing over four hundred thousand crore rupees of corporate assets, filed wordlessly to the small table in a corner and put their signatures down. A photographer recorded the signing. The little ceremony concluded with a group picture after Manwani had added his own signature at the end.

When they had all resumed their seats, Manwani took up the thread again. 'It remains for me to report to you on the progress of the subcommittee on the Indo-Uzbek howitzer project. Our proposal to the PM met with a less than enthusiastic response, gentlemen. We had hoped that a financial package backed by the leading industrial houses of the country would have cleared the last remaining stumbling-block for the project. We pointed out that our coming together – quite unprecedented in form and composition – was geared especially with a view to protect Indian security interests from the vagaries of Western geopolitics. I am sad to say that our best efforts were fruitless. The PM seemed to feel that it was too late to reopen the case.

'Some of you had, quite rightly, anticipated this. But as we had decided an effort needed to be made notwithstanding, such an effort was made.

'As this board had suggested, we subsequently met with the foreign minister. I am gratified to report that his reaction to the formation of our consortium to finance the Indo-Uzbek howitzer's production was encouraging. Extremely so. I might add that he was surprised at the PM's lukewarm reaction to our proposal.' The two men seated on either side of Manwani nodded in agreement. 'Well, gentlemen, we must redouble our efforts to salvage this project for our country.'

Vishnu Bansiwal from Calcutta spoke up, 'There is every reason to believe that the ruling party will get re-elected. We've got a problem.'

'True. Before we discuss anything further, I must bring to your notice some rather disturbing information which has come to my notice only today. One of my closest aides has a close friend in one of the military intelligence organisations. The source, he says, is authentic.'

He held up a slim plastic folder with about a dozen or so typewritten sheets of paper.

'This information was deliberately leaked to my aide by this intelligence officer, since he felt it was the only course of action open to him as a patriotic Indian. I have made copies for each of you in this room, no more. In sum, gentlemen, this report speaks of a conspiracy at the very highest levels of government to foist a foreign make of howitzer on India. The advent of this gun has been lubricated,' Manwani's lips curled in distaste, 'by what I will only term "irregular financial practices".'

The men gathered around the table were stunned into silence. They reached for the slim folders in front of them with trepidation. The central air-conditioning hummed softly as they went through each detail in the report. It was clear, concise and damning. Facts, figures, events were all set down in stark language which rang with a conviction that dispelled all doubts about its authenticity. Hardened as they were by years of dealing with Delhi's labyrinthine government departments, nothing in their experience had prepared them for this. The trust the country had reposed in its leaders was being betrayed in the worst possible manner.

The meeting went on until late in the evening. They discussed the material threadbare. Several incidents which had puzzled political observers and defence experts during the past few months became clear in the harsh light of the report.

The conclusion that the Fort Club reached that day was grimly momentous; a campaign would have to be mounted to unseat the present government and put a new leader for the country in place. They decided that the Club would back the present foreign minister as the prime ministerial candidate. The exercise would have to be delicately managed to ensure that the ruling party retained power at the Centre, because no other political party appeared qualified to maintain the momentum of India's economic liberalisation.

But the man at the top and his caucus would have to be replaced.

◆

Sam Bannerjee stood wearily at the open balcony door of his fifteenth floor suite at the Oberoi Towers. Far below, the lights of Mumbai's Marine Drive were strung in a golden crescent along the shoreline. It had been a long day for him. He had taken the first flight out of Delhi and had been at back-to-back meetings until six p.m. But he had been steeling himself for the most important meeting of the day – with Rubita, in his suite. He would have to break the bad news to her. The thing had gone on long enough, the stress building up each day until it had become unbearable. He knew that if he didn't bare his soul to the one person in the world who mattered to him, he would break down.

He turned around and looked at his daughter as she finished reading the letter, the latest in a long series that he had been receiving for the last year. It was, to him, the last straw.

Sam Bannerjee had got entangled with a young lady half his age. She had played a cameo in a theatrical production that had been staged in the capital some three years before. They had met when he had dropped into the greenroom after the show to congratulate the director, an old friend of his. Sam and the young lady had spent a long time discussing her part and had ended up going out, later that night, to dinner. Over the next few weeks, Sam Bannerjee had found himself becoming infatuated with her. Playing upon the loneliness of the powerful old widower, the young starlet had managed to set herself up as his keep and quit the tiresome troupe.

Soon getting bored of the older man, she had started an affair on the side with an ambitious young denizen of Delhi's numerous five-star hotel bars. It had not taken long for the two to work out that, in his position as finance secretary, Bannerjee represented a route to quick riches. They had applied the squeeze. He dreaded the potential effect of the exposé on his daughter. Despite her strong-willed nature, he knew that Rubita held him in very high regard and loved him deeply. Her world, and his, could be shattered. Sam had capitulated meekly.

The duo gradually increased their demands until they ran into lakhs of rupees. Having scraped out the last of his considerable family fortunes, a desperate Sam had approached his old friend Kalidoss, who was uniquely placed and, for reasons he chose not to reveal immediately, only too willing to help him out. Kalidoss put Sam in the way of making money on the side, for the first time in his long and unblemished career. That was the only way Sam could have paid the blackmailers but it was taking a heavy toll on his soul.

The story of blackmail and betrayal had played out until finally Sam decided that life was not going to be worth living given this state of affairs. He would have to face up, sooner or later.

That moment had arrived. His eyes were sunken and his cheeks had a pallor that Rubita had never seen before. There was much in her father's life that she was seeing for the first time, ever since the episode of the howitzer had begun. And now there was this letter – from a blackmailer to her father! She knew, as she looked at his drawn face, that he must have been through an agonising ordeal, dreading this encounter but forcing himself to go through with it nevertheless.

'Oh, Sam! How lonesome you must have been all these years in that old bungalow! I don't blame you for having sought this woman's company. Remember, I told you the last time we met that there would probably be many women who would die to hook you.'

Sam perked up visibly at her words. 'You mean,' he stuttered, 'y-you mean you don't mind what I've done?'

'Oh, Sam, you poor darling!' Rubita sprang up and threw her arms around her father. 'No, I don't mind. Not your having a fling or two, I mean. What do you take me for? I'm only sad that you thought I would be ashamed of you and allowed this slut to blackmail you. Why didn't you trust me?'

'It's not so simple, Rubes. It gets a bit more complicated.' His voice quavered. 'It…it has got really out of hand.'

Rubita saw the despondency in his face. 'How bad is it, Sam?' she whispered.

Sam's face turned ashen. 'Rubes, they wanted a few thousands at first. Then it was lakhs. Then…then it went up to a crore. I had nothing left. Even the flat in Calcutta was gone. It was too late. I was too deep into it.' He dropped onto the sofa and covered his face with his hands.

Rubita went to him and threw an arm across his shoulders. 'Shhh. Tell me everything. No matter what, you're still my Sam and I love you. Whatever it is, we'll face it together.'

'No, Rubes. It's too much to ask, even of you. Especially of you. You didn't deserve this.' He took a long moment to pull himself together and continued, 'I had nothing more to give them, yet they pressed on. Finally, they suggested that I go to Kali. And I went to him. He said he would help me out; he gave me one crore.'

Rubita was stunned. One crore rupees! There was only one way a civil servant like Kalidoss could get that kind of money.

'I took the money. I haven't yet given it to them. But I'm already a traitor to my country, Rubes. I don't deserve to live anymore. Kali even told me where it was coming from – the gun money. He's also told me the price I would have to pay. Cooperation. In the end, it's all so simple, isn't it?'

She thought of the many occasions in the recent past when she had felt that her father was being less than frank with her, those twinges of melancholy when she felt that a wall had sprung up between them. Now she knew the cause. Her heart filled with compassion. She lifted his chin and looked into his eyes. Then she kissed him gently on the cheek.

'Shhh, shhh. You've told me. Now you don't need to worry anymore. Not about this trashy slut anyway. Nor her friend, whoever he is. Nor Kalidoss. We'll get the bastards. All of them. You've still got the evidence, because that's what the money is. How else could you have got so much money if you had nothing left? Come on, Sam. Chin up. We'll get the scumbags. All of them.'

Then the floodgates crashed open and Sam Bannerjee wept like a small child. Rubita held her father tightly, rocking him back and forth for a long time until, exhausted and cleansed, the old man relaxed, relieved of a terrible burden.

Later, as she turned in for the night, Rubita realised that her journalistic instinct should have caught some nuance in the conversation, but she had been too deeply affected as a daughter learning, for the first time, shameful secrets about her father to spot it. She went over the conversation again and again but could not pin down the thing lurking at the back of her mind. She tossed and turned in her bed, but it was futile. Hoping that it would flash into her consciousness in the morning, she drifted off, happy that she had her father back.

11

The drive to Pandey-ji's farmhouse some five kilometres off the Hindon Air Base through the starlit December night was biting cold. Another grey winter was at its peak and only those who had pressing business ventured out at this time. The traffic was quite thin as they left the capital and they made good time. A light breeze from the south played with wisps of mist as they turned right off State Highway 57. Satyan hunkered down in his seat, rubbing his arms to get warmer. Butt was at the wheel of a regulation white Maruti Gypsy, and had maintained a steady hundred kmph ever since they had cleared the Wazirabad Bridge over the sluggish waters of the Yamuna.

When Satyan had received an invitation from Pandey-ji to dine at his farmhouse, he had called Rubita. This much was apparent to them, that the Minister of State for Home was the man behind Gulab Chand and that he had now been forced to show his hand. Since he had no official standing in the howitzer affair, he couldn't summon Satyan for a discussion overtly. Pandey-ji had therefore set up the meeting far from prying eyes. The question was – why?

More intriguing was the latest discovery that Pandey-ji was rumoured to be quite close to Arnaud Leconte who, amongst the wheeler-dealer crowd in Delhi, was said to be the real 'foreign hand' rather than the usual bogeyman most people suspected – the US. What was more, Rubita had got a clear indication from Sam Bannerjee that FIAM was tipped to bag the howitzer contract. The French company had no official liaison officer in Delhi and yet was the frontrunner in one of the largest howitzer deals in the world. Given Delhi's corruption-riddled corridors of power, there had to be a fixer doing the job and it seemed very likely that Leconte was the man.

With so many possibilities and so much mud being slung around, it was becoming difficult for the young entrepreneur and his fiancée to get to the bottom of the scam. That a huge scam was under way was not in doubt anymore, it was just a question of separating the different threads to find the one that would lead them to the real culprits. Satyan's meeting with Pandey-ji would be a good opportunity to figure out whether he was acting as an agent of the Americans, the Russians or the French.

Rubita had voiced an anxiety that had been gnawing at her nerves. 'But, Satyan, you're going to be all alone in that farmhouse, baby. We've seen that Pandey-ji can be ruthless and he employs violent henchmen. What if you have an argument with him out there? How will you protect yourself?'

Satyan had reassured her that he had already thought of that. 'I'll get Butt to come along. He's quite competent and will surely smell trouble in advance if there's any.'

'Yes, that's a good idea!' Rubita had replied enthusiastically. 'And he's quite a senior officer; maybe he can even sit in on your talk with Pandey-ji.'

When Satyan called Butt, the intelligence officer had been as mystified about Pandey-ji's move as Satyan. He agreed that the minister was probably acting as an agent of one of the foreign powers. He himself had come to the conclusion that Pandey-ji was acting for the Russians but, given the current frontrunner for the howitzer contract, he agreed that a French connection couldn't be ruled out. And he had no hesitation in agreeing to come along. He had been about to suggest it himself. Satyan had no difficulty in getting Pandey-ji to extend the invitation to his 'official bodyguard'.

It was pushing nine by the time they drew up at the imposing wrought-iron gates of the minister's farmhouse. The place was crawling with 'Black Cat' commandos of the elite Special Protection

Group. In the status-crazy crowd of the capital's cocktail circus, a VIP's standing was most visibly measured by the number of assault-rifle-toting commandos surrounding him. Pandey-ji had been able to commandeer more than his fair share of security, and he enjoyed publicly wallowing in his black-togged entourage. Butt rolled down the window and handed over his ID card and pass for scrutiny by the guard at the gate. The man flicked the pasteboard with his fingers as he scanned the photo on it and compared it with the face behind the wheel. He glanced over at Satyan who handed over his pass. After scrutinising it, the guard walked over to his booth and called in to the main house. A moment later he came out, handed the passes and the card back before releasing the main gate. He did not utter a single word the whole time.

They drove up a flagstoned driveway which led straight to the portico about fifty metres from the gate. On the other side of the portico, the driveway skirted a wide, beautifully manicured lawn before rejoining the main drive to form a 'P'. To their left were banks of flowerbeds bounded by a twenty-foot high wall topped with naked electrified wire. The wall stretched away into the darkness behind the house and returned on the other side. The returning wall also had a flowerbed running alongside. They could see one segment of an L-shaped lawn reaching out almost fifty metres to their right. The other segment of the 'L', they guessed, would probably be at least as large. The grounds could perhaps host a party for five hundred guests. Presumably there was a farm somewhere, but that was not important. The house itself was an imposing three-storey structure fronted by spacious open-air terraces, each smaller than the one below. The massive structure of glass and wood glowed dully through the thin winter mist in the light of dozens of lamps standing about the grounds.

Butt drove the Gypsy through the portico and into a vacant slot in the parking bay on the far side. As they got down, two commandos stepped out of the front door to wait for them. They showed their papers again to one, while the other watched, silent and alert. Satisfied, the commando handed back the papers and strode wordlessly into the house, signalling that they were to follow him.

The second man brought up the rear. They were escorted into a drawing room which had a large oaken desk in one corner, beside an open fireplace. An electric fire warmed the sofas and chairs nearby. Indicating that they were to be seated, the guards left them to wait for the minister.

Pandey-ji walked in some ten minutes later, wheezing with the effort of having to move his great bulk. Over his white cotton clothes, he had on an overcoat of 'politically correct' homespun wool. Satyan allowed his hand to be engulfed by the minister's soft pudgy paws. Displaying his broad paan-stained teeth in a smile of welcome, Pandey-ji drew his guest to a sofa by his side.

As if noticing Butt for the first time, Pandey-ji said with a wave of his hand, 'You can go now. You are not needed. Wait for us outside. We will have dinner in about half an hour.'

The intelligence man was taken aback. 'But I was told that...'

'How dare you contradict your superiors?' said the minister. Soft though it was, his voice carried an unmistakable note of command. 'We are going to discuss confidential matters here.'

The intelligence man stood his ground. 'With respect, sir, I have been assigned to watch Mr Sharma night and day. Please ignore my presence. Since I am under official oath, any matters you discuss will not be leaked from my end.'

Pandey-ji had dealt with government officials for years. He flashed Butt a reassuring smile. 'My dear fellow, I am as concerned about security as you are. This room has nobody except the three of us. Now tell me, who would dare attack us here with so many SPG commandos around? Don't worry about your precious Sharma sahib. Why don't you sit outside the door? I have no objection. Your dedication to duty is commendable. I shall put in a word for you with your superiors.'

Butt withdrew reluctantly. With a chuckle, the minister settled his ample girth into a chair and gestured to Satyan to seat himself. 'Just because he was invited to have dinner with us, he thinks he can sit for top secret discussions. What is the bureaucracy coming to nowadays, eh, Sharma sahib? Achha, leave all that. What will you have to drink – some Scotch?' Pandey-ji pressed a tiny button under the arm of his sofa. A faint rustle was heard and a waiter appeared. Satyan ordered a Scotch and soda for himself. With quiet efficiency, they were served. The minister kept up a steady flow of small talk while they were waited upon. After the waiter disappeared, he broached the main subject.

'Sharma sahib, I know that you are always in a hurry, so I will come straight to the point. As you might have guessed, it is about the howitzer contract.' Seeing a hard edge to Satyan's expression he ran on hastily, 'Don't think that I have called you here to discuss anything underhand. What I am about to suggest you may seem somewhat unusual, which is why I wanted to talk to you privately and at leisure before making it public. But I assure you that it is in the best interests of the nation.'

Satyan grunted noncommittally. He sipped his Scotch and waited.

'It is like this, Sharma sahib. The PM has had several consultations in the last few days on this subject and all aspects of the matter have been carefully gone into. All the secretaries of the empowered group of ministers have given their reports. Great care has been taken to ensure that a consensus emerges among everybody on this critical issue relating to the nation's defence.'

With an uneasy sense of foreboding, Satyan guessed that the decision had already been taken. He knew that sometimes key decisions were taken by forming a consensus of ministers beforehand, so that the formal cabinet meeting itself could be projected to have taken place unanimously. Why else would the man tell him all this? What was more puzzling was why, if the decision had in fact been taken, he had been called here to be given the bad news when a cursory letter in the usual governmental style would have been the procedure? Yet, here he was. Obviously Pandey-ji had some kind of deal in mind.

'Ah, Sharma sahib, I can perceive that your keen mind has already leaped forward to grasp the essential aspects of the cabinet's likely decision. Truly, I must now believe all that I have been told about you. Yes, I must regretfully inform you that the empowered group, after several meetings, is inclined in favour of the FIAM gun. I can understand how disappointed you must be since you have been so closely involved with this project.'

So there it was at last. Years of struggle, the hopes of some of his best people – in fact, of some of the best software brains in the world – and his own dreams of setting into motion a software juggernaut to challenge the mightiest multinationals, of taking Pure Space to heights not achieved by any Indian company so far, were about to receive a major setback. Satyan's fingers tightened around his glass as he considered the news. Shakily, he took a swig. He stared into the middle distance, wondering how he would break it to his men back in Mumbai.

Pandey-ji cleared his throat gently. He watched disappointment shadowing his guest's eyes. He knew that this was a good moment to move in for the kill.

'The FIAM gun has, on balance, the best combination of features in the long run, Sharma sahib. Technically it is on par with the Uzbek prototype, the supply track record of the European company is impeccable. And various other considerations have made it the better choice in this case.'

Satyan sneered. 'Yes, Mr Pandey, I fully understand the various other considerations which may have played a role. We did not have any of those considerations to offer the people who would take this decision, but the FIAM company had plenty of them. How many considerations did they offer you, Mr Pandey?'

Pandey-ji looked suitably angry. 'What are you trying to say, Sharma sahib? Here I am, taking the time and trouble to explain to you personally what the cabinet's decision is going to be even before it has been taken, and this is the way you thank me! Do you know the risk I am running by discussing national secrets with a private party? Are you trying to cast aspersions on the elected representatives of the people of India? I can understand that your frustration is making you say these things. But be careful, Sharma sahib. Use your words cautiously here.'

◆

The morning was going badly for Matthews. The India operation was slowly but surely turning into a fiasco and the Secretary of State had been on the phone, first thing in the morning. He had been far from gentle in his choice of words. A few months before, Mad Matt had expected to present a simple but telling show of US intelligence power across the world. And now, instead of receiving kudos for a job going well as he had hoped, he was receiving increasing flak from DC. The last meeting in the Pentagon with Hawthorne still rankled and the pressure had grown more intense during the past few weeks.

Matthews couldn't understand it. He had got the operation planned so beautifully. Picking Connolly for the job had been right – of that he was sure. And now it was this very decision that was being criticised by the armchair generals up at the Pentagon.

From the corner of his eye, he saw the little red light under his desk begin to flash. Prudence had dictated that Matthews install a totally private phone line which could not be tapped even by the CIA. The number had been given to a very select list of people whose personal loyalty he could implicitly depend on. Not more than twenty people in the entire world – and not every one of them American – knew of the existence of this phone. There was no ring, just a little red flasher hidden from the sight of anyone visiting him at the office. An electronic code activated the instrument when he wanted so that even incoming calls could not be registered unless he was in the room.

He was startled, therefore, when he heard the voice at the other end. On several occasions in the past, he had listened to this voice in conversations monitored by his operatives in Kremlin. But he had never expected to hear Major General Aliakhin of the FSS on this particular line.

'Good morning, Mr Matthews,' boomed the general. 'I assure you that I would not have used your privileged phone had the situation not called for it. But I needed to talk to you man to man, away from the prying and insensitive ears of our respective colleagues. I think you know what a soldier feels in the midst of bureaucratic officials in the corridors of power, eh, Mr Matthews?'

Mad Matt finally found his voice. 'How the fuck did you get this frigging number?' he asked in a hoarse whisper.

'That, my dear Mr Matthews, is not germane to the issue. Suffice it to say that I have a similar facility at my end, and it seemed logical to me that you would not overlook so elementary a device. It only remained for me to find out the number and it has been my experience that a seeker always finds what he is looking for, if he knows what he wants.'

'What do you want?' asked Matthews.

'Mr Matthews, Matt – may I call you Matt? I feel that I know you so well. Please call me Yegor, by the way. I am calling you entirely in my personal capacity, as a Russian and a citizen of the world speaking to another man of the world. My intention is to preserve the truce that has existed between the CIA and the FSS for the last few years because my country cannot afford to break it. There, you see, I am being frank with you. No one in Russia knows that I am making this call. No one else, in fact, knows your telephone number and you may depend on me not to divulge it. I know that your first reaction was anger, but I am sure you will overlook that when you hear what I have to say.'

Aliakhin knew that he had Matthews' undivided attention. He continued, 'Matt, even as we speak, one of my operatives is seeking to eliminate the young Indian businessman, Satyan Sharma, who is involved in the howitzer which has occupied so much of our time and energy these past few months. My operative knows that the man posing as an Indian Intelligence Bureau officer and accompanying Sharma on the pretext of guarding him is, in fact, an operative of yours. A good man, may I say, but hardly up to the current situation.

'My man sent me a message that he was moving in to a rendezvous that Sharma is having with Mr Pandey, a minister in the Indian cabinet. This minister was supposed to help us obtain the designs of the Indian howitzer. This is a business arrangement which he has, unfortunately, seen fit to make with the US as well. Naturally, we were quite upset and sent him a friendly warning. This warning, Mr Pandey has chosen to ignore. The designs are of no use to us if everybody has them. In fact, it will serve us better if no one has them. Therefore, I have ordered my man there to eliminate Pandey at this farmhouse meeting. Two birds, as you people say, with one stone, eh? You will surely appreciate that this is an opportunity we cannot afford to miss. My man is moving in even as we speak. Naturally, I waited until now to tell you this so that you wouldn't be able to mount a counter-operation. I'm sure you understand.'

'But why are you telling me all this?' asked Matthews.

'Because there is a strong possibility that your operative will also meet with an unsavoury end as he is present on the spot right now, Matt. I want you to know that Connolly is not the target.' Matt's sharp intake of breath at the mention of the field operative's name brought a quick chuckle in response from Aliakhin. 'It is unfortunate that he will be caught in the line of fire. If anything should happen to Connolly, please don't react in any untoward manner; that is a request from me. Matt, the cold war is over and I think that is to Russia's benefit. We can't afford to carry on as before. We need to spend our resources in building a stronger economy. I want you to view any accident that takes place as merely that – an accident.

'I am calling you to appeal to one of the more pragmatic members of the opposition in the name of peace. Mother Russia is a proud nation, Matt. Foolishly so. There are enough people of the old guard left in the Kremlin who will join battle with the US with relish. But I know that we cannot afford to break our truce. So, before anything happens to set us at each other's throats again, I plead with you to exercise restraint in case there is an accident in India.'

'Why in the name of god do you goons want to start a shoot-out then? What the hell was this guy doing shooting us up in Mumbai? In broad daylight, for crying out loud! Why have you sent such a trigger-happy operative? If you didn't want the Indians to win the contract, couldn't you have tried other methods?'

'The incident in Mumbai was a sad lapse in judgment, Matt. I had immediately instructed my operative to desist from such attacks. But now, we find that there are no options left. What other methods were you referring to, Matt?'

'Hey, that's a no-brainer. Frame the minister with charges of corruption. Paint Satyan Sharma as the villain of the piece. His fiancée's father is on the bankroll too. Simple enough to blow the whole shebang to kingdom come through a public scandal played out on tv. That's the power of democracy working for you.'

'You may have to reconsider the power of democracy, Matt. Especially in an underdeveloped economy like India. The masses of peasants, who provide this democratic power you talk of, neither understand nor care about the scandals their leaders get into. You see, Matt, your cherished democracy is a Western value which has been artificially transplanted on Indian soil. A scandal about the gun will interest only ineffectual intellectuals and the effete middle-classes of India. There are so many scandals anyway, what is one more or less? And as for the poverty-stricken masses that make up the majority of the voters in India, they are too busy fighting for their two square meals a day to worry about the fate of a distant multinational involved in a business deal. Issues like this are too far removed from their daily subsistence for them to know or care about.

'The Russian peasant has the same indifference, arising from the same preoccupations. In this, I think, lies the reason why we Russians have been able to understand the Indians better than you Americans.

'No, my dear Matt, the only way to put an end to this business is our way. Eliminate the key players. And we have Sharma and Pandey at one place right now. Please heed me when I say that Connolly's presence is an unfortunate coincidence and that he is not the target. Do I have your word, Matt?'

'I'm warning you, Connolly is one of my best guys. He can take care of himself, even against Konstantin.'

Aliakhin chuckled. 'Touché, Matt. It would have disappointed me greatly if you hadn't known my operative's name. Well, I take it that we are agreed, then. I hope we can talk again in happier circumstances.'

◆

Satyan leaned back, pondering his next words. Pandey-ji watched his guest. They could hear the ticking of the clock hanging on the wall.

'Well, Mr Pandey, we have done the best we can in the service of the country. I have myself witnessed the field tests at Lakhimpur, Kumaon and Ladakh. Our gun has passed all tests surpassing the expectations of the Indian army. Now we await the decision of the elected leaders of this country. If this is what you have to tell me today, will you kindly excuse me from the dinner and allow me to return to my hotel? I see no purpose in staying on here.'

Pandey-ji smiled his broadest, most conciliatory smile. 'Now, Sharma sahib, you don't think I am so insensitive that I would have called you here just to tell you this disappointing news? No, no, Sharma sahib, you misunderstand me. You see, it is because of the excellent work that your company has put into the fire control unit that the cabinet is finding it so difficult to arrive at a decision. For two reasons. One, the party that has developed it is Indian and two, it is considerably superior to the one in the FIAM gun. The people of this country are proud of you, Sharma sahib.'

'It's not just the FCU that is superior,' said Satyan with asperity, 'so are the ballistics and the dependability of performance under the most adverse conditions. The gun can continue firing for days together without getting overheated. It is a brilliant piece of design and engineering and you people know it. And as for the people of this country being proud, I don't see how they can be proud about something they don't know.'

'Ah, here they will no doubt be helped to a large extent by your beautiful and charming fiancée, Sharma sahib,' Pandey-ji said with a sly smile.

So, it had worked, Satyan thought with grim exultation. The minister was admitting indirectly that Pinnacle TV's exposé of the scandal could affect the ruling party's chances in the coming elections. The consequences for everyone involved with the project, Pure Space Networks included, might turn out to be disastrous. But Satyan had decided that if his dream had to be sacrificed in fighting the ugly corruption he was seeing, then he would sacrifice it. He would have to switch gears. The game had changed. The gun itself was merely one of the pieces on the board. Sam Bannerjee had sent him ample warning about it – here was the hard evidence. He composed himself to listen carefully to what the minister was going to say.

'But we are men too busy to worry about actions that cannot be undone, Sharma sahib,' said Pandey-ji. 'Let me get to the most important thing I want to discuss with you.

'What the cabinet has asked me to explore, is the feasibility of a somewhat novel idea. In fact,' said Pandey-ji, lowering his voice, 'no less a person than the deputy PM, Shri Panduranga Rao himself, suggested this in order to ensure that dynamic Indian entrepreneurs like you are encouraged. So you see why I am happy to be the one to convey this suggestion to you. I have been asked to sound you out in private before making it official. That is why I have requested you to meet me here rather than in the office. But this conversation must remain strictly confidential until I give the clearance. What I am about to say must stay within the four walls of this room.'

'That depends on what you tell me, Mr Pandey,' said Satyan, not wanting to seem too willing a convert.

Pandey-ji knew that Satyan had a low opinion of politicians. Proof was the sullen and intransigent attitude he was now showing. Inwardly, Pandey-ji sighed. How many years, he thought, did the young need before they realised the futility of sticking to empty ideals? Why did he have to waste his time with these misguided upper-class hypocrites when this matter could have been smoothly and quickly worked out just like any other business transaction?

Containing his irritation, Pandey-ji continued, 'You see, Sharma sahib, the cabinet is very impressed with your FCU. They feel that it would be a pity to see all this effort go waste. Now, unfortunately, we have decided not to go ahead with the Uzbek proposal. That should not in any way mean that you will go unrewarded. What we are simply proposing, Sharma sahib, is why don't we see if you can work on an FCU to fit into the FIAM gun? That way we can retrieve the Indian contribution in this project. The Indian people will be proud of such an achievement. And you will also make a good profit, no?'

It was all so absurdly simple. And the man was right, it seemed to benefit everybody. Everybody except the Uzbeks and old Barkhatiev, that is. And Rajan. But perhaps he could see to it that Rajan at least remained on the project. That his skills would continue to be considered valuable by the government. Satyan felt a twinge of remorse at the thought of the old man. But what the hell, he thought, somebody or the other would be the loser in this game. The FIAM gun was not a bad choice anyway. It had been shortlisted by the army from a field of more than half a dozen. He couldn't find a fault with this new angle. Unless there was something else happening here. Unless the wily minister was not playing straight with him.

And then it struck him. The decision probably had not been taken yet. Pandey-ji was just trying to hoodwink and push him. His fire control unit must be the stumbling block. The deputy PM must have figured that if it could be made a part of the French gun, the deal could be swung and the scam quietly brushed under the carpet. If not, they knew that Rubita and he would not rest until the scam and its perpetrators were exposed. With the parliamentary elections looming, the kickback money was desperately needed but a scandal would be fatal to the ruling party. The timing must be bugging the hell out of everybody in Delhi.

Technically, it wasn't going to be easy to achieve but, with Pure Space Networks working closely with FIAM's engineers, it could be done. If the Indian government put pressure on the French company, it might agree to discuss things with Satyan's company.

Satyan considered. The deputy PM seemed to be the kingpin of this whole rigmarole. He and his cronies, definitely Pandey too, would by now have worked out their share of the loot from the deal. He and Rubita could go on tv with details of the scam and there would be a huge uproar. But would that help? If he did expose the scam, the ruling party might get a rude jolt but the government machinery could be relied upon to drag things on for years. New shames and scandals would replace this one in the public memory. Time and the great Indian bureaucracy would hush the whole thing up. Rarely if ever were the high and mighty of this country brought to book. Corruption in Indian politics had become so common that throwing charges at people like Pandey-ji was like throwing pebbles at a sandstorm.

All of a sudden, a barrage of unexpected questions began assaulting him. Was he actually trying to rationalise here by mentally working through a potential collaboration with FIAM? Was he really above all this muck? Why was he even considering this kind of partnership with the French company? With all that had happened over the past few months, was he also descending to the level of these bastards? Was their power so subtle, the appeal of their contorted value systems so inescapable, that they were able to even turn his mind? Damn the bastards, could they even subvert his own fucking soul?

Pandey-ji sensed that Satyan was undergoing some kind of deep soul-searching and smiled indulgently. The young man was facing his moment of truth and he would bide his time.

Satyan caught that smile and all the worldly wisdom it represented. Yes, he told himself harshly, you're no better than these fucking blood-suckers. The bile rose in his throat. His mind was torn half in horror at the abyss he had almost slipped into and half in revulsion at the bloated bastard smirking away at him. He realised that he was on the verge of allowing his inner turmoil to overcome his rational mind. To cover his emotional struggle and to allow himself time to push them deep into his subconscious, he rose on his shaky legs to pour himself another drink. Pandey-ji remained still, waiting patiently for Satyan's inner demons to work themselves out.

With his back to the minister, Satyan fought a hard battle within himself. Unknown to his conscious mind, a vengeful creature had uncoiled itself and begun to rise from the depths of his being, sensing that its moment was approaching.

As the ice cubes splashed with little tinkles into the Scotch, Satyan began to map out the angles. He decided to play along for a while to see how the ground lay. Turning, he leaned his tall frame against the table, forcing the fat man to twist his neck painfully around and look up at his prey.

'Mr Pandey,' Satyan said slowly, his expression displaying the thoughtfulness of a man trying to reconcile himself to a new reality, 'I can see the possibilities in what you are suggesting. Suppose I tell you at this stage – without any commitments, mind you – that

I am willing to listen to more details of your proposal, there would still be another angle you have to take care of.'

'What is that?'

'The FIAM company. Why should they agree?'

'Ah, you are quick, Sharma sahib. But we have anticipated that. No problem. I have sounded them out through their representative in India and received a favourable response. If both parties can agree on the terms, then your company stands to make huge profits. But they have been as tentative as you are now. There are commitments they must have made to their own software consultants which could complicate the picture. This is why this matter has to be handled with great care and delicacy. But leave it to me. I will take care of everything. And I must warn you again, please keep this matter totally confidential.'

Satyan remained silent, thinking the thing through. There was some mystery behind this whole picture that needed to be figured out, but he wasn't able to put his finger on it. He felt it in his bones. Pandey-ji was not levelling with him.

Then he had a sudden realisation. Why was this initiative not coming from the defence ministry? How come Pandey-ji, from the home ministry and of second-level rank at that, was taking the lead? Maybe the really big guns in the government didn't want to get directly involved just yet. Maybe they wanted him to commit himself to this double-game before coming out into the open, in case the whole thing backfired.

But Satyan wanted to hear Pandey-ji's version.

◆

Satyan leaned forward to probe Pandey-ji for more details when the door to the room burst open and Butt strode in without bothering to ask for permission.

'Pandey-ji, have you dismissed the SPG? The commandos are leaving. They say that they have received orders to relocate immediately.'

The effect of this announcement was instantaneous. Pandey-ji's face turned ashen. He began to stammer. He gripped his chair and his eyes rolled around. Cold sweat had broken out on his face. The two men stared at him, wondering if he was going to suffer a stroke.

Finally, he was able to speak coherently. 'Call them back,' he croaked. 'Call them back! They can't leave without my permission! Whose orders? Whose orders? I am the minister, don't they know? Call them back now!'

They could hear the grinding of gears as the commandos' vehicles began to assemble in the portico. Pandey-ji was struggling wildly to get his bulk out of the depths of the sofa. The man was positively frantic. Satyan watched with fascination – the cool composure of the consummate politician had been blown away completely.

He glanced over at Butt. The IB officer was looking speculatively at Pandey-ji. He seemed to be more interested in the changed demeanour of the minister than on the mystery of the evacuating commandos. It dawned on Satyan that this new development was perhaps not as big a surprise to the minister as they expected. It was almost as if Pandey-ji had been anticipating something like this , though his reaction was not any less panicky now that it had actually taken place. That was puzzling Satyan. Maybe it was puzzling Butt, too.

When Pandey-ji managed to extricate himself and went panting and puffing out of the house, Butt walked to the windows of the study which overlooked the portico. Parting the curtains, he watched the minister rushing about in the dust raised by the jeeps, crying plaintively at the commandos, begging them to stay back until he could sort out the 'mistake'.

The last of the Black Cats piled wordlessly into their transport and drove away. Satyan watched them in silence from the window. They had their orders, he supposed. But the minister seemed to be overreacting. He saw him stand and stare after the vanished vehicles for a long time, clutching his 'Gandhi' cap, hair askew, shoulders drooping, looking like a man who had lost everything. Satyan couldn't understand why he was making such a song and dance about this. If he felt so deeply about the loss of what at the end was merely a status symbol, then why wasn't he on the phone, bawling out whoever was responsible?

The minutes stretched out. The minister remained rooted to the spot, head hanging low. Everything had gone still. Satyan and Butt stood at the window, looking out into the darkness.

On the road beyond the compound wall, the silhouette of a lone vehicle emerged from the mist, inching along only on parking lights. They watched as it drove slowly past the farmhouse gates, now that there was no one to guard them. This seemed to galvanise the minister, who went rushing into the drawing room. Satyan and Butt exchanged looks.

'The minister seems to be taking this badly,' said Satyan in a bemused voice. 'He looks quite pitiable, don't you think?'

Butt's expression seemed to have hardened further in the past few minutes. There was a cold, calculating glint in his eyes that Satyan couldn't fathom.

'Don't waste your pity on scum like him, Mr Sharma,' the IB man said grimly. 'This is what he gets for playing dangerous games. Play dirty, eat dirt.'

'What's that supposed to mean, Javed? Are you saying that you have definite evidence about Pandey taking kickbacks from FIAM? And is that connected to this withdrawal of security in some way? But why?'

The barrage of questions snapped Butt out of his reverie. He looked at Satyan – a shade nervously, thought the young businessman – and answered quickly, 'Yes, Mr Sharma, we have known about Pandey-ji's FIAM games for some time now. But no evidence. Something must have happened in Delhi. Maybe Pandey-ji has become *persona non grata* in the government. Whatever it is, I think this place is going to get too warm for our health very soon. I don't think we should stay here. Let's get moving.'

'No,' said Satyan, grabbing hold of Butt's shirt. 'We are not going to leave this man in the lurch. No one deserves to be left to face danger by himself and I think that you are implying that there's danger around the corner for Pandey. And what's more, aren't you, as an intelligence officer, supposed to hold him in your sights until he can be brought to justice? How can you shirk your responsibility like this? What's going on? I know you are a very brave man, Javed, so obviously you're not about to run away just to save your skin. There is something more to all this. You are hiding something from me. Tell me what it is now!'

Butt tried to shrug off Satyan's grip, but it was too strong. Then Butt relaxed. 'You're right, Mr Sharma. The police are likely to make an appearance soon. Maybe that's why the commandos were asked to leave immediately. But yes, we'll stay on until they get here.'

Satyan released him and they went into the drawing room. Pandey-ji was punching the numbers of his cellphone in frenzy. He wasn't able to raise anyone at this time of the night. When he looked up at them, they could see that he was wild-eyed with terror. He was babbling incoherently and his face and body were drenched with sweat.

'Calm him down, Mr Sharma,' said Butt. 'Give him a drink. I'm going to take a look around the place.' He went for the wide circular staircase which led upstairs.

Satyan walked up to the minister and asked him why he was so terrified. 'Have you received any threats to your life recently?'

Pandey-ji gulped. Running a soaking handkerchief over his forehead, he tried to control his heartbeat. Hand on his chest, eyes closed, he seemed to be willing himself to calm down. Finally, he opened his eyes and looked at the younger man who handed him a glass of water.

'Sharma sahib, what can I say? Ever since this gun business has started, I have been under constant threat. I have had to send my family back to Bihar. And today morning I got not one but three phone calls from terrorist groups saying that they will kill me. And now look at this; my enemies in the party have removed the security, under god knows what pretext, knowing fully well that I can be attacked at any time. I tell you this is a conspiracy!'

'Save your breath, Mr Pandey,' said Satyan roughly, 'you'll need it later.' Satyan hadn't been taken in by the reference to Pandey-ji's family. He suspected that they had been sent off to the ancestral village to allow Pandey-ji to score with his choice of young and willing social ladder-climbers in the capital.

The looming physical danger was palpable while Satyan was deep in thought. Butt had said so, that it would be unwise to stay on in this isolated farmhouse. He looked around as the intelligence bureau man came down the stairs at a run.

'Looks like whoever is behind this isn't wasting time. A jeep has been parked about a hundred metres up the road and three men are coming on foot towards the gate. They look like they are carrying guns. I couldn't make out for sure in the darkness but I feel certain by the way they are walking. I'm definitely not waiting to find out.

'Pandey-ji, where are your cars? We will need something faster than the Gypsy I drove from Delhi.'

Pandey-ji gestured towards the back of the house. 'Through the side door there,' he wheezed, 'there is a small room which has a direct exit to the garage.' Panting and puffing, he followed the sprinting Butt and Satyan.

'Quick, the Mercedes,' said Butt, unhesitatingly making his selection from the four cars in the garage. He scanned a board near the switches where several bunches of keys hung. Turning to Pandey-ji he asked, 'Which are the keys to the Mercedes?'

'I don't know!' wailed the minister. 'I don't know how to drive!'

'Here, this looks like it,' said Satyan, tossing a bunch at Butt. 'But we'll take all of them, just in case.'

Butt took the driver's seat without a word and tried the key. Satyan ran to open the garage doors and Pandey-ji squeezed into the back. Butt could hear him muttering to himself as the engine purred to life. Satyan dove into the car as it came abreast the doors. He too heard the muttering from the rear seat. With a start, both men realised that Pandey-ji was praying.

Butt drove the car slowly towards the gates, the high-precision engine emitting a low whisper. Though it was night-time, the mist would deaden sounds and the car would probably not be heard from too far away. He had not switched the headlights on. The gate was clearly visible in the bright lights around the grounds. The big car gathered speed as it moved silently through the night. A few metres short of the gates, he threw the gear and jammed the accelerator down hard. The three intruders had been approaching the big villa cautiously and were about ten metres shy of the gates when the car burst out without any sound or light to warn them. They scattered when they saw it hurtling towards them. Butt swerved, heading straight for the man in the lead, trying to mow him down, but he jumped nimbly out of the way. The car roared down the road towards Delhi.

As they neared the jeep parked by the side of the road, Butt slowed the car down to a smooth forty kmph and rolled the window down. Taking careful aim with his automatic pistol, he let off a single shot. At barely ten metres, he did not miss. The jeep jerked as the near front wheel ruptured. A flurry of shots erupted behind them, the bullets missing by miles.

'That should hold them down for a few minutes, enough to give us a good start.'

'Good shot, Javed,' said Satyan, marvelling at Butt's intrepidity. Behind them, Pandey-ji shouted with glee.

Satyan twisted around to see the three men making a dash for their jeep. 'Looks like we've bought ourselves some time, Javed. And something else, I think I've seen one of them before. Yes, I know! It's the Russian agent who chased us in Mumbai!' Satyan peered again through the rear window. He could see one of the men reach for the stepney attached to the back of the jeep before the darkness swallowed them. 'They planned this thing well,' he said. 'Let's hope we can make it into the city before they catch up.'

'Don't get complacent yet, Mr Sharma,' warned Butt. 'If these guys are smart, they would know that there's only one place we'll be heading for – Delhi. They must have a team watching out for us at the entry point into the city. They can radio on ahead with the car's number and description and follow us as soon as they have the tyre fixed. We're boxed in unless we can come up with a good plan.'

That got Pandey-ji yelling again. 'Go faster, driver! If we can reach the city before them, we can change into a taxi or another car. I shall call for a car on my mobile phone. Or at least we can lose them in the traffic. Go faster!'

Satyan shot an angry glance at Pandey-ji over his shoulder. Up until tonight, his responsibility to his team had forced him to keep his emotions bottled. But now, having seen the blustery minister turn into a blubbering coward so swiftly, he felt revulsion fill his heart.

And the dark demon inside his soul continued rising steadily to the surface.

◆

The silence of the library of the Delhi's Willingdon Institute was punctuated by intermittent clicks of billiard balls from next door. John Kalidoss stretched his legs out on the chaise lounge in the alcove and lighted an after-lunch cigar. He looked across fondly at Sam Bannerjee. They had been served coffee and left to themselves.

Sam had wondered all through the meal why he had been invited – almost summoned – to this 'meeting' at the club. Making up a plausible reason to explain his absence for two hours on a busy working day had been a difficult task. Kalidoss had quipped that it ought not to be too difficult, given Sam's experience. Sam had swallowed the intended dig quietly. He realised that he was in no position to reply strongly to such barbs, least of all to Kalidoss. But he had expected better from his urbane colleague.

During the meal, his host had studied him patiently. Sam had played along. He had acted the part of a thoroughly contrite and chastened sinner trying to put up a brave front to the world. The man was apparently satisfied and ready to broach the main subject of the meeting.

They had been discussing the forthcoming parliamentary elections over lunch and the prospects of various political parties. Sam had, like Kalidoss, always tacitly supported the ruling party and they had desultorily evaluated the key candidates and their likely influence on the polls. Now, relaxing over their cigars, Kalidoss gave the discussion a more tangible direction.

'Sam, old boy, now that we seem to be in agreement that the insidious Rashtriya Party has a good chance of rocking the boat, I think it is high time that all right-minded people, like you and I, should put our shoulders to the ruling party's wheel.'

'Only too glad to be of any help I can, John,' Sam said. 'All you have to do is to say the word. Do you have anything particular in mind?'

'As a matter of fact, I do. It wouldn't exactly harm the party if it were to feature positively in the news on tv regularly from now on. Most channels are already doing their bit, only too happily, considering the outlays to their newscasters. But I'm told that one channel hasn't been exactly cooperative. Pinnacle tv. I was surprised to hear that because five years ago it had come down quite heavily in favour of the PM. Of course, at that time he wasn't the PM. The impression is that Pinnacle is being anti-establishment merely because that is their policy, no matter who is in power.

'I was wondering if you would be able to discuss this with Rubita the next time you speak to her. It's not right for a leading tv channel to appear biased, as I'm sure you'll agree.'

Bannerjee couldn't help admire the smooth way in which Kalidoss had put across the thing. That he had thought it fit to spend so much time to build up to this proposition meant that the ruling party recognised Rubita's sway over the audience. And they had sent Kalidoss to collect the bill on Sam.

This was just what Rubita and he had been planning and hoping for.

Sam had met covertly with Pinnacle TV's top brass twice after confessing to his daughter. He had documented and presented to them a detailed, blow-by-blow account of how hundreds of crores of slush funds were being built up by the people close to the highest executive in the land to finance the ruling party during its election campaign. Together, they had planned to start featuring senior party leaders in a run-up to the elections until they reached the deputy PM himself, as a climax. Each successive episode would paint a stronger picture of the ruling party's chances until the unsuspecting deputy PM would be set up for a devastating interview on various scams – the howitzer deal taking pride of place – live on Pinnacle TV. He would be shown up to be a mercenary who had sold out the country's most vital interests for dirt money.

The snag in the plan had been Pinnacle TV's well-known animosity for the ruling party in its current avatar – an animosity that was mutual. Rubita Bannerjee had been at the forefront of many an embarrassing investigation into the party's affairs and was *persona non grata* at the party HQ. Their plan called for what would seem a sudden and inexplicable change in Pinnacle TV's attitude. How to do this credibly had been a problem that senior Pinnacle executives had tossed into Sam's lap. Pressure had been building up for weeks as each passing day brought the nation closer to the elections. So far, he had drawn a blank. And now, out of the blue, he was being offered just the opening they had been hoping for.

His mind raced ahead while, outwardly, he retained a faintly servile expression. He seemed only too eager to demonstrate his gratitude. It wasn't too difficult an act. In the experience of Kalidoss and his masters, money could buy anything in the world, even men's souls. And limitless quantities of money could buy souls limitlessly. All Sam had to do was to lean forward eagerly to reinforce the impression.

'You're absolutely right, John. Pinnacle TV does seem to operate with a chip on its shoulder. I have thought so several times myself. And I think you have made an excellent point. A channel perceived to be biased by the public will soon cease to be taken seriously. I'll try and get Rubita to see that. But you know that's no mean task. You've met her often enough to know how headstrong she is. And her ability to convince other people in Pinnacle is something I'm not able to assess at present. I'll need some time.'

'Sam, old chap, we're two old foxes at this game,' Kalidoss said conspiratorially. 'I'm sure you'll find a way to work around these fellows.' He lowered his voice to a barely audible whisper, 'There's plenty of Vitamin M, if that'll do the trick. And, Sam, I'm sure I don't have to tell you that many important people in the capital are going to press for quick action. The elections are not far.' He held Sam's gaze long and hard.

Bannerjee suddenly felt as if the room had become suffocating. He averted his eyes, focusing on the ashtray by his side as he stubbed out his cigar. 'I don't think that's the style at Pinnacle, but I'll make sure that window's open,' he replied.

'Good. Very good. I'll talk to my contacts at the cabinet secretariat immediately and have them standing by. Why don't you chalk out a plan of action and run it past me in the next two or three days? We must do our bit for the party. It's our way of contributing. Our way of ensuring that an enlightened vision guides the destiny of our country. I'm so happy for having talked to you today, old boy. Really happy.'

The two old friends parted ways on the steps of the club.

◆

Butt focused on the road ahead, oblivious to the change in Satyan's mood. He could not see that Satyan's face had acquired a wild look, as if he was losing possession of himself. Butt was thinking about how quickly the Russians could get back on the road. 'I hope they take a long time fixing that wheel,' he remarked. He laid his automatic on the dashboard and concentrated on getting the maximum distance possible between them and the intruders.

They sped through the night in silence. A housing colony flashed by in the darkness as the big car topped a hundred and fifty kmph without straining. The night was biting cold and everybody was indoors. They couldn't go any faster because the state highway, like most Indian roads, was in disrepair. The only consolation was that their pursuers would be up against the same road.

All the time Satyan was brooding on the moment of self-revelation back at the farm house. That self-knowledge had hit him like a hammer out of the blue. His horror at the realisation that he could, if given the right kind of shove, maybe sell his soul to the devil like the whining fat slob in the back seat, had resurfaced.

'What the fuck was I thinking,' he told himself, squeezing a fist hard into his thigh. 'How the hell could a dirty fucking pig like Pandey get to look at my inner self, as if he knows me better than I know myself. A part of me that even I didn't know existed? How did that happen? Damn the son of a bitch.'

His chest was feeling tight, as if steel ropes were tied around it and being tightened by some unseen machine. He felt that he was on the verge of losing his sanity. The wild twists and turns of the past few months were finally taking their toll on him. It had all begun with the attack on old Mr Agarwal. Then his meeting with those two swines in that restaurant, the manic encounter with Ashank Kumar up in the Kumaon, the desperate run for safety in Film City and all the other incidents of violence that had peppered the trail this gun project had run. But these things had not upset him, he felt, as much as the ugly facts of life he had been hit with in the corridors of power. It was the discovery that everybody in the government seemed intent only on making money by fair means or foul, swindling the public shamelessly at the cost even of the country's very security, which had begun to eat into his mind. Even guys like Sam and Kalidoss who had the benefit of education and a comfortable life were not immune to the plague of corruption. And now, in a sudden flash, he was made to realise that he wasn't above scumbags like Gulab Chand and Pandey, pitiful bastards he had looked at superciliously until so recently. That was what he couldn't accept. He felt an unreasoning madness taking control of his body.

A truck sped past them going the other way, its huge headlights and blaring horn jerking his mind back to their current situation. They sped along, the trees flashing by in a blur.

Suddenly a thought struck him and he spoke up. 'I've been wondering how the Russians got here. This was supposed to be a secret meeting, right, Mr Pandey? So secret that even your fucking cabinet colleagues did not know about it!' Butt glanced sharply at the younger man. He had never seen Satyan lose his cool and use four-letter words before. This could become dangerous, he felt. 'So what the hell are the Russians doing here?' Satyan continued. 'How did they know I was here?'

'They've been tailing you for six months now, Mr Sharma,' said Butt, cutting in sharply. 'I figured we had shaken them off at Mumbai. I reckon I was wrong. But we've lost them for now. When we reach the city, they'll have no chance of catching up. Sit tight!'

'But that wasn't the reason they came. They knew that Pandey's guards had been removed. It was too much of a coincidence for them to turn up like that. They were after him, not me! Mr Pandey, tell me if I'm wrong.'

'Damn! You may be right, Mr Sharma,' Butt cut in once more. 'We'll figure it all out when we get to safety. For now, let's concentrate on getting out of here.'

'There you go, butting in again. I think you are hiding something from me. I want answers, dammit, and I want them right now!'

Satyan lunged for the automatic on the dashboard. The car swerved wildly as Butt, caught unawares by the sudden move, cut down viciously with his right hand to try and stop him. Satyan parried the blow and grabbed the automatic. Transferring it to his left hand, he leaned over the seat and pointed it at the terrified minister's midriff, poised barely six inches away. Pandey-ji stared wide-eyed at the barrel, transfixed.

Butt tried to regain control. 'OK, Mr Sharma, there's no need for that. Give the gun back to me before there's an accident.'

'Right, Javed. Stop the car. Let's get all this straightened out and I'll return the gun.'

'Pull over? You've got to be kidding, Mr Sharma! Those Russkies are minutes behind us and will shoot first and ask questions later. Do you want to get us all killed?'

'Okay. So, tell me. Why are they after Pandey?'

Butt remained silent. Satyan stared at the intelligence man. Ever since the Russians had shown up at the farmhouse, he had been behaving strangely. He had been willing to desert Pandey-ji at a time when his duty dictated that he stay and protect the minister. Satyan's mind flashed back to the ham shop in Bangalore. Corbett had detected something phony in Butt's manner. Satyan was becoming convinced that Butt was not levelling with him.

'You! Pandey!' Satyan turned to the minister. 'You tell me! The game is obviously up. Your backers in the government have decided to leave you to your fate. That's why the commandos were removed just before the Russian team came in. I know all about you and the kickbacks, Pandey. Why should the FSS want to eliminate you? It's not as if the Russians have anything to lose if France gets the contract. Tell me quickly, your best chance for survival is to tell me the whole truth right now.'

Pandey-ji licked his lips as he peered fearfully at the automatic. For once, he was at a loss for words. His eyes nervously met Satyan's gaze. 'You would not kill an old man, Sharma sahib?' he whined. 'I have children and a wife,' he added with a weak, ingratiating smile. 'Please, please don't kill me.'

Butt snorted. 'It will do the dirty double-crosser good, Mr Sharma. Good riddance for all of us.'

'No, no, no!' Pandey-ji's whine rose several notches. 'Please! Please listen to me! I can make you both very rich if you save my life. Yes, Sharma sahib. Richer than you can ever be, even with your Pure Space company. I have very rich friends, and I can see to it that both of you are covered with gold, diamonds, anything! Hundreds of crores for each of you! Riches beyond your every dream! Bank accounts in Switzerland! Just name your fancy, Sharma sahib! You too, sir,' Pandey-ji said, turning with a sly look towards Butt. 'I can make sure that your next three generations will never have to care for money! All you have to do is, see me safely to Delhi. I will tell you the address of a close and powerful friend of mine. You will be a multimillionaire! Eh, Sharma sahib, what do you say? Why throw away the chance of a lifetime?'

Satyan was staring at Butt. Something about the intelligence man was not ringing true. And it wasn't anything to do with keeping official secrets from civilian ears or anything like that. No, it was the intelligence man himself. What had he called the minister? Double-crosser. That was it. Pandey-ji was not being loyal to his country, that much was obvious. But double-crossing? That implied something more than treason. Double-crossing whom? And Butt was part of the double-crossed party. So, if he was fighting the Russians – he was working for the Americans!

Suddenly he found his gun-hand engulfed in the minister's paws. Pandey-ji had taken advantage of Satyan's preoccupation and made a desperate lunge for the automatic. But the younger man's reflexes were too sharp. Satyan tightened his grip on the gun and with his right hand tried to break the minister's grip. Butt saw his chance. With one hand on the steering wheel, he struck hard at Satyan's face.

◆

It was each man for himself now.

A deep, all-consuming rage had welled up inside Satyan. He had had enough of Pandey-ji and the sleaze he represented. Enough also of Butt and whatever deception he was playing at. Enough of being a gentleman in a world populated by cheap gutter rats. The demon inside had finally risen to the surface, breathing an infernal fire that was overwhelming his head, full of venom and primed to strike.

The Mercedes was doing well over one-hundred-and-fifty kmph. The grim struggle continued as the big car, guided only by Butt's left hand, swung violently from one side of the road to the other. In the far distance, off to their right, the red marker lights of the Wazirabad Bridge appeared, their tiny pinpoints flickering through the gaps in the mist.

Visibility beyond five hundred metres wasn't too good, but Satyan remembered that after a right turn followed by a straight stretch rising gently for about a kilometre, they would hit the bridge. The black stretch of asphalt flashed silently by under the headlights. The light bounced off the trees lining the highway. At each curve of the road, Butt had to grab at the wheel with both hands to steady the car before returning to the struggle for the gun.

The abrupt glare from an oncoming truck's headlights as it straddled the middle of the road caught the grim tableau inside the Mercedes. Pandey-ji was terror-struck, his thin hair askew. His lips were drawn back from his teeth in desperate concentration. His soft hands were no more effective in loosening Satyan's grip than those of a child. Beads of sweat hung like raindrops on his face. Butt was squeezing hard on Satyan's right forearm, his fingers digging deep into the tendons. The fingers of his left hand, gripping the steering wheel, were white with strain. His eyes were set in steely determination.

Butt had been at the point of giving a convulsive jerk, which would have caused Satyan to let go of the gun, when the truck burst upon them. Butt grabbed the wheel again with both hands. Free of his vise-like grip, Satyan leaned further into the back of the car and cuffed Pandey-ji sharply on the head. Still the minister hung on to the barrel.

With a wild swerve, Butt brought the car around as they passed the truck, bouncing heavily on the rough shoulder. The gun in Satyan's hand jerked and went off. The bullet grazed Pandey-ji's palm and, plowing through the upholstery, drilled straight into the petrol tank.

Pandey-ji yelped in pain and fell back in a corner. Blood was coursing from his flesh wound, flowing all over his white khadi kurta.

After a minute there was a muted thump from behind.

'Did you hear that?' yelled Butt. 'You've shot through the gas tank, Mr Sharma! The car can catch fire any time now!'

Without a word, Satyan leaned over backwards and yanked mightily at the door handle, next to the cringing minister. It broke off with a sharp snap. Giving the dazed minister a backhanded whack across the face, he leaned over to the other door and wrenched the handle off that as well.

By now, the first tiny flickers of flame were teasing the upholstery. Pandey-ji screamed as he saw them. Satyan knew with a glance that the last of Pandey-ji's fight had been knocked out of him and he lost interest in the man.

Butt was cursing freely as he fought to bring the car under control. They were now close to the straight stretch leading to the bridge. The little red lights had grown larger. Butt slowed the car for the sharp turn onto Wazirabad Road. He brought the car to a sudden halt and grabbed the door handle, meaning to leap out of the burning vehicle.

'Don't jump out of the car, damn you,' yelled Satyan, jamming the nose of the automatic onto the IB man's neck. 'Keep fucking driving on!'

'You've gone crazy!' Butt screamed. 'The car's burning! It's going to explode any moment! Do you want to die?'

'Drive on, you Yankee bastard,' Satyan replied in an even voice. 'Or I'll kill you.' The tone of Satyan's voice and the unrelenting pressure of the automatic jammed onto his neck silenced the American spy.

'I've finally got onto your fucking game, you son of a bitch. Russkies, huh? When the pressure's on your American slang comes through, huh? An Indian would never say "gas-tank" like you just did. And remember back in Mumbai, on the way to the helicopter? You were dishing out American slang mighty freely. I should have caught on to you, back there. Chicago is closer to your hometown than Mumbai is, huh? Your game is up. We'll see what stuff you're made of before the night is over. Right now,' he growled, pushing the automatic deeper into Connolly's neck, 'one false move and I'll blow your bloody head off. I don't give a shit if we all die in this car right now. So don't fucking mess with me!'

The demon in Satyan's soul had taken complete possession of his being. He had metamorphosed into a cold-blooded killing machine. In the flickering light of the flames, his eyes were bulging and his lips were drawn back, baring his teeth. Every sinew in his body was flowing with power and the pressure of the automatic on Connolly's neck unrelenting. Satyan was utterly unrecognisable in this state.

'And get the fucking move on,' he continued, 'you've got no chance in hell running for it in these parts. Look around, damn you! There's no cover anywhere and the Russians will hunt us down like dogs. The only chance is to hit the Delhi roads and lose ourselves in the traffic. Come on, we're losing time!'

Beads of perspiration on his face, his cover finally blown, Connolly weighed his options. He stared straight ahead at the road, not daring to turn his head. He cursed himself silently for having given himself away. He must have gotten complacent to have slipped up so badly. And there had been no inkling whatsoever of this vicious side to Satyan. Connolly had made a grave error of judgment and now found himself totally outwitted by an amateur.

His brain cast desperately about for an opening. The automatic was pressing deep into his throat. Pandey-ji was screaming his guts out in the back seat. With each passing minute the Russians were narrowing the gap and closing in on them. He realised that he had run out of options and threw the car into gear. Jamming the accelerator hard as the car hit the sharp turn on to Wazirabad Road, he sent it flying down the straight stretch.

Grimly, Satyan watched the bridge get closer, while keeping an eye on the face framed by the leaping flames reflected in the rearview mirror. He became aware of the terrified screams from the backseat. The minister's fingers were scraping ineffectually at the door panels. The bridge seemed some eight hundred metres away, straight down the road. It would take little more than half a minute to reach it, Satyan calculated. He glanced at the flames in the mirror, judging the moment when they would finally erupt and send the car into oblivion. The seconds were ticking by. Very little time was left.

'Pandey!' Satyan bellowed. 'You have one last chance to survive! Give me the bank name and account number where Leconte makes payments for the gun.' At the mention of the Frenchman's name Pandey-ji jerked his head and Satyan knew he had hit the right spot. 'And give me the private phone numbers he operates. Give this to me right now and I will let you live!

The flames were getting hotter by the second and in their light Satyan could see that he was losing what little was left of his self-control. Pandey-ji felt a deathly shudder down his numb spine.

'Quick! Do as I say or be ready to die!'

Pandey-ji was trying desperately to think. Satyan held all the cards. He had no option. He fumbled in the pockets of his kurta and drew out his cellphone. 'Are the details in the phone?' Satyan asked.

Pandey-ji nodded vigorously several times. Butt was unable to turn his head. Satyan had shoved the gun deep into his neck. Satyan looked behind. The minister was fumbling with the buttons, trying to retrieve the stored information – a difficult job because his hands were clammy. With a quick swipe, Satyan grabbed the instrument from the fat man's hands and shoved it into his trouser pocket. There would be time enough later for this. Right now, it was a question of survival.

The flames were now all around the boot of the hurtling car, whipped up by the rushing wind. They were licking at the rear doors. The men inside could feel the interior get hotter. The car was doing over a hundred again.

Two hundred metres to go – seven or eight seconds at most. Could he make it?

Satyan glanced again at the rearview mirror. Through the flames he saw the distant pinpoints of a pair of headlights. The Russians were approaching the straight stretch to the bridge.

He knew he didn't stand a chance if he got out of the car and made a run for it across the flat land surrounding them. There was no cover. The bridge and, more importantly, the river flowing far below it, gave him the only chance for an escape. He would make a break for it on the bridge.

But first he had to dispose of the minister and the American spy. His timing would be critical.

One hundred metres. Another three or four seconds.

Pandey-ji was screaming continuously. Connolly glanced at Satyan from the corner of his eye, trying to gauge his intention. The pressure on his neck was rock-steady. Sweat glistened on his face. It would take very little to set Satyan's nerves off and there was no way the bullet could miss.

Fifty metres. Any time now.

Satyan looked into the mirror again. The headlights were maybe forty-five seconds behind. He glanced at the secret agent. 'Faster! Go faster!' he yelled.

Surprised, Connolly opened his mouth to protest. At that moment, Satyan brought the gun down hard on Connolly's temple. Momentarily dazed, the secret agent slumped forward on the wheel, jerking it to one side. Satyan whipped his leg out and jammed the brakes. The car spun around as it shot onto the bridge. Still spinning wildly, it skidded along for ten or fifteen metres before bouncing on the pavement and slamming to a halt against the steelwork. The whole body was now burning fiercely.

For a long minute, nobody moved inside the car. Then Satyan willed himself to get moving.

He ignored Pandey-ji's continuous wailing. In fact, the man hadn't stopped screaming for what seemed like ages. The secret agent was stirring slowly, barely conscious. Satyan himself was only half-conscious, faintly aware that he must get away from the car soon. The flames were leaping high into the night sky and the interior of the car had already become hellishly hot.

The door handle seared his hands. Flesh burned off his fingers as he willed himself to ignore the pain. He pushed the door open and staggered out.

The headlights on the highway were still some two or three hundred metres from the bridge. He broke into a stumbling run towards the struts of the bridge, as far away from the burning car as possible, remaining in the shadows of the superstructure.

The Russians slowed down when they saw the car spin out of control, not wanting to run into the fire-ball. They could see, through the surrounding mist, the orange flames leaping up into the darkness. They saw a man tumble out from the driver's side. His clothes were on fire. Konstantin brought the vehicle down to a crawl, intently watching the burning figure in its macabre dance.

The jeep was about ten metres away from the bridge when Satyan stepped away from the strut, still in the shadows, the automatic aimed directly at a point just above the steering wheel. Holding the automatic steady, he swung his body to lead the vehicle's motion for a second before squeezing the trigger.

He watched with detached calm as the face behind the wheel shattered in a burst of crimson. In a convulsive jerk, Konstantin's leg jammed down harder on the accelerator. The jeep swivelled and rammed into the bridge, not ten metres from where he stood. He moved silently and rapidly, half crouching to stay hidden, coming up to the jeep on the driver's side, Konstantin's slumped body giving him the cover he needed. The other two men inside had still not fully recovered their orientation. They hadn't expected anyone to survive in the Mercedes. They were gaping at Satyan when he shot them at point blank range.

The explosion from the Mercedes blasted him off the ground and threw him some distance away. After a while, he raised himself and turned to look. Through the leaping flames of the wreckage he could barely make out the tangled mass of twisted metal. The stench of burning flesh tugged at his senses. He remained sitting on the pavement for a while, waiting for the flames to subside. A dark charred mass lay propped against the bridgework. Connolly had not made it over the side. Nothing stirred. No vehicles passed.

Some five minutes later, he got up and began walking across the bridge towards Delhi. He tossed the automatic into the waters of the Yamuna.

12

The next day's front pages carried news of Ram Niranjan Pandey's death in a tragic car accident. His Mercedes had been engulfed in a mysterious fire. His driver was also reported to have perished in the flames. No collision seemed to have occurred. The police were investigating the possibility of sabotage. In fact, the investigating official said that, at this stage, no possibility could be ruled out. Pandey-ji's home district had declared a holiday in his honour and his ashes had been sent to his native place.

There was no mention of a second vehicle.

Satyan was seated with Sam Bannerjee and Rubita for breakfast at their Pandara Road bungalow, briefing them about the previous night's incident. They had now eliminated one more link in the chain of corruption and had established for certain that Leconte was playing a pivotal role in this drama. They also had confirmation that Kalidoss was deeply involved.

The dead minister's cellphone had turned out to be a treasure trove of information. Both Leconte and Kalidoss were using several numbers. The cellphone also had four numbers listed under the name of Chintamani Rao, the deputy PM's son. Interestingly, there was an international number amongst these – the International Subscriber Dialling code located it to the British Virgin Islands. More interesting still was the fact that one of the numbers listed for Leconte also had the same ISD code. That tiny territory in the middle of the Caribbean Sea obviously held an important piece of the jigsaw puzzle. A lot would become clearer once they found out where exactly in the BVI these two numbers were located. Were these residential numbers? And, if so, who owned them and what connection did Chintamani Rao and Leconte have with them?

Rubita was ecstatic. 'My god, Sam, this is beautiful!'

'Yes, Rubes. But we're running out of time,' her father replied. 'The cabinet is meeting in two weeks to decide the contract. And I know that FIAM is getting it.'

'We need to get Leconte,' Satyan said. 'The question is – how?'

Sam had an answer. 'I'll get phone taps organised on all these numbers. It'll take me a day or two but I'll go straight to the vigilance commissioner. He has the authority and he's a good man. Tough, too. He won't take nonsense from anyone. If he's convinced, then there's no problem. I'll also requisition logs for all the calls made for as many days as the phone companies have.'

'But, Sam, you know – I mean, won't that put you in a lot of trouble?' Satyan asked, throwing a glance at Rubita.

Sam nodded. 'Well, that will have to come sooner or later. And, anyway, we're talking of national security here. I can't live with myself if I feel I let my country down in this.' His face betrayed his pain but his voice was firm. There was no doubting his resolve. Rubita slid her hand over his and gave it a squeeze. He smiled wanly.

Whatever the outcome, however mildly Sam Bannerjee would be judged, his career was going to be finished. Years of stellar performance would be ground to dust in the mill of public opinion. He would be dishonourably dismissed. Had this episode not marred an otherwise brilliant career, he would certainly have got the chairmanship of some corporation on retirement. With luck, he could even have landed an international appointment. Now, he would have to give up these hopes and retire into obscurity, hoping that sooner or later the public would forget him and allow him to spend his remaining years in peace.

Then Sam shook himself out of the despondent mood and snapped his fingers. 'Enough of this. We've got work to do and very little time,' he said. 'The director of the counterinsurgency unit of the IB is a good friend of mine. He'll put me in touch with the best people to organise the phone taps.'

Satyan broke in. 'We'll also have to be prepared for rough stuff. The payoffs run into several hundreds of crores and many political reputations are on the line here. We'll have to line up some official muscle to protect us.'

'Yes,' said Rubita thoughtfully. 'We can't go to a private detective unit. They will never be given access to official phone taps, and that will be needed by whoever we use to protect us.'

'Good point,' Sam agreed. 'This thing is not going to be easy. If there are too many people in the know, then it increases our enemies' chances of being tipped off.'

'Why not contact Gupte uncle, Sam?' asked Rubita. 'He's a major general in the Black Cats, isn't he? I'm sure he knows you too well to doubt your integrity. If you tell the vigilance commissioner about him, he can do his reference checks and then I'm sure he'll agree.'

'But why will the vigilance commissioner drag the Black Cats into this? He has no authority over them and they are not in any way related to this thing.'

'That's their advantage, Sam,' said Satyan. 'Nobody will expect them to be involved and they'll hold the element of surprise. No harm in trying.'

'No harm indeed,' said Sam. 'Yes, since we're dealing with the most powerful leaders in the land, we need unconventional means at our disposal. My career is finished anyway, what do I stand to lose?'

He flashed a rueful smile and flipped open his cellphone.

◆

Sam was successful in pushing all the right levers. In the next few days, he met both the vigilance commissioner as well as the head of the Black Cat commandos. The clinching argument in both cases was that a senior bureaucrat with an impeccable record was willingly laying a lifetime's reputation on the line. He had carried signed affidavits that clearly laid out his personal role in the affair and could be used against him in court. In effect, he was signing his career's death warrant. It was unprecedented in the history of the civil services, and that simple act overcame all objections. Both men agreed to get the necessary clearances, keeping the details in Sam's affidavit out of it for the present. That meant that both these officials were putting their necks on the block as well, being accessories after the fact. They carried on regardless.

It would need skill and patience before he, Rubita and Satyan could get enough information about Leconte's operations and his connections with the deputy PM's son for them to figure out the exact modus operandi. And once names of people on the payoff list started emerging, the vigilance commissioner would have to be approached for permission to tap more phones. The circle was bound to be wide, reaching the highest echelons of the armed forces, the defence ministry and, quite possibly, several of Delhi's socialites acting as conduits for both information and kickback funds. These would be the hardest to pin down because they had no official standing and, hence, no rules and regulations to worry about.

And all this information would be of little use unless hard evidence of treason could be gathered from Leconte and Chintamani Rao. Names could be collected but that exercise would be futile unless evidence could be produced in a court of law. The need for secrecy made things more difficult; the proper authorities couldn't be depended upon to prevent information leaks about their operation.

To make things worse, time was running out. They needed the evidence before the cabinet met to decide the contract. Or else the French gun would win.

◆

They met again in Sam's bungalow three days later, for a council of war. Sam began the proceedings with a report. 'I've been able to get some info on the bank accounts in the British Virgin Islands. Both Leconte and Chintamani Rao have accounts at Barclays' Road Town branch. An old friend of mine from Harvard is Under Secretary of the Treasury in London. He got me some figures as a personal favour.

Rao has nearly seventy million dollars stashed away in his account. And he's built himself a Spanish-style villa on a hill overlooking the capital. He's got a sailing yacht moored in the harbour and he goes on a two-week sailing trip around the Caribbean every six months. He's also part-owner of an art gallery in town. Apparently the best of the jet-set are among his clients.'

'So if he wants to, he can settle down there and live the rest of his life in leisure with a going art business to pay his bills,' said Satyan.

'There's more,' Sam added. 'The other partner in the art gallery is none other than Arnaud Leconte.'

Satyan whistled.

Sam nodded. 'By the way, Leconte is in Paris right now. He has probably been called by his bosses there for a last-minute conference on the gun deal. I'm told he's returning on Friday night, on the company jet – that's the day after tomorrow.'

'I've been doing some checking up on the world art trade among my media contacts in London,' said Rubita. 'The British Virgin Islands are a big centre for trading in the masters – Van Gogh, Renoir, Picasso, everybody who matters. Especially paintings that have disappeared from the public eye and gone into the underground circuit. BVI is a big draw among wealthy art collectors who want to stay away from the media's glare. Because they don't want too many questions being asked about how they came across some of their acquisitions.'

Satyan snapped his fingers. 'Okay, I've got it! What we need is an authentic-looking report going to Rao that a famous painting has surfaced in the BVI and is up for sale to the highest bidder. The price should be more than the seventy million dollars he has in his account. The only condition is that the seller wants the money fast, say, within seventy-two hours of the auction. If Rao rises to the bait, then he'll have to act fast. The only way he can raise the money so fast is to go to his good friend and partner, Leconte.'

'Yes, that should do it,' Sam said. 'Chintamani Rao would like nothing more than a feather in his gallery's cap. It will get him entrenched more than ever in the art market.'

'Okay then,' Satyan said. 'Rubes, you need to dig around some more among your media friends. Find out which paintings costing more than seventy million dollars have disappeared from public view in the last four or five years. I've got a feeling we're on to something here.'

'Satyan, that's a great idea,' she replied. 'But who will tell Rao? We need someone whom he will trust. Someone who would be expected to know these things. Someone with taste and refinement and access to confidential information.'

'Someone like John Kalidoss,' Sam pointed out.

'Rubes, get the phone lines going and let's meet again in the evening,' Satyan said.

Several hours later they had worked out the plan down to the last detail.

Sam would encash various favours people in different ministries owed him. Rubita would do the same among her contacts in the media and art worlds. The thing needed global orchestration. Timing would be crucial.

◆

The phone rang at the Art Masala gallery on Road Town's placid waterfront, breaking the afternoon's languor. Karl Hoogens, the manager whom Chintamani Rao had hired when he had set up the gallery three years ago, reluctantly put his can of beer down and ambled to the front desk. The beer haze evaporated the moment he heard the voice at the other end.

'May I speak with Mr... Hoogens, please,' the voice said, obviously referring to a piece of paper. When Hoogens identified himself, it continued, 'Ah, then may I take a few minutes of your time? This is Chris Chapman calling from London.'

Chris Chapman was a legendary expert on impressionist painters who had held key positions in Sotheby's before striking out on his own as an art consultant. He worked discreetly from the sidelines for an exclusive clientele, advising them on how to invest millions of dollars in art. Seldom seen outside of London and New York, his reputation made him a revered figure among art dealers in the Caribbean.

'Mr Hoogens,' said Chapman. 'I'm calling a very select list of people on a matter of extreme sensitivity. Before I do that, may I request you to confirm that there is nobody else with you in the room? If need be, I can call later.'

Hoogens' antennae were up and buzzing. If Chapman was involved, it had to be big. He hastily assured his caller that they were alone. The information his caller conveyed made his heart leap with excitement. One of Van Gogh's masterpieces, *Portrait of Dr Gachet*, was going to resurface after years in some unidentified collector's vault, and was going to be put on display for inspection by a very select list of potential buyers. The auction was slated to happen in three days' time, in the British Virgin Islands. The bidding would start, Chapman told him, at eighty million dollars. The caller wanted to know if Chintamani Rao was interested. If so, he could get in touch with Chapman on arrival any time before the auction. As was normal practice in such transactions, he explained, the transfer of funds in exchange for the painting would have to take place immediately. The caller rang off without wasting time on further civilities.

This was an opportunity for Art Masala to enter the big league. Hoogens and his employer had been waiting for just such an opening. And now, one of the biggest names in the underground art market had called up. The last three years of painstaking effort seemed to have placed the gallery within striking distance of the very top.

Hoogens' fingers trembled with excitement as he punched Chintamani Rao's number.

◆

It was afternoon and Sam Bannerjee was catching up with files in the office when his cellphone rang. Paris was on the line. He listened wordlessly to the short communication. Leconte had just left for Mumbai in the FIAM company jet.

At quitting time that evening, he called Kalidoss. 'Ah, John, hope I didn't catch you in the middle of a meeting. No? That's good.'

The two friends exchanged small talk before Sam broached the topic. 'Our young friend Satyan Sharma has come around, John. It looks like he met Ram Niranjan Pandey at the farmhouse, on the day of his accident. The poor boy was quite frazzled by what happened to Pandey. He seems to think that it was not an accident. That Pandey paid the price for some kind of indiscretion.'

He paused as Kalidoss asked a question and replied, 'No, no. This is obviously some speculation on Satyan's part. But the boy is in quite a tizzy. Anyway, more to the point, John, it seems Pandey hinted to Satyan that the contract was almost decided in favour of the French. One thing Pandey seems to have convinced him about is that, whoever gets the contract, the Uzbeks are definitely out. But that the Indian government would like to see Satyan's fire control unit integrated into the howitzer.'

Kalidoss had been expecting this. He knew that Satyan Sharma's business instincts would get the better of emotional arguments. That was precisely why he had got Pandey to talk to him. The accident at the farmhouse was unfortunate because he had lost his front-man and would now have to emerge from the shadows, but it seemed to have had some positive influence too. Satyan had realised the consequences of non-cooperation. He told Sam that he would see what could be done and rang off.

Half-an-hour later, when Kalidoss rang Chintamani Rao and told him about Satyan Sharma's willingness to discuss a tie-up with FIAM, the deputy PM's son was beside himself with joy. Ever since Karl Hoogens had called him about the Van Gogh he had been casting desperately about for ways of raising another thirty million dollars within two days, to add to the seventy million he already had. Here was the opportunity he had been seeking to get into the exclusive circles of the global art market. One big deal like this, and the doors of the truly wealthy would open for him. But without a hundred million dollars at hand to back his play, he may not be able to match other bids and the opportunity would slip out of his hands.

The only way he could see to raise the money was to approach Leconte for an advance on the gun contract. But would Leconte's principals in France agree to such a large advance? Would he be able to raise the money in three days and get it to the British Virgin Islands? The deputy PM's son had been frantic because the man who could answer these questions was jetting his way to India from Paris and out of reach of cellphone signals. He would have to wait until the Frenchman landed before being able to talk to him. The suspense was almost too much to bear.

So when Kalidoss' message came to him, it seemed to Chintamani Rao as if manna had dropped into his lap from heaven. With Satyan Sharma willing to talk turkey, one of the major stumbling blocks for FIAM would be removed. Chintamani Rao would be seen as the one who was bringing a hitherto intransigent Satyan in line, and an extra payment would be easy to negotiate. All that remained was to get Leconte to move fast. With the cabinet meeting a week away, that would not be a problem. Once the money was in the bag, there remained only the little matter of arranging transport to the Caribbean.

Leconte would be landing at Delhi's international airport at two a.m. Chintamani Rao called Satyan Sharma and told him to be ready the next day for a breakfast meeting with the FIAM representative. Satyan was to come to the deputy PM's residence and they would make the half-hour drive to Leconte's house together.

That done, Chintamani had nothing to do but wait. He was so excited he barely slept a wink.

13

Satyan Sharma started out for the deputy PM's residence on Akbar Road at 6:30 a.m. the next day. The meeting had been set up for half past seven at the Leconte residence.

As the wide avenues swept past his window, Satyan became acutely conscious of the cold sweat on his hands and under his armpits. It wasn't because of the blazer he was wearing; it was the sweat of raw fear. Deep down, Satyan knew that the high-stakes game was drawing to its close. And today was judgment day. Pure Space Networks and all the dreams it had held seemed so distant to him. The sweat and toil of his boys in the bull-pit seemed trivial, now that he was up against the powers that really mattered in the real world. The drive back from Pandey's farmhouse that night had opened his eyes to this other, sinister, infinitely dangerous system that existed in the corridors of power.

And now he was entering the lion's den, wires taped to his torso, his head swimming with all the details of a careful set-up to trap both Chintamani Rao and Leconte at one go.

He ran his mind over the possible hitches and the back-up plans that had been discussed at length the previous night with the commando brigadier and the young but battle-hardened Captain Mahendran who had accompanied him. The captain had been through some tough street-fighting in Sri Lanka and Kashmir, and his skills were well suited to this environment. He would be in charge of the field operations, but Satyan would really be on his own most of the time.

More unnerving was that the army team had been expressly forbidden from carrying out any action. It was only for surveillance that they had been called in. That, and the fact that the whole affair was of direct interest to the army. In fact, if things went according to plan, the involvement of the army would be completely invisible, even to official scrutiny. As both Captain Mahendran and his brigadier knew so well, things seldom went according to plan. But they kept this opinion to themselves.

Satyan would have no reinforcements to count on if things got sticky.

Sam and Rubita had been present. They had gone over every inch of the way, time and again, reviewing every possibility of things going wrong.

And now Satyan was on his way.

Satyan's car was halfway down Maulana Azad Road, barely a kilometre from the deputy PM's residence, before he saw the checkpoint. A police van was parked ahead, blocking traffic in the direction of Akbar Road. There had been reports of terrorist movements in the city and the police were inspecting all vehicles passing specific points. Even this early, there was a long line of cars that had been pulled over. There were two teams of policemen doing the checking while another team stood by, watching over the proceedings. Satyan counted at least ten cars in front of him.

He called Chintamani Rao and told him about the police checking all cars. 'It looks like we'll be held up for at least fifteen minutes, Mr Rao,' he said.

'Damn those fuckers! Did they have to come up right now?' came the screaming reply. 'Tell them you're coming here, damn it. They have to let you through.'

'I told my driver, sir, but he's too scared to try. I believe the cops are extra strict nowadays.'

'Ah shit! Man, oh man! I don't have the time to play these silly games! Why can't you pull out, do a U-turn and come another way?'

'Sir, you know how it is in Delhi. If the cops see us going off...'

'Okay, okay, I know. Don't teach me about Delhi, damn you!' yelled Chintamani, boiling with rage and frustration. He had spent a sleepless night, waiting. And now, even a minute's delay was enough to make him apoplectic. 'Fuck it, then. I'll come that way and pick you up. We're losing time arguing about this. Where the devil are you exactly?'

When Satyan explained his location, the PM's son told him to stand outside his car and wait for him. Within ten minutes, a greyish blue BMW drove abreast of his car across the road and a gun-toting security man ran up to the police checkpoint to flash his credentials and have a quick discussion. Then, trotting up to Satyan and slinging his rifle over his shoulder, he got ready to frisk him.

The BMW's door swung open and Chintamani Rao screamed at the guard, 'Forget the damn search and bring him here, you idiot! I'm running out of time, man, can't you see? I know he's not a terrorist, you bloody nincompoop! Come on, come on, hurry up and get here on the double.'

Flustered, the security man gestured to Satyan and sprinted across the road. Satyan followed at a flat run and got in the back. The security man got in next to the driver and they were off.

Rao pushed a button and a soundproof glass partition slid up between them and the front seat. 'Bloody incompetence of the highest order! Following rules just to cover their backsides, the bastards! No wonder the actual terrorists get away scot-free!' Seeing Rao in this excitable state, Satyan held his tongue and waited.

Chintamani Rao remained silent for another ten minutes, drumming his fingers on the armrest. Then, in a more sober tone, he asked, 'So, Mr Sharma, tell me more about this fascinating new invention of yours that the whole goddamned world is desperate for. What exactly does it do?'

Over the next few minutes, Satyan explained the essentials of the FCU. Chintamani Rao's quick intellect grasped the basics very quickly and his incisive questions made Satyan delve deeper into its fundamental principles. Caught up in the technical beauty of the design, his mind began to calm down.

'Hey, Satyan – may I call you Satyan? Call me Chintu, by the way. We're going to be doing business soon, so let's ditch the formalities. Okay? So, Satyan, look. Your unit looks out of the world, man! But tell me, are you saying the French haven't got this kind of gizmo on their gun?'

'They have, um – Chintu,' Satyan replied. 'But it doesn't have the sophisticated features that my unit has.'

'Which is why they're itching to buy the design from you, man? Okay, look, let me into the game. What is it worth to the Frenchies to get the designs from you? Like I just want a ballpark, man, so that I can figure out what my cut should be, eh?'

When Satyan showed hesitation, he rushed on, 'I mean everybody in this town is on the take, man. That's the way this town operates and that's why we're going to Leconte's pad, right? And I don't want to get shortchanged, okay? So do me a favour and give me a number, man.'

When Satyan told him, Chintamani whistled.

◆

Leconte's sprawling residence in the stately neighbourhood of West End was accessed through twenty-foot high gates that swung open electronically. Chintamani Rao's presence was enough to get them waved in without questioning.

There were two security booths, on either side of a twenty-metre long driveway. Chained to each booth was a huge black Rottweiler with jaws that could tear a man's chest open within minutes. The chains looked too flimsy to Satyan and the dog on his side of the car – just seven feet away – looked ready to spring in through the open car window.

The sight of the Rottweilers had revived in Satyan a heightened awareness of the danger that surrounded him. The mansion and its beautifully laid-out grounds, the manicured bushes and the gracious porch did little to calm his nerves. The building had three floors and was built on the lines of medieval homes of the aristocracy of Europe.

At the crenellated double doors, a uniformed butler in a white jacket waited to escort them to Leconte. Chintamani struck up a rapid conversation with the manservant in fluent French that Satyan followed with some difficulty. They were led into a passage that ran past a library and a billiards room to the garden at the back.

Leconte was pruning a bush. A table was laid for three, beside the swimming pool. The Frenchman turned to greet them with a smile and waved them to the table.

'Won't you take off your jacket, Mr Sharma?' he asked, gesturing to a servant nearby. 'It'll get rather hot for a jacket and tie as the sun rises.'

Satyan waved the servant away and said quickly, 'No thank you, Mr Leconte. I carry a lot of things and the pockets are quite handy. You know – my cellphone, some tablets for my blood pressure, a PDA and some notes for today's discussion. I'm fine, thank you.'

'Ah, your office follows you, eh? You must be a hands-on manager? Well, have it your way. But please feel free to remove it if it gets too hot.

'So tell me, what kind of PDA do you have?'

Satyan and Leconte spent the next fifteen minutes exchanging notes on personal digital assistants and, from there, launched into a discussion on upcoming gadgets from Apple. The game was on between them. Each wanted to find the right opening and rushing things wouldn't be good negotiating practice. Leconte would expect no less and Satyan wanted a diversion to calm his nerves. Chintamani watched this for as long as his patience allowed.

'Hey, Arnie, you know this guy's fire control unit is something else, man! It even does health checks on the gun by the minute, you know?'

Leconte froze. He eyed Chintamani sternly and turned his back on him. Gazing at Satyan's sweat-soaked shirt he said, 'Mr Sharma, I think you really must remove your jacket before you melt in front of our very eyes, eh? Look at you. Your shirt is completely soaked.'

'No, no. It's all right, Mr Leconte,' Satyan said, shrugging his shoulders. 'I'm fine, really.'

The Frenchman's voice suddenly acquired a hard edge. 'I must insist, Mr Sharma. It's not natural. You can hang it on the back of your chair if you need it close to you.'

'No, Mr Leconte…' Satyan started as Leconte leaned forward and twisted his tiepin off.

It trailed a wire and, as Leconte tugged, the wire came off Satyan's chest with a ripping sound as the tape gave. Wild with fury, the Frenchman stood up and yanked off all the wiring until, finally, he had the transmitter unit in his hand. It looked like a mobile phone and had nestled in Satyan's trouser pocket. Satyan's shirt buttons had got ripped out and he stood there, looking like something the cat had brought in.

'So, a transmitter disguised as a mobile phone? Very ingenious, Mr Sharma. And, may I add, very brave of you to have carried it. I don't know how you managed to get it past Chintu's security guards.' He glanced at Chintu, who winced. 'Ah, I see, somehow you tricked Chintu into overruling a security check on your person. How you did so is not important, Mr Sharma. What is important is – what shall we do now?'

Satyan was stunned by the suddenness of his exposure. It was over now and he was trapped. He was in dire physical danger and all alone. Making a dash for it was out of the question; the two Rottweilers in front wouldn't let him get out alive and the walls surrounding the garden at the back were nearly twenty feet high. Not to mention the security guards – Satyan had no idea how many were there, where they were positioned or how they were armed.

He needed to talk his way out of this.

'Fucking shit! You had this on your body all the time, you bastard! You must have got every word I said in the car. Oh shit!' Chintu hopped about in rage. 'Man, what do we do with this guy, Arnie? The bastard knows everything!'

Leconte was examining Satyan closely. 'What exactly did you discuss in the car, Chintu? Quick, tell me exactly what was said.'

'Huh? Well, like, he told me the FCU's features – circuitry, software – you know, all the technical stuff. Fucking thing was, Arnie, we needed something to pass the damn time and the way this guy spoke, I kind of got involved, you know.'

'Was there any mention at all about a possible deal? With FIAM?'

Chintu got a little cagey. 'Ah, let me think. No, nothing specific, you know.'

'Chintu, my friend, come clean with me. I need to know exactly what was said about FIAM. Now try and remember.' Leconte's stare was unrelenting.

'Well, okay. I guess I was curious how much this thing was worth. Like how big this was to FIAM. I mean like…'

'Enough! I have heard enough!'

'The fucking bastard! He's ruined us! Shit! I'll be dead meat in this country now because of this asshole!' Chintu raged, kicking at Satyan, who evaded the assault and stepped behind his chair to preempt another.

'Control yourself, Chintu. This is not the time for childish tantrums,' the Frenchman said. Satyan looked at his coldblooded expression and a chill ran down his spine. Leconte, calculating his next move, was the more dangerous of the two. Chintamani Rao was just raving and ranting. Turning on his heel, the deputy PM's son stormed petulantly off into the house.

'Well, well, well. This looks like it has been carefully planned, Mr Sharma. I doubt if there is any truth in that Van Gogh story, now is there?'

Satyan was silent.

'Ah, I have my answer. So, what's the next move, then? Where will your police strike? Here, in my house? No, they have nothing on me except some rambling from Chintu. Rambling that I can easily say are speculations. But who is behind this eh, Mr Sharma? That is an important question. Is it the IB? Or the army? Well?'

Standing there in the shade of the mango tree, his blazer slung over one elbow, Satyan was thinking fast.

'Leconte, our little chat in the car is right now with the vigilance commissioner. Chintu is *persona non grata*. Even his father will not be able to help him now. Maybe his father will be out of politics for good before the day is out. And as for FIAM, the taint will be too strong for any government to give the contract to them. The game is up and it's best if you come clean, cooperate with the investigation that's sure to follow and get out of India. Cut your losses, Leconte, before you get deeper into trouble.'

Leconte smiled thinly. 'You're no pushover, my friend, I can see that. Stronger measures will be needed, eh?'

Satyan did not miss the intent behind those words. He was about to respond when Chintu came dashing back and thundered, 'Okay, you fucking piece of shit, this is the end of the road for you!'

Satyan blanched when he turned around. Chintu was waving a pistol about in maniacal frenzy, a few feet from his face.

'What say, Arnie? Shall we end this bastard's trip right here? That will teach him not to fuck with me!' Chintu was hopping mad. The slightest move on Satyan's part could push him over the edge.

'Hold it right there, Chintu my friend. Keep the gun trained on Mr Sharma, that's a good idea. Shoot him only if he moves. And now let me think. He has told me that a lot of information is with the vigilance commissioner already. You should have been more discreet. In fact, you should have allowed your guards to check him before letting him into the car. But what's done is done. Mr Sharma was about to tell us the next moves planned. It is of great interest to us, Chintu, if we want to survive this. And Mr Sharma will have to tell us more if he wants to survive this. So, Mr Sharma, the choice is yours. Tell us, or die.'

Chintu's face wore a wolfish grin. His lips were drawn back in a grimace, exposing gleaming white teeth. Satyan could see Chintu's canines. They seemed more prominent than was human. Satyan glanced sideways and Chintu's eyes swung with his to rest on Leconte, who was waiting, still as a statue, for Satyan to start talking.

At that moment, Satyan took a wild gamble and swung his blazer at Chintu's face. Following through, he lunged forward and grabbed the gun hand, twisting it upwards so that it was no longer pointing at him. Desperation lent an almost superhuman strength to his grip.

Taken by surprise, Chintu staggered back, his eyes widening with fear as the barrel turned up and got wedged against his chest. The two were evenly matched in height and weight and they struggled for the gun, toe-to-toe.

Leconte wavered, unsure whether any interference from him would cause harm to his friend. He looked around and found a heavy vase on the table. Emptying it, he stood by, waiting for an opportunity to strike.

The two men were staggering to and fro, grunting with the effort to get control of the gun. It was wedged somewhere between them, hidden under Satyan's blazer and Leconte had difficulty in locating it.

There was a sudden bark, muffled by the two bodies and the blazer. For a moment, the two men were as if turned into stone, frozen in the midst of the action.

Then, Chintu slid down to the ground.

Satyan stood staring at his hands, stunned, before Leconte swung the vase at the back of his head and he blanked out.

◆

'Damn, he's stopped transmitting,' Captain Mahendran muttered under his breath. But, within the confines of the closed van, it was loud enough for Rubita to catch.

'Why? Has your equipment developed a hitch?' she asked anxiously.

'No, ma'am. We've checked all the meters. There's some hitch at Mr Sharma's end, not ours. Firefly One, do you read me, over?'

'Firefly One, sir. Loud and clear. No transmission for last seventy seconds. I think transmitter out of action, sir. Over,' the man stationed on a forty-foot high water-tank in the line of sight from Leconte's residence whispered into his microphone in reply. He was lying prone on the service catwalk around the tank, out of sight from anyone at ground level. He had watched as the BMW had been cleared through the gates and, for the last twenty minutes, had listened as a steady stream of voices had been transmitting from Satyan's unit, to be instantly amplified and relayed to the van parked near the gate of the enclave.

'Let's go in!' Rubita urged the captain, fearing that Satyan had somehow been exposed. He might be in grave danger and she was deeply worried. When they had planned this morning's sequence, she had been the only one to protest because there were too many things that could go wrong either at Chintamani Rao's residence or at Leconte's. Satyan had insisted on doing it this way, assuring her that the younger Rao's psychology would play in their favour. They had already seen how the inability to communicate with Leconte in his frantic state had played tricks on Chintu's mind. He was a pushover. What gave Satyan's argument urgency was the fact that there was no time.

They had had two days to prepare the set-up and it had worked splendidly even up to the point where Satyan had gained smooth access to Leconte's mansion. So Rubita's worries seemed to have been unnecessary. But, now, was it all unravelling? Was Satyan hurt or wounded? Or worse?

'Come on, Captain,' she repeated, 'let's go in! God knows what's happening in that house! You said there are huge Rottweilers inside. Those dogs are killers. We shouldn't delay even for one more minute.'

The captain was sympathetic but firm. 'Ma'am, that's against the plan. We discussed and dismissed the possibility of taking direct action in any eventuality, remember? We need to be ready when they emerge, as they're bound to, ma'am. And we still haven't got our second objective – the evidence from Leconte himself. I cannot jeopardise the operation until we have that, ma'am. I'm sorry, but this was agreed upon with my commander.'

'Oh god, but this is different! We didn't expect transmission to stop suddenly like this.'

'It could have stopped for any number of reasons, ma'am. And we're in a battle zone, in a manner of speaking. So I request you to remain silent, else I may have to evacuate you, ma'am.'

That stopped any further argument and Rubita sat in her chair, chewing her nails in anxiety. The minutes ticked by excruciatingly.

There were three of them in the van: Rubita, the young commando captain and his radio operator. She had been allowed there with great reluctance by the army officers, only when she had convinced them that since she had been part of the whole affair from the very beginning, she may add value by providing crucial information on the spot in case something unexpected cropped up. Now the commando captain was wondering if it had been a wise move. Offloading her from the van in the middle of the road, in front of the West End enclave's main gate, might attract unwanted attention.

As the clock's hands moved silently across the dial, the heat and the tension inside the small space grew. Nobody spoke. They waited.

The radio crackled to life. 'Firefly One calling Angel One. Do you read me? Over.'

'This is Angel One. Go ahead, Firefly One.'

'Car coming out, sir. Black limousine. Different from the car that went in. Windows are up, sir, too dark. I can't see how many people inside. Sir, it has CD number plates. AL 52. Coming towards colony gate now, sir. Over.'

'Firefly One, stay there until further orders. Over and out.'

The captain turned to Rubita and said, 'Looks like they're making their break. Let's see if they do what we expected and go to the airport. They should be out of the enclave gates any time now.'

They waited for a few minutes and the Mercedes emerged on the main road, turning in the direction of Palam airport. Using infrared glasses, the captain counted four occupants in the car, two in front and two in the back. He reported this to his colonel and listened intently to the orders he received from the other end. Tapping the window in front, he told the van's driver to get going. They did not follow the black limousine.

◆

Satyan regained consciousness in the car. His head was throbbing. It seemed like there were a hundred heavy bells ringing in every corner of his brain.

The back of his eyes hurt badly and it was all he could do to focus on the situation. Slowly, he took in his surroundings. He was in the back seat, behind the driver. It wasn't Chintu's BMW but something in the same luxury class. There was a glass partition, which was up. Satyan's hands were bound with nylon cord. Another length of nylon cord tied him to the window armrest so that he couldn't move from his position.

Next to him, Leconte was speaking urgently in French to someone on his cellphone. Satyan gradually began to make out the words. Leconte was issuing instructions to the pilot of a plane.

'Tell them I will be there in half an hour and will sort out the paperwork. My diplomatic identity is with me so there won't be any problem. You get the takeoff slot allotted now. Make a flight plan for UAE, destination Fujairah. There will be three passengers. One of them is an invalid who needs to travel urgently to his home in Fujairah, got that? I need a wheel-chair standing by.

'Get the fuel and the engine check-ups done and have everything ready quickly. Now go, don't waste time.' He listened for a minute while the voice at the other end uttered something. 'Well, we can't wait for him now. You can surely fly the plane alone until Fujairah. I'll make arrangements for another company pilot to come from Dubai or Bahrain to take over from you.'

Leconte glanced at Satyan, who dropped his eyes quickly, but not quickly enough. The Frenchman must have caught on that Satyan knew the language. He had a gun in his hand – not the Walther that Chintu had brought out from the house. Remembering Chintu, Satyan glanced around and saw him slumped in the front seat next to the driver, held in place by the seat belt. There was a baseball cap with a large peak on his head and his face was almost obscured by a pair of dark Ray-Bans. He had been put into a loose windcheater that had been zipped up to his chin. The image of the body slipping down from his grasp returned to him. Chintu's eyes had stared intensely into his as he died. There had been so little blood. Satyan remembered looking down to see the gun smoking slightly in Chintu's hand. And then his head had exploded and he had blacked out.

The Frenchman must have hit him with something heavy. Now he was sitting behind Chintu, keying in another number. He appeared in total control. Cold-blooded and ruthless. Only such a man could have thought of putting a dead man in the front seat. Only such a man could have convinced the driver to take them like this to the airport. Unless the driver was trained to handle such exigencies, which made the whole set-up more intriguing.

Leconte was still speaking in French, but he was pouring treacle into his voice now. He had someone from the embassy at the other end and was asking them, as a personal favour, to apply pressure on air traffic control in Palam to clear his pilot's flight plan on priority. He, Leconte, would only just have time to drive to the plane and take off. It was on business connected with the gun deal and, as everybody knew, the Indian cabinet was going to meet very shortly to take the final decision. Time was of the essence. He had two others with him – one was an invalid who would be taken on board on a wheelchair. Leconte was all charm and Satyan could hear a female voice at the other end. With a bit of flirtatious banter, Leconte thanked the woman and promised to make this up to her on his return.

Satyan's blood turned icy cold in his veins. He didn't have to wonder why Leconte was allowing himself to be overheard. He could guess. The game, as far as the Indian howitzer deal was concerned, was over. Leconte's days as a fixer and mover in this town, too, had met a sudden and unsavoury end. Chintamani Rao was dead, killed in his house by a gunshot wound. His presence there had been established in the transmitted conversation. Then there had been silence, followed by Rao's death. There was no way that Leconte could continue in this country. In all probability, he wouldn't ever be able to step into India without being arrested on arrival to stand trial for the murder of the deputy PM's son.

So, Leconte was arranging his escape. This country was becoming more dangerous for him by the minute.

When Sam, Satyan and Rubita had thought up this plan, Leconte was expected to take the same route. The difference was that, according to that plan, Chintu was to have been alive and kicking, accompanying Leconte on a treasure hunt in the Caribbean. An accident in mid-air soon after their plane took off would have tied all loose ends and brought the whole matter to a close. Instead, Chintu was already dead. And Satyan was probably soon going to be. Disposing these two inconvenient bodies would be easier for Leconte in the deserts of Fujairah, or in the waters of the Arabian Sea.

Leconte flipped his phone open once more and dialled. 'Fiona, my love. I'm so sorry to spring another one of my surprises on you. Darling, I've got a call from De Villiers. He's got some kind of last-minute thing to discuss about next week's cabinet meeting, and I had to agree. He's in Dubai and I have had to rush off. I'll be back tonight in time for the party, darling. I promise.'

After exchanging a few endearments he rang off.

Craning his neck, Satyan could look over the driver's shoulder. The tree-lined boulevards flashed by. He couldn't identify the make of the car. He peered desperately through the side windows, but the tint on the glasses was too heavy and nobody could look inside. At a traffic light, he found himself looking directly into the eyes of a motorcyclist who arranged his hair in the reflection from his window and then drove on, oblivious to the tense scene inside the car.

'Don't even try to yell or scream, Mr Sharma,' Leconte told him, lounging comfortably against the cushions. 'This car is soundproof and bulletproof. You had your chance and you threw it away. So unwise and so typical of youth.

'And now, I see that you have understood everything I said on the phone and have figured it all out for yourself. You are my insurance cover to get out of this country alive, Mr Sharma. I'm being very frank with you. I need you. My chauffeur,' Leconte inclined his head forward, 'is a highly trained soldier. Ex-Foreign Legion. You are in safe hands, Mr Sharma.

'As Confucius said, when the rape is inevitable, lie back and enjoy it, eh?'

◆

At the airport, they drove straight to a private hangar and halted just inside the doors, hidden in its dark shadows from casual passersby.

The plane was outside, bathed in bright sunshine, its engines emanating a low whine. A team of engineers was at work, getting it flight-ready.

The pilot came up to them at a brisk pace. Leconte brusquely ordered him to get a wheelchair and the man went to fetch one. Leconte and the chauffeur waited for it before opening the doors to lift Chintu's body out of the car. While the chauffeur was loading the wheelchair and strapping the body into it, Leconte gestured to the rear door and the pilot opened it for Satyan to step out. He didn't bat an eyelid when he saw Satyan trussed up. Unbidden, he untied the cord at the armrest without releasing the knot tying the prisoner's hands together. It was done very smoothly.

As the pilot worked, he remarked to Leconte that he must have pulled a lot of strings – the full team of engineers had arrived within minutes to check the engines and fuselage even before he had started out for the air-traffic control office. The papers had been ready and he only had to sign. The refuelling truck had also arrived promptly.

Satyan could see that this news wasn't received too well by Leconte. Leconte told the chauffeur to watch over Satyan and walked towards the plane, calling out to the group of engineers who had finished their job on the plane and were piling into their van. They began to move off. He ran forward a few steps, yelling louder to catch their attention. They didn't look back. In fact, Leconte spotted an officer in an olive green uniform nearby who was waving them off vigorously.

The officer then approached Leconte. Squinting against the bright glare outside, Satyan spotted the brass pips of an army captain. He looked more closely and, with a wave of relief, recognised Captain Mahendran.

But what was he doing here? Satyan had been told that there would be no scope for the army's direct involvement. But Captain Mahendran's presence was a godsend; he didn't feel like questioning too closely.

Leconte hesitated. The presence of an Indian army officer by his plane was completely unexpected. He swung around to where Satyan and the chauffeur were standing beside the wheelchair carrying Chintu's body. Then, looking over their shoulders, he saw a contingent of six commandos silently forming a cordon around them. Leconte fingered his tie, thinking of drawing his gun from its shoulder holster. The commando captain, who had by now come up behind him, quietly urged him to refrain and gently relieved him of the weapon.

'I've been ordered to allow your little group to depart expeditiously without any incident, sir,' he said. 'Please don't create one.'

He jerked his thumb to indicate to the pilot to go in and get ready for takeoff. Two of the soldiers escorted the pilot, taking the wheelchair along with them.

The captain asked Satyan to step behind the cordon. That was the moment when Leconte realised fully what was about to happen – why the group of engineers had been there, and why they had almost run when he called out to them. His face crumpled up and he wore a desperate expression. He looked at the captain, ready to plead with him, but that officer had a cold, stony, unyielding look about him. He nodded to his men and two of them stepped briskly up to frisk Leconte and his chauffeur, retrieving a Luger and a vicious-looking hunting knife from the latter. Leconte was declared clean of any other weapon.

The Frenchman glanced towards the plane. Chintu's body was being hoisted up the stairs by two commandos. He hesitated for a moment, turned and said to Satyan, 'Listen, Mr Sharma. Fiona wasn't involved in anything, okay? Promise me she'll be unharmed. Please promise me that. And tell her that I love her.' Tears were welling up in his eyes.

Satyan considered. Finally he nodded an okay.

Captain Mahendran stared rigidly into the distance and his men stepped forward to escort the two Frenchmen to the waiting plane. Already, the engines were revving up.

When the door closed on Leconte, the little group moved to one side to watch it taxi and takeoff. Climbing sharply, it banked and turned swiftly out over the plains. It would probably head due south-west over the Thar Desert and fly over Pakistan before crossing the shoreline of the Arabian Sea. Off to one side of the airport, an army helicopter took flight after it.

About five minutes later, Satyan and his escort reached their vehicles in the parking lot. The captain drove the lead vehicle, nudging it past the morning rush out of the airport complex. He pulled up at a roundabout and parked to one side, waiting. Satyan was about to ask him what the matter was when the radio set burst into life.

'Bravo Three calling Angel One. Bravo Three calling Angel One. Do you read me? Over.' Even with the static, the excitement in the voice was unmistakable.

'Angel One here, Bravo Three. Read you loud and clear. Go ahead.'

'There has been an accident. Repeat, there has been an accident! The aircraft has exploded, sir. Estimated ninety kilometres due south-west of Delhi airport, sir. Altitude approximately five thousand metres and climbing. It was a fireball, possibly an engine failure. I'm afraid there is no chance for any survivors.'

The young captain stiffened a bit and remained silent for a moment before acknowledging curtly, 'This is Angel One. Roger. Over and out.'

'I hope we don't have too much collateral damage,' Satyan heard him say in an undertone.

Switching the engine to life, he gunned the vehicle out onto the main road, heading into the city.

14

The happy throngs flowed along the capital's streets. Satyan, Rubita and Sam Bannerjee watched the parade from the terrace of Sam's bungalow. The crowd's passage was punctuated every so often by firecrackers, filling the night sky with brilliantly coloured starbursts.

At first, the crowds had come in tens and twenties and then, as the evening had progressed bringing in more results from ballot-counting stations across the country, the numbers of revellers had swelled into hundreds, then thousands.

Satyan and Rubita stood near the balustrade holding their drinks. It had been a long journey. Sam stood nearby, quiet tears glistening in his eyes.

The nation had given its verdict. The twelfth parliament was clearly going the way of the ruling party, which had already won two-hundred-and-forty seats and was leading in seventy more. In a house of five-hundred-and-forty-two members, nothing could stop it from retaining the mandate to rule the country for another five years. The masses had voted for stability and status quo.

But there was a difference – already, the PM and his closest associates had lost or were in retreat in their constituencies.

The PM had referred, time and again, in his campaign to a 'foreign hand' behind a political conspiracy to destabilise him and unseat his party. He had repeated, *ad infinitum*, the tremendous progress the country had made under his party in the last term. Playing to the wish-fulfilment of the moneyed class, he had highlighted the professional team which ran the country, with him as the CEO of India Ltd. Playing to the illiterate masses, he had banked on the personality cult and the name of his dynasty to sway the voters. Financial scandals didn't bother him. The older politicians had weathered many scandals in the past. Public memory had always been short. Petroleum, sugar, cement – every large industry had witnessed financial fiddling by the country's leaders. Fingers would get pointed. Everybody would know who was doing what. Yet nobody important ever got caught. At least not for a long time after such scandals broke out. And the punishment was invariably minuscule compared to the crime.

This time, however, the old guard had underestimated the significance of the scams that had emerged like worms from the rotten woodwork of the party framework. The accuracy and speed with which information had surfaced left many observers puzzled. Detail after gory detail on the shenanigans of key members of the ruling party played out in the newspapers. Uncannily, the right propaganda always seemed available at the right time to the opposition. The picture that emerged was of a ruling party which had been shortchanged by its own leaders over the years. There seemed a larger power at work – many political commentators, even among the PM's opponents, felt that the 'foreign hand' theory was true.

But the voting public had not let the ruling party down; they had faithfully put their stamp on the all too familiar party symbol on the ballot paper. Nothing had changed there.

What had changed were the opposition party's tactics. They had targeted those constituencies where the established leaders had stood for election. The calculation had been that, with the top guns biting the dust, the candidates who did get elected would be unsure of the party's future and have little cause to refuse their money to cross the floor after the polls. In this way, the opposition could win the numbers game and gain a majority in the Lok Sabha – the more powerful of the two houses of representatives in the Parliament. Paradoxically, what emerged victorious was a new-look ruling party, with even greater strength than before. What the opposition had not bargained for was a new leader to rise to the occasion.

The foreign minister was young and personable. The latest in a long line of glamorous Rajput maharajas, he had enough charm and presence to offer the people an alternative figure to worship. He and his loyalists had won their seats with thumping majorities and his faction in the party had won the upper hand. The Indian multitude loved dynasties and the ruling party was miraculously offering them a new one to substitute the old. Nothing had changed and yet everything had changed.

Sam Bannerjee's manservant came to the terrace with the cordless phone. 'Call for you, sahib. Mr Manwani from Mumbai.'

The voice at the other end was vibrant. 'Sam, old friend! How's the situation in Delhi? Mumbai is absolutely bursting with joy.'

'Ditto for Delhi, Ketan. It's almost as if the whole country is pouring into the capital to celebrate. We've made it!'

'Is Satyan there?'

'Right here, Ketan. When you're in Delhi next, we must get together for a celebration.' He handed the phone to Satyan.

'Satyan, my boy,' said Manwani. 'I've got great news for you! Once it was pretty certain that the thing was in the bag, the Raja himself called me. Not ten minutes ago, to be precise. He wanted to consult me on a couple of names for the finance and industry ministries, basically. But you know what else? He also told me to get the Fort Club and Pure Space Networks standing by. You hear that, my boy? Cheers!'

◆

Three days later, a smiling Satyan Sharma acknowledged the greetings of the workers as he nosed his car through the EMMG group's compound. He paused as the gates to the Pure Space enclosure were opened for him. Glancing across at the Next Gen building, he saw Mr Agarwal turn and wave to him. He smiled cheerfully and waved back. The old man had recovered fully and returned, fighting fit, to his post some four weeks after his brush with Lakhan Singh's thugs.

Satyan drove around the sweeping curves of the Pure Space buildings, humming to himself. The Indo-Uzbek howitzer would be going into full-scale production soon. Pure Space Networks could turn its attention to marketing the Epsilon-6 software, which was the brain of the fire control unit, to the rest of the world. He reckoned the potential revenue would be at least a hundred million dollars over the next three years. More importantly, it would catapult Pure Space – and, with it, the entire EMMG group – onto the world stage. He ran his eye over the campus, imagining the towering edifices that the future held for his group of companies.

Satyan parked the car in the bay and ran up the steps. The entire PSN team had partied late into the previous night. He had given them the day off but had hauled himself out of bed early as usual. Eager to get started on the business plans for Epsilon-6, he pushed open the doors of the 'bull-pit' a few minutes past eight a.m.

He had expected to find the place all to himself that morning and was surprised to find his vice-president, Jacob Mehta, sitting there with a mug of coffee in his hand.

'Hey, Jake, what gives? I thought all you guys would be sleeping the party off today. Looks like I'm not the only one who can't stay away from Pure Space, eh?' Satyan thumped Mehta heartily on the shoulder.

'Hi, Satyan. I hadn't expected you to be in today either.' He looked down at the floor and stroked his stubble. He seemed somewhat shamefaced.

Satyan noticed that Mehta had not changed out of the clothes he had been wearing the previous night. Satyan took in the unshaven chin, the dishevelled appearance and sunken eyes. Mehta had, obviously, not slept at all.

Satyan's brow clouded over with concern. He pulled up a nearby chair and sat down straddling it, propping his elbows on its back. 'Hey, buddy, what's wrong? What's happened?'

'I – I'd wanted to collect my thoughts before talking to you. I wouldn't have been able to sleep, so I came here straight from the party.'

'Thoughts about what, Jake? I'm here now, so tell me.'

'Satyan, look,' Mehta began hesitantly. 'However I do this, it's going to come out sounding bad to you.'

Satyan's mind snapped and he lost control. Unbidden, black thoughts came storming into his head. The questions flew at him in a blinding maelstrom, as if swirling out of the vortex of corruption and violence he had been through during the last few months.

What the hell was this, he thought to himself, wasn't the fucking world done with him yet? He could not take any more shit now, he'd been through too much.

And now, he asked himself, what more was there in this goddamn circus? Could his trusted lieutenant have been involved in any of the games he had seen in the past few months? It was too horrible to contemplate. But could it be that his closest colleague had been spying against his own country? Could it be that fifteen years in the US had subverted Mehta's loyalty to India? Could it possibly be that in all the years that Mehta had been with Pure Space, Satyan had been blind to this aspect of his character? Had his loyalties shifted to serve American interests, perhaps at Maggie's insistent urging? For the past few weeks he had not been able to spend much time in his office, had the bloody wheeler-dealers been busy here behind his back?

For so many weeks he had been unable to share his innermost thoughts and feelings with anyone, not even Rubita, and some circuit deep in his brain exploded without warning.

The demon inside his soul burst onto the surface. Satyan went berserk. His lips curled back in a brutal snarl. He lunged out of the chair, sending it flying. He grabbed Mehta's shirt and lifted the startled man bodily with uncharacteristic strength so that his toes were trailing on the floor.

Thrusting his face close, Satyan growled, 'Sound bad to me? Jake, I've been to hell and back on this one. I've been fucked around with so badly by so many people, you don't want to know. Sound bad?' He continued in a paroxysm of rage, 'Nothing can ever sound bad to me again, do you understand? Unless,' he laid his other hand on Mehta's throat, 'unless you're going to tell me that I've been let down by a fucking friend.' He began shaking the frightened man back and forth with the strength of a man possessed. 'I've seen dirty games being played these past few months, Jake. I've aged many years since this project began. I've seen men betray the trust their country has placed in them. I've seen grown men cross all limits of civilised behaviour.' His eyes bored steadily into Mehta's. 'I've crossed some limits on my own, Jake. I've done things the world will never come to know about.'

Unable to comprehend the demonic look in Satyan's eyes, Mehta clung speechlessly to the sinewy hands that threatened to choke the life out of his body. The Satyan he had known was a gentleman to the core. The Satyan he now saw three inches from his face terrified him.

Satyan continued, 'I've also seen a man kill his friend's soul while leaving his body untouched, Jake. I swear if someone mocks my friendship, my vengeance will know no limits.' Mehta's blood ran cold. 'So, what is it that you wanted to tell me?'

When Mehta recovered his wits, he found his heart filled, not with anger but with compassion. He looked deep into Satyan's eyes and shook his head gently. He took Satyan's hands in his and extricated his shirtfront from the clenched fists. He saw the dark light in Satyan's eyes dying away, as suddenly as it had appeared. Satyan now had a bewildered look on his face. Both men righted their chairs and sank into them. Jake placed his hands on Satyan's knees and waited, gasping while he recovered his breath. Patiently, he waited for the rage to die down. The minutes ticked by. Satyan flicked his glance several times at his deputy and looked away every time, not finding the words to express his emotions.

Finally, Mehta broke the silence.

'Satyan, I want to quit.' To Satyan, the words seemed to ring out in that vast room. Somewhere deep down, he instinctively knew that in those few mad moments, he had crossed a point of no return. 'I can't take it anymore, Satyan. I've been watching the way you have to do business in this country. And I don't like it. I waited until we had the howitzer project tied down before telling you of my decision. I owed you and the team that much. Now I want to go back.'

'But what about Pure Space, Jake?' Satyan pleaded in contrition. 'You and I created it together. Surely you knew that you were going to become president soon. And now we're on song, you're on the threshold of a great future.'

'The future, Satyan? Here in India? As president of Pure Space?' Mehta smiled. 'Let's be rational about this. I was okay handling the technical stuff, but I'm not cut out to be head honcho. You kept all of us sheltered from the dirty tricks department; I've been watching you do that. And you've done a tremendous job. I won't be able to handle it. But you've got to watch yourself, Satyan. Look what it's done to you – flying off the handle like that. To hell and back, like you just said.'

Satyan winced.

'Look,' Mehta continued in a softer voice, 'I've always known that you wanted me to take over at Pure Space. And I appreciate that. But my mind is made up. I can't accept this mantle. You'll get others to take my place; you know how many top notch guys have been sending us feelers lately.'

'But, Jake, none of them can take your place. I don't want to lose a friend, goddammit!'

'You almost did, Satyan,' said Mehta gently. 'You almost did, back there.'

Acknowledgements

Stories do not exist without an audience. My very first audience was my younger sister Preetha, who listened with rapt attention to stories I cobbled together on the fly in our childhood during long and lazy Sunday afternoons. She thus started me off on my career as a storyteller. I thank her for giving me those unforgettable moments.

That career waited a few decades before producing this debut novel of mine. So to the present, I thank my editor and literary agent, Kanishka Gupta of Writer's Side, who believed in me almost more than I did myself. His perseverance played a large role in putting this book in your hands, dear reader. Kanishka as well as Rahul Soni gave me insights that helped me to raise the storyline to a higher plane. So did Shikha Dimri of Rupa Publications, and I thank her also for the care with which she edited the manuscript.

I thank many friends who read the different versions of the novel and declared it readable, motivating me to keep at it.

I am grateful to my wife Roopa and daughter Anushya, who gave me their frank opinions about the novel over relaxed cups of tea of a morning. Above all, I thank my mother and my father who gave me an abiding sense of values, the perspective and the encouragement to find myself through good times and bad.